R02

LIBRARY SYSTEM
3650 Summit Boulevard
West Palm Beach, FL   33406-4198

Who
Do I Run To?

Who Do I Run To?

Anna Black

www.urbanbooks.net

Urban Books, LLC
300 Farmingdale Road, N.Y.-Route 109
Farmingdale, NY 11735

Who Do I Run To? Copyright © 2022 Anna Black

All rights reserved. No part of this book may be repro-
duced in any form or by any means without prior consent
of the Publisher, except brief quotes used in reviews.

ISBN 13: 978-1-64556-331-0
ISBN 10: 1-64556-331-6

First Trade Paperback Printing May 2022
Printed in the United States of America

10 9 8 7 6 5 4 3 2 1

*This is a work of fiction. Any references or similarities
to actual events, real people, living or dead, or to real
locales are intended to give the novel a sense of reality.
Any similarity in other names, characters, places, and
incidents is entirely coincidental.*

Distributed by Kensington Publishing Corp.
Submit Orders to:
Customer Service
400 Hahn Road
Westminster, MD 21157-4627
Phone: 1-800-733-3000
Fax: 1-800-659-2436

Also, by Anna Black

Dedication

This book, as always, is dedicated to my readers, whom I really appreciate, and I hope that I'm able to make you laugh, cry, and reflect. I am so excited to release this book for you guys . . . Wow, I'm fortunate. I am pleased to entertain with words, and I am excited that you decided to read *Who Do I Run To?* This one is for you, my readers, the ones who give me a reason to do what I do.

Enjoy.

Acknowledgments

My source: my Lord and Savior Jesus Christ. He has blessed me with a creative mind, and I thank Him. I would especially like to thank my family, friends, and supporters; thanks for the encouragement, the compliments, and for just giving me a chance to entertain you with words.

I am grateful to God for so many blessings. To have an inventive mind is a gift, and I thank Him. To allow my stories to be enjoyed by others is also a blessing. Thank you, my readers, for giving *Who Do I Run To?* an opportunity to be read by you.

Just always remember to
"Be You, Do You & Love You."

Prologue

"Damn, K.P., what is your problem?" I said out loud, looking at his gorgeous picture on my desk. He was my type, desire, and everything I wanted in a man . . . but he was still another woman's husband.

"Promises, promises are all you ever make me," I said, picking up the photo. I never pressured him about leaving Kimberly, but he would always mention the day he would make me his new wife. For a long time, I believed him, but now, I was starting to think he was playing me. "When are you going to leave her?" I asked the photo and then put it back in its spot next to a picture of my sister, Janelle, and me.

"Janelle is so wrong about you," I said, shaking my head and shaking the thoughts of my sister's words of how big of an asshole K.P. was. "She doesn't know you like I know you, and I trust you," I said and smiled.

"Trust who?" a voice asked, taking me by surprise.

"Shawnee!" I said, looking up, wondering how long she had been standing there outside of my cubicle.

"Who are you talking about?" Shawnee asked.

This nosy bitch. "What?" I asked with my head tilted, wondering why Shawnee was asking anything because we were not friends, and she was definitely not one of my favorites.

"Awww, never mind," Shawnee said, coming in and sitting in the chair against my cubicle wall. Now I wished I had taken the chair back down the hall after my supervisor and I had our afternoon meeting.

"Listen, my brother and I are having this little get-together this weekend, and I wanted to know if you'd like to come," she asked nicely—not the Shawnee that I was familiar with.

"Get-together, huh?" I said suspiciously. "What's the occasion?" I asked, leaning back in my chair.

"Well, believe it or not, it's my birthday weekend, and my brother wanted to give me something at his house. So he told me to invite a few of my girlfriends, and since, you know," she said and flung her weave and batted her fake eyelashes, "most of the bitches up in here are jealous, and I don't have many girlfriends to invite," she said . . . I wanted to laugh in her face. I was definitely *not* one of Shawnee's girlfriends, nor did I think that the women in our office were jealous of her. Shawnee was just an evil, backbiting bitch, and women couldn't stand her.

"Well, Shawnee, you and I are not exactly girlfriends either," I pointed out.

"Nonsense, girl—you and I have been cool since we started. Remember, we came out of orientation together," she said as if that made us buddies.

"Yes, and most of the time when you see me, you turn your nose up."

"Janiece, I do not." Shawnee protested like that was far from the truth. "You have always been one of my favorites," she said with a phony smile. I could see right through her fake-ass green contacts and ten-inch artificial lashes. At that moment, I felt sorry for her because I knew Shawnee didn't have any friends up in our office, so I decided I *might* go, but I was not sure if I would.

"Look, I'll think about it, see if I'll be free, and let you know."

"Okay," she sighed. "Here's the address, just in case you decide you wanna come," she said, handing me an invitation. "And you are welcome to bring that fine-ass man of yours if you do."

I *knew* she was up to something. I heard the rumors that Shawnee called K.P. "The Invisible Man" because no one in our office had ever seen him in person during the years I worked here.

Their office had a party for every occasion, and although Janiece claimed to be the woman of the stud in the pictures she had on her desk, no one had actually met him.

"I'll see, Shawnee—K.P. is an extremely busy man."

"You don't say," Shawnee said sarcastically.

"As I *said,* I'll see," I said again and stuffed the invite into my purse. I knew right then *that* was the reason why Shawnee invited me. She just wanted to see if I really had a man.

"Fine. See you Saturday," Shawnee said and sashayed back to her cubicle. I wished I could invite my sexy-ass man to go with me, but I knew he'd say no like he always did, afraid he'd run into someone he and Kimberly knew.

I went back to thinking of being Mrs. Paxton, and my day went by fairly quickly. At the close of the day, I grabbed my stuff and headed straight for the train station. I stood to get off the metro and looked down to see who was calling again. It said Private, so I dropped my phone back into my purse.

I made my way to the doors, got off, then stood to wait for the train to clear the tracks. When the rails went up for me to cross, my face lit up when I saw his SUV. He was at my condo to share fleeting moments of bliss that Friday evening, and I was anxious to get inside to see him.

I climbed the steps, and when I opened the door, I saw that he had set up my place beautifully and romantically with candles and soft music. The scent of food hit my nose. I knew it was from my favorite restaurant.

"Oh my, K.P., this is nice," I said when I entered the living room.

"Hey," he said, getting up from the sofa.

"Wow, K.P., you did it up, baby." I was very impressed with his surprise candlelit dinner.

"Why, thanks, babe. Come on, have a seat, and let your man serve you," he said and pulled out my chair. He grabbed the bottle of chilled wine and poured me a glass.

"This is so sweet," I said and took a sip. Then I noticed there was only one place setting on the table. "Hey, why is the table only set for one?" I asked, wondering what was going on.

"Listen, babe, please don't be mad, but Kimberly's parents are having a big dinner tonight at the main house, and I can't stay."

"But, K.P., this is my weekend. *My* Friday night," I replied, disappointed.

"I know, babe, and I'll make it up to you. But you know, my wife can't go alone."

"K.P., damn, baby," I said, putting my glass down and holding back the tears in my burning eyes. I anticipated my weekends, and now instead of his two a.m. departure, he was leaving before seven.

"Come on, Jai, no dramatics, okay? Now, I ran you a bath. I got your grilled chicken, mashed potatoes, and steamed veggies just the way you like it, warming in the microwave. I want you to enjoy your evening."

"How, K.P.? My evening was supposed to be with *you*."

"I know, Jai, but Kimberly sprang this on me at the last minute, and you know how it goes. Duty calls," he said and glanced at his watch because he didn't have much time.

"Forget it, Kerry. Just go," I said and pushed the empty plate away.

"Jai, please, you know I hate to leave you upset," he said.

"But you always do," I whined.

"I can't help it, Jai. When I tell you I gotta do stuff with my wife, I don't want you to get this way. You know damn well I'd rather be here with you than at some uptight, uppity party at Kim's parents. But her dad is my boss, okay? And Kimberly is my wife."

"I know, K.P. Damn. I don't need you constantly reminding me that Kimberly is your wife," I yelled, and he had to go.

"A'ight, Jai, fine," he said and kissed my forehead. "I gotta go, baby, and I really would like to see you smile for me," he said. I gave him a faint smile. "That's my girl. Now, I'll see you tomorrow, okay?" I nodded. He went over to the coffee table and grabbed his keys. Then he gave me a quick peck, and I held back the tears.

"I love you," he said, walking toward the door.

"I love you too," I stated once he shut the door.

Chapter One

So many questions ran through Janiece's mind while she was sitting in her dimly lit bedroom. Candles were burning, and Joe's soft sounds, "Worst Case Scenario," repeatedly played for the fourth or fifth time. She looked over at the clock. The minutes were ticking by fast. Soon, it would be time for him to make his departure. She rubbed his face, gently caressing his chocolate skin. Then she leaned over, kissed his shoulder, and then slid back under the covers to enjoy her final moments of having his warm body in her bed.

She wished he would take a courageous chance and stay past his usual two o'clock departure hour, but not one night in five years did he change his routine. For five years, she has been his "other half." "The completion of his life," he would say. She gave him all the things he couldn't get from Mrs. Paxton. He was the only man she wanted, loved, desired, and adored. But, as much as she wanted to be, she wasn't the first lady in his life. The truth is, he was married with two kids, but Janiece was his "more than a woman," he would say.

She was the listener with no back talk or disputes. He told her that her home was a place of peace and relaxation. She had no kids, no pets, and no loudmouthed girlfriends hanging around. Instead, she offered a quiet, peaceful, stress-free environment, with good eating and good loving.

She would only get in his ear when she felt she wasn't getting enough time. There were times when she got plenty of his attention, and then there were the dry moments when she barely saw him. She tried dating and seeing other men to occupy the lonely times in her life a few times, but that didn't work because K.P. would get upset. He wouldn't actually come out and say it, but he would make comments or find a way to ruin the relationship, like coming over when he knew she had company.

One time, she had a date that she brought home with her, and when she got to her condo, K.P. was sitting outside on the steps waiting for her. He didn't make a scene. He just politely asked her date if he could speak with her for a moment in private, and, of course, her date obliged. They stepped inside her door, and she was waiting for him to say something, but he said nothing. Finally, after a few moments of silence, she asked, "K.P., what is it? I can't leave him out there too long. Why are you here? You knew I was going on a date." And he just stood there looking at her like she had been caught doing something wrong.

She could see how bothered he was, and she felt terrible, so she said, "Look, baby, I'll get rid of him, and I'll call you when he's gone," because K.P. didn't budge. So she finally brushed by him to tell her date she would call him later, but he was already gone.

When she came back inside, K.P. was standing there looking at her like he had done nothing wrong. After that, she gave up dating completely. She had no interest in other men because she had gotten so deeply involved with K.P. that he was the only one she made herself available for. So she fell into a regular routine of being his "other woman," and that was how things were.

She thought he was the sexiest man she had ever hooked up with. From day one, she was caught up on him.

Even though their time was limited, she had gotten pretty comfortable with him over the years. He was tall, had chocolate skin, and was built like a freight train. She was turned on by his style, the way he dressed, and that beautiful, bright smile he was blessed with. Unfortunately, that was his weapon against her.

When she would be pissed or upset because he'd either stand her up or not answer his phone for days, all he had to do was turn on the charm, but when she pissed him off, he'd be an asshole. The sad thing is, he was only pissed when he was jealous and thought some other man was sniffing around. So she would purposely lie and say she had plans with a guy and instead, be out with her sister so that she could get extra time and attention from him. He'd only put in work when he thought he had competition, so she used that to her advantage.

After a moment of pulling the jealous card, she promised him that she wouldn't mess with anyone else. He got a key to her place, and he has been her only man for the last three of their five-year relationship. Now he answers her phone, comes and goes as he pleases, and has all the privileges that a married man shouldn't have her sister Janelle would tell her. Janelle would always shake her head at some of the things Janiece would say about their relationship. Janiece just felt that Janelle didn't understand or know K.P. like she knew him, but in Janelle's mind, he was a low-down, dirty bastard, and she couldn't stand the sight of him.

She told Janiece too many times how she felt about K.P. and the whole situation with him, and Janiece would simply reply, "What's good for you ain't good for everybody. When I get tired of the situation, that's when I get tired, and that's that." Janelle would just shake her head in astonishment. She wanted better for her one and only sister, but you can't tell grown folks anything, so she tried to stop pushing the issue. It never changed anything, and for five years, Janiece has played second to Kimberly Paxton, a woman Janiece didn't have a positive or negative attitude about.

Janiece sometimes felt that Kimberly was just as bad as she was, being in love with a man she had to know was cheating on her. There were times when he and Janiece would be together, and his wife would call his phone ten times, and he wouldn't answer. What he told his wife later, Janiece had no clue. There were times when they'd be making love, and he would pick up his phone and tell his wife that he was busy, and he'd call her back. He'd say to her that he'd be home in an hour and didn't leave Janiece's condo until three or four hours later sometimes.

That made Janiece feel his wife had to know something. Maybe Kimberly was just like her . . . in love with him and had accepted things for what they were. Janiece loved him just as much as his wife, she assumed, and she continued to love him and be right there for him because that was where she wanted to be, and that night was no different.

Although she dreaded the two a.m. hour, it was approaching quickly. The alarm would be waking him soon to leave her again, and she wasn't ready for it to sound off.

K.P. was so anal about getting up on time. He also set his alarm on his phone so that he wouldn't oversleep. She lay back in his arms and snuggled close to him. The clock read 11:29 p.m., and it's like she blinked, and the alarm was sounding off. Mechanically, he got up. He hit the OFF button on the alarm clock, and then he turned the alarm on his phone off. After that, he stood up and leaned over in the dark, looking for his boxers.

"Jai," he whispered like he would wake up someone else in the house.

"Yeah?" she responded, annoyed.

"Where are my boxers?" he asked, feeling around and under her as if she hid them.

"Man, I don't know," she said and nestled back under the covers.

"Come on, Jai, stop fucking around and help me. You know I gotta go," he said, feeling around like a madman.

"Look, dude, turn on the lamp and leave me alone," she snapped. She didn't have pleasantries to exchange when he had to go. Her attitude was completely different from when he first arrived.

"Fine," he said and turned on the lamp that sat on the nightstand. "I thought the light would bother you, bighead," he said and proceeded to look for his shorts. He found them and quickly started to dress.

"No, that loud-ass alarm bothers me. The fact that you can't give me one night at my place in five years bothers me," she snapped.

"Jai, baby, come on. Don't, baby, please. Don't do this tonight. Don't trip out on me. You know I don't like to leave when you're upset," he said, putting on his socks. It seemed as if he was in a hurry because he was dressed before she knew it. His shirt was unbuttoned, but he was dressed faster than he had ever dressed before.

"If you hate it so much, why do you leave me by myself all the time? All I asked is for you to just stay past two for one night, K.P.—just one," she whined.

"Janiece, stop it, baby. No dramatics tonight," he said and bent over and kissed her forehead. "Now, go back to sleep, and I'll call you tomorrow. I'll let you know early if we can get together and maybe rent a movie," he said.

"I'm tired of renting movies. Chicago is a big city. Why can't we go *out* to a movie? You're not going to get caught," she said, to him, frustrated because they hardly went out anywhere. Instead, they spent their time indoors, and if they went out, it was to the local bookstore or park near her condo.

"Look," he said, raising his voice. Then he looked at her face and changed his tone. "Baby, I promise I'll try to get over here tomorrow, and if you want to go out, I'll take you out," he said softly and caressed her face. "Okay, baby? I promise. Now, get some sleep, beautiful, and I'll work out something special for us tomorrow evening," he said, laying on the charm. In times like this, she couldn't stay mad at him.

"You promise?" she asked.

"Yes, you know I will. I love you, babe. Now, come on. Smile for me," he said, smiling at her. She returned the smile but still didn't want him to leave.

"I gotta go," he said, backing away.

"I know, and I love you too," she told him.

"That's my girl." He turned off the lamp and then headed for the door. It didn't matter if she smiled at him or not. He still had to go. The tears started to flow as soon as she heard the back door shut. Why on earth did she let him have so much power over her? Why couldn't she just tell him to get the hell on and find a man of her own? She couldn't figure it out.

She knew she was tired of the "two a.m. got to go home to wife and family" crap. Why did she love someone else's husband? She didn't know the answer. Why did she get this deeply involved with K.P.? What she did know was that something had to change for her—and soon.

Chapter Two

It was Sunday afternoon, and she hadn't heard a word from Kerry. Janiece text messaged him five or six times, and she didn't get any response. She was hungry but didn't want to eat in case he called and wanted to take her to dinner. She peeped out the kitchen window for the hundredth time, hoping to see his black Escalade in her guest parking stall because he'd sometimes just show up instead of calling.

She wasn't sure why he would do that from time to time. She just figured that made him feel good to be able to walk in unannounced with his key, guaranteeing she wouldn't have a guy over. She stared at the clock, and it was still ten after four, and it seemed to be stuck on that time, she thought to herself. She reached for her phone again to text him, but it vibrated in her hand, and she immediately got excited, thinking it was him finally calling or returning her text, but it was her sister, Janelle, instead.

She really didn't want to talk to her at that time, but she figured she'd kill some time if she chatted with her sister while she waited for Mr. K.P. to call or come by.

"Hello, Janelle," she said after finally picking up.

"Well, hello, little sis. How are you?" Janelle asked, upbeat. She was always in good spirits. She lived a life that Janiece only dreamed of living. She had a fine-ass husband who made a lot of dough and lived in a huge, six-bedroom home with a gourmet kitchen to die for.

She was self-employed and got to work out of her family room. Her husband was a successful banker and worked for one of the largest banks in Chicago.

Janelle went all the way in school. I mean, all the way. She was in school for so long that Janiece thought school was her career choice. When she finally did graduate, and so-called started working, it was from her home, and Janiece, to this day, didn't get what her job was, although Janelle had broken it down to her five or six times. But Janiece figured it sure was a great-paying career that allowed you to work in your pj's. So she understood why Janelle was always perky and happy.

"Hey, Nellie, what's going on?" she asked, trying to sound just as cheery as Janelle was.

"Nothing too much—I was just calling to see what you were up to and to see if you wanted to hang out for a minute. You know, go to the movies, dinner . . . I want to see that new Sanaa Lathan movie that's out."

"What—you wanna hang out with me? Where's Gregory?" she asked sarcastically.

"Greg is out with the fellas at the game, and I finished some work sooner than I thought, and I wanted to get some air. Why do I have to explain why I wanna spend time with you, Janiece?" she asked, sounding a little upset.

"Calm down, Janelle. Damn, I was just joking," she said quickly. Janelle was older, but she was a big sensitive baby. She would cry at the drop of a hat.

"Oh, okay. So how about it? Are you up for a movie?"

"Girl, I would, but I'm waiting to see if K.P. is gonna call. He was supposed to have something special planned for us tonight," she said, but she wished she had not.

"Again . . ." Janelle said and clicked her tongue. "Janiece, when are you gonna stop waiting around for this clown? He's a two-timing loser," she said, with anger in her voice.

"Come on, Nellie, don't start. You know how I feel about K.P., and you know we've been through this a million times. What I do is my business."

"Yeah, I know, and you know how I feel about my baby sister fucking someone's husband," she said unsympathetically.

Janiece really didn't want to continue the conversation if they went through the same old sermon about her and Kerry.

"Okay, Janelle, here we go. You wanna reprimand me again, go right ahead. You wanna bash K.P. again, go right ahead. It's not like you're gonna say something new," Janiece said, rolling her eyes. She wished she hadn't picked up the damn phone and was about a minute from hanging up.

"You are so stubborn and thickheaded, just like your daddy was."

"Aw, please, Janelle, he was *your* daddy too, you heifer, and I've never disregarded what you've said. I just want you to know that I will leave K.P. alone when I'm good and ready. There's nothing you can say to make me change. I love him, and that's that, so leave it alone."

"And if he loved you, you wouldn't have to sit around waiting to see if he is or if he isn't gonna call. If he loved or respected his wife, he wouldn't be fucking around with you. So if you want to continue to wait for that loser, go right ahead; be my guest. I have nothing more to say about it," she said and blew out a breath of air.

"Good," Janiece said, relieved and hoping she'd leave it alone. She thought that would be the end of it, but, of course, it wasn't.

"I just can't understand for the life of me why a beautiful young woman like you would settle for such crap. You can have any guy you want, but you put up with K.P.'s stank behind. I don't get that, Jai," she said, now, sounding like their mother.

"So stop trying to get it, Mrs. Perfect. We all can't be like you. Do you feel better now that you've told me straight?" Janiece asked, irritated.

"Come on, Jai. Don't, sweetie. I didn't call you to argue or tell you straight. I just wanted to hang out with you. I want you to be happy, and I just think you deserve way more in a man than being on standby," she said tenderly.

Janiece knew her sister meant well, but her life was her life. Janiece couldn't help that she was in love with K.P. She never meant for that to happen, but since it had, she stayed with him. She didn't have any intentions or schemes to ruin his marriage. She just accepted things for what they were, and she would keep going until she couldn't go anymore. All the scolding in the world from Janelle went in one ear and out the other.

Her girlfriend Tia didn't lecture her. Tia stopped bad-mouthing K.P. two years ago when she realized Janiece would do what Janiece wanted to do, and Janiece wished her sister had taken the same approach to her life choices.

"I know where you're coming from. I've heard you the last 2,000 times you have told me, but please, leave it alone. I wish I could just walk away. I wish I could just stop messing with a married man. I wish I could just turn my feelings for K.P. off, but that is not the case. Shit is just not that simple. Understand that I'm not proud of my relationship with him, Nellie. I'm not walking down the streets broadcasting I'm in love with a married man who is two-timing his wife. I just love him, Nellie, and I'm sad without him. I know you think I sound pathetic and stupid, but that's how I feel," she said, speaking honestly to her older sister.

No matter what approach she took with Janelle, there was no common ground with that situation. Janelle wasn't going to show her sister any type of approval or support for her lifestyle with K.P.—she totally hated that about her sister, and she wasn't going to change.

"So the answer is no? You don't wanna go? You wanna wait for Mr. Dawg to call you?"

"No, the answer is not no. Just give me a little while longer to see if he calls, and if he doesn't, I wanna go, okay? Please, sissy, don't give me a hard time," she whined like a little sister would.

"Okay. Fine, you little nutcase. I love you so much, and I just can't comprehend how we came from the same parents. You are twisted, you little retard," she said jokingly. But deep down, she thought her baby sister was crazy to be in love with such a loser. "But you better not take forever. Unlike you, I have a life, and I'm hungry, and K.P. is not gonna put my life on hold too."

"Thanks, Nellie. I'll call you back soon," Janiece said, smiling. She loved her sister and knew that if K.P. came up in any conversation, it would be the same argument, and it didn't make her so angry anymore.

"Yeah, yeah, whatever. Bye," she said and hung up before Janiece could say goodbye. Janiece hopped off the couch and ran to the window again, and still, there was no sign of him. So she redialed his phone, and it went straight to voicemail. She didn't leave another message this time. Then she opened the fridge and fought the urge to fix a sandwich or eat a piece of fruit because she didn't want to ruin her appetite if he came by or if she went out with her sister.

Janiece went back to the sofa, grabbed the remote, and flipped through the channels. She landed on the Encore channel and decided to watch *Love Jones,* one of her favorite movies. It had already been on, but she wanted to finish it anyway. Once the film was over, it was 5:44 p.m., so she reached for the cordless and dialed K.P. once more, but again, the voicemail came on.

She walked to the kitchen window while dialing her sister back and looking through the curtains. Her guest parking stall was still empty. When Janelle picked up, she was glad that her sister didn't wait until seven or eight o'clock for K.P. to call. She was actually surprised that she called back that soon. That was good for Janiece.

"Hey, girl, you're getting better," Janelle teased.

"What are you talking about?" Janiece asked in confusion.

"I thought you'd be waiting for the dawg longer than an hour," she joked.

"Ha-ha, funny—you always got to go there, don't you?"

"I'm just playing. You wanna go? There's a movie that starts at 8:40. We can go to dinner and make that one."

"Yeah, that's cool. I'll be ready in about twenty minutes," Janiece said, looking out the window with a sad look on her face. She was disappointed again that he didn't call like he said he would.

"Okay, then, I'll be there shortly."

"Okay, bye," Janiece said, and they hung up. Janiece went into the bathroom to brush her teeth and fix her hair. She unwrapped her hair, looked at her roots, and shook her head. Then, quickly, she plugged in her flat iron and started dressing.

She put on her jeans, but not her shirt, because she had to put some heat on her roots, so her hair could look halfway decent. She washed her face, then put on some powder and lip gloss. As soon as she put on her shirt, her sister knocked on the door. She looked at her clock and thought, *Damn, she must have done ninety,* but then she realized flat ironing her hair took some time.

Chapter Three

"You're dressed," Janelle teased when she opened the door.

"Yes, I am. Just let me grab my boots and jacket," Janiece said, walking back into the other room and opening her hall closet. The layout of her condo was nice. It's just that the hall closet was near the front door, and she never used the front door unless she checked the mail or wanted quiet with a nice breeze. The parking stalls were in the back, so the back door was used for convenience. She grabbed a pair of tan boots and went into her room to put them on.

"Your place is immaculately clean, as usual. I wish I were as creative as you," Janelle yelled.

"Thank you, and you know I get it from Mom."

"I know. I wished you were this brilliant when it came to picking men," she added.

Janiece rolled her eyes and went back to the living room to say something about her sister's last remark, but she paused and took another look at her sister, thinking how good she looked with her casual clothing, fresh curly hairdo, and French-manicured nails. Her diamond wedding ring sparkled underneath the dim light, and as usual, she had on name-brand boots, a matching handbag, and a nice camel-colored leather jacket. Her makeup, not the cheap stuff Janiece used, looked like a professional did it, Janiece thought as she checked out her sister.

"Hey, are you ready?" Janiece asked with purse and jacket in hand. She was ready, but after taking a good look at Janelle, she wished she had chosen a different outfit.

"Yeah, I'm starving, girl," she said and started to walk toward the door.

"Girl, me too," Janiece said, walking a step behind her. As they made their way to the door, Janiece heard keys on the other side. Someone was coming in. It was the one and only K.P., and they both paused when he entered. When he opened the door, he stood there for an awkward moment before she said anything. He was dressed nicely and had flowers in his hand.

"Hey, baby, we were on our way out for dinner," Janiece said, breaking the silence.

"These are for you," he said, handing her the flowers. "How are you, Janelle?" he asked.

Janelle gave him a weak smile and merely replied that she was good. She didn't bother to ask him how he was doing, but he disclosed the unwanted information to her anyway.

"I'm doing well myself," he said, volunteering conversation. Even though he wasn't one of her favorites, that never stopped him from trying to be friendly. "Look, I can see that I came at a bad time. I was just trying to surprise you," he said to Janiece. He looked at her like he wanted her to forget about her plans with Janelle and allow him to do what he came to do.

"I know, baby, and I am happy that you came, and the flowers are beautiful," she said, admiring them. Janelle sucked her teeth and rolled her eyes. She didn't bother to hide how irritated she was around K.P., but Janiece didn't pay her any mind.

"Look, baby, you can come with us. We all can go to dinner," she said like that was an excellent idea, and Janelle looked at her like she was insane.

"Look, I'll be downstairs," Janelle interrupted and opened the door. "And hurry up, Jai, because I'm hungry," she barked and shut the door behind her after giving K.P. another evil look.

"Look, K.P., I'm sorry about her," Jai said, apologizing for her sister's behavior.

"It's okay. You don't have to apologize for her. I know and understand why she hates me. I told you in the beginning not to tell her that I was married, Jai."

"I had to tell her. I can't lie to my family. Not to my big sister. It's bad enough my father died with that lie. He was crazy about you, and if he had known—"

K.P. cut her off. "Baby, don't go there, okay? Just go to dinner with your sister, and I'll be here when you get back," he said and kissed her on the forehead.

"You'll wait for me?" she asked, surprised. Although she waited for him all the time, she never pressured him to do the same.

"Of course, I will. Dinner shouldn't take that long," he said.

"Okay, baby, I'll be back soon. Do you want me to bring you something?"

"No, thanks. Kimberly cooked today," he said.

"Oh," she said and headed for the door.

"Hurry back, baby. I miss you," he said, coming up behind her and touching her waist. He kissed her neck, and Janiece knew what he wanted.

"I won't be long," she said and walked away. She wasn't smiling anymore because the name Kimberly thundered in her ears and jabbed into her stomach.

When she got in the car, Janelle didn't say anything. They rode to the restaurant in silence. Once they got there, they ordered their drinks, and the conversation came alive. Janiece knew not to mention or say anything about K.P., so she refrained from bringing up his name.

Although she wanted to vent about him telling her nonsense about his wife cooking for him, she declined.

They were on their second glass of wine, and the server hadn't taken their dinner orders yet. Janiece was starting to get a little edgy. She didn't want to make it obvious, but she didn't want to keep K.P. waiting too long. She kept looking at her watch and looking around.

"Where's the waitress?" she asked, searching the room once more.

"Calm down, Jai. He'll be there when you get home. You waited all day for him; he can wait a couple of hours," Janelle said and sipped her drink.

"I'm not worried about him, Nellie. I'm just hungry," she lied. Her appetite was the last thing on her mind. She *was* worried about K.P.

"You're a liar. I know you," Janelle said, laughing. "There's the waitress. I'll call her over." She waved her hand to get the server's attention. She came over, and they ordered their food. They talked and laughed, but Janiece was getting anxious because the food still hadn't arrived.

They ordered another glass of Merlot, and Janiece excused herself to go to the ladies' room. She didn't have to go, but she wanted to call K.P. and give him an update. She tried her condo, but he didn't pick up. Then she called his phone, and it went straight to voicemail again. She redialed her home and almost broke into a sweat when she got no answer. Finally, she calmed herself and checked the mirror because she did not want to go back to the table looking stressed.

When she got to the table, their meals were there. She nibbled and poked at her food, and then she asked the server for a box to go. Janelle began to shake her head.

"What, Nellie?" she asked, wondering what she was doing wrong.

"You're pathetic, you know that?" she asked, looking at Janiece like she was a loser.

"What, Nellie? What now?" she asked.

"You waited all day for that sack of shit, and you can't allow him to wait a couple of hours for you to have dinner with your sister?" she asked, trying not to raise her voice. Janiece knew her sister well and could tell that she was incensed.

"Janelle, why do you have to intensify everything? I came out with you, the service was slow, and yes, I don't want to keep him waiting too long. What's wrong with that?" she asked, and Janelle looked at her like she wanted to slap her simple face.

"There's nothing wrong with not wanting to impose on someone's time, but you've waited more than he has in this relationship. What . . .? I'm supposed to be grateful to you because you made this small sacrifice to come when all you've been doing is looking at your watch ever since we sat down. I couldn't enjoy our time together because your body is here, but your mind is on Ninety-Fifth Street.

"Our parents didn't raise us to be so needy and dependent. Yet, you walk around like you haven't a clue that this man is walking all over you. How could you enjoy living with such bullshit? I mean, sitting around all day waiting for him to call you, and he drops by when it's convenient for him, and you have to stop what you've planned to cater to him.

"I can't believe you, Jai. You couldn't even sit here and taste your damn food," she said, and then she stopped midsentence and shook her head. "You know what? Forget it. It's useless even to try to get through that thick skull of yours," she said and waved for the server.

She didn't make eye contact with Janiece. She just waited for the server to come back with the bill. Janiece

tried to hand her forty dollars for her part, but she didn't take it. She looked over the bill, put ninety dollars in the black case, and then stood up. She didn't take her unfinished meal, and Janiece left her food too. They rode back to her condo in silence.

When they got there, to Janiece's disappointment, the Escalade was gone. *Damn,* she thought to herself when she opened the door to get out of her sister's Benz. She held the door open for a moment to see if Janelle would say anything, but she didn't. As soon as she shut the door, Janelle pulled off, something she'd never done before. She would always wait for Janiece to get safely inside, but she was so appalled and disgusted with Janiece that she didn't wait this time, Janiece figured.

Janiece climbed the steps to her floor and opened the storm door. She unlocked the dead bolt, went inside, and she hoped K.P. only ran to the store or something like that and that he'd be back. She took off her jacket and sat at the dining room table to remove her boots. Then she looked up and noticed a note hanging on the television, causing her to smile. She undressed and showered, then put on her pajamas. Finally, she snatched the message from the tube and climbed into bed to read it.

She reached over to double-check the alarm to ensure it was on and set for the following day. Then she got cozy and comfortable to read what she thought would be a sweet love note from her baby, but instead, it was the actual words of a selfish asshole that read:

Oh, so I guess you expected me to wait all night for you. I guess hanging out with your sister is more important than our time together. I'll remember that when I try to get out on a Sunday to do something special for you the next time. I hope your long dinner and outing with your sister was better than spending time with yo' man. See if I ever get out on another Sunday night for you. You know Sundays are for my family.

K.P.

She was in tears when she finished reading that nasty note he had written. She wasn't gone that long, she thought to herself, and it wasn't her fault that it took as long as it did. The restaurant was crowded. She sobbed and wished she had someone to talk to. She tried calling her girlfriend Tia, but she wasn't home. She tried her phone, but, of course, she was over at her man's house and couldn't be there for her.

She knew damn well not to call Janelle because Janelle was the last person she could talk to about K.P., so she got up and poured herself a glass of wine. Frustrated, she hit the PLAY button on her mini system in her room to listen to her favorite 112 CD. She read the note several more times, wondering how on earth she could be so madly in love with this man, and finally ripped it to pieces. After finishing her glass of wine, Janiece buried herself under the covers and cried herself to sleep.

Chapter Four

That week dragged, and it was a depressing workweek for her too because she hadn't talked to her sister or K.P. She called him a few times and even took a chance calling him at his office. She left him a ton of messages on his voicemail, and she never heard a word back from him.

She was too afraid to call her sister. She didn't know what to say to Janelle. She had a hard time apologizing to her sister when she felt she didn't do anything wrong. Why her sister was letting her lifestyle make her so angry was beyond her, so she didn't know what to say to make Janelle lay off.

She wasn't breaking up with K.P., or at least she hoped they were not breaking up, so she didn't have the answer to make Janelle feel better. Janiece just couldn't stand when they were not talking, especially then, because her weekend would be extra lonely with her and K.P. not speaking either.

She called her girlfriend Tia, but she had plans to go to Joliet with Rick to a wedding for one of his family members. She was depressed and sad and didn't look forward to her weekend. She checked her phone all day, hoping K.P. would call.

On her train ride, Janiece imagined going home, and he'd be there waiting for her like he usually would be on Fridays, with dinner and soft music playing. But, although she hoped, she knew deep down inside that that was a fat chance.

She got off the metro and waited for the rails to go up. That's when she saw a truck in her guest parking stall, but it wasn't K.P.'s truck. *Maybe he got a new vehicle,* she thought and smiled as she got closer to her building. Just then, the aroma of grilled meat penetrated her nose. As she got closer, she realized one of her neighbors was having a cookout or a party.

There were people outside on the back porch and standing around. It was warm for that September evening, so they were grilling, and it smelled fabulous. She walked up the steps of her back porch, and everyone spoke and gave friendly smiles. As Janiece got up to her door, she dug around in her purse for her keys.

She felt everyone's eyes on her, so she put her bags down so that she could search for her keys with both hands. She wanted to hurry and get on the other side of the door because she was starting to feel like an idiot standing there, not being able to find her keys.

She suddenly remembered they were in her work bag, so she grabbed that bag and quickly retrieved her keys. She unlocked the storm door, but before she could get the dead bolt unlocked, she heard an unfamiliar voice from behind her say hello.

"Hi . . . How are you?" she stuttered after turning around and seeing who it was. He was gorgeous, fine as hell—beautiful if truth be told, she thought to herself.

"I'm fine," he said, and she thought, *You can say that again.* "Do you need some help?" he asked because it looked apparent that she was having a little trouble getting into her place.

"No no no, I'm fine. I got it," she said and unlocked the dead bolt and opened the door.

"Are you sure? You look like you could use a little help," he said, offering her some assistance again.

"No, I'm certain. I got it," she quickly replied and gave him a friendly smile. She had to get inside of her condo before she took him up on his offer to help her have an orgasm. She stepped inside and quickly shut the door. Then she realized she had left her work bag outside. Next, she heard a little tap on the door, and, of course, it was Mr. Too Fine with her bag.

"Here—you forgot this," he said, handing over the bag.

"Thanks, I was gonna come back for that," she said, trying not to look so stupid for forgetting the bag he had offered to help her with in the first place.

"Sure you were," he said smiling. He stood there and smiled, and after a brief moment of awkward silence, he spoke again. "My name is Isaiah, and this little cookout is for me. If you're not doing anything, I'm sure Iyeshia wouldn't mind if you came over," he said, offering an invitation to a party that his woman was throwing for him. Not only was he fine, but he was also cocky, she thought.

"No, no, thanks. I don't know Iyeshia too well. Plus, she may not like you inviting other girls to a bash she's putting down for you," she replied, giving him that *you got your nerve* look. She already had one man that she loved that belonged to someone else in her life. She didn't want to start a list of unavailable men, plus this one's woman lived right across the hall. That would be just pushing it to the limit.

"Why would she mind?" he asked like he was clueless.

"Duh, this looks like a jamming shindig. A girl wouldn't go through all this trouble for her man to be asking other chicks to his party," she said, giving him the *get-lost* nod, and he laughed. What was funny? She didn't see the humor in what she had said.

"Well, first, Iyeshia is not my woman. The dude over there by the cooler is her man," he said, pointing at someone else at the party, and she peeped out the door a little to see who he talked about.

"Second, I'm her twin brother. I know you can't tell because we're not identical, but I think we favor," he said, flashing that beautiful smile again. "Lastly, this party is my welcome home party. I just recently came home from Iraq."

"Oh, my bad," Janiece said, looking foolish.

"No, that's cool. You didn't know. I can see you and my sister don't talk much," he remarked, and her thoughts were . . . *Not at all since I never knew she had a fine-ass brother like you.*

"No, not really. I mean, we speak and chat on occasion, but with our schedules, I guess we barely see each other."

"Well, I think it's time for you to get to know your neighbor, Miss . . ." he said and waited for her to give her name.

"Jai . . . I mean . . . Janiece, but . . . most people call me . . . Jai," she said, with stuttered words.

"Janiece, I like that, but if you'd prefer Jai, I can call you Jai," he said as if he would be talking to her regularly.

"Jai, or Janiece, whichever you'd like. I don't mind either way."

"Well, Janiece, will you be joining us?"

"Thanks, but I think I'll pass. I'm a little tired, but welcome home, Isaiah. I hope you enjoy your party," she said, pushing the door to signal him to leave, but he kept going.

"I'll try, but you know, I'd enjoy my party a little more if you'd come. Anyway, can I change your mind? My mom makes a slamming potato salad. It would be a crime if you missed out on some good food and free liquor," he joked. She was so tempted to say yes, but she was tired. And she wanted to call K.P. again. And on top of that, she knew she was looking torn up. He looked so good, and she really wanted to say okay, but still, she resisted.

"No, I'm sorry. Maybe another time because I had a rough week, and today was not good either. I just wanna relax," she said, giving him a fake yawn, and then she guessed he got the picture that she couldn't be persuaded because he backed off.

"Okay, Janiece, I can see that you're dead set on staying in and missing out on a great social event, but—I'll tell you what. I'll bring you a plate. Can I at least feed you?" he asked so sweetly.

You can feed me, you can lick me, you can spank me, you can do whatever you want to me with yo' fine ass were the thoughts going through her mind, so she couldn't turn down the plate. For one, she was starving, and the food smelled so damn good.

"Okay. A plate would be great; just make sure no pork or beef."

"No pork or beef? What else is left if there are no ribs or steak?" he asked, looking at her like she were insane.

"Chicken," she smiled.

"Oh yeah, of course," he smiled back at her. "Whatever works for you . . . I'll be back with that plate soon," he promised, finally allowing their conversation to end. He smiled a beautiful smile and then walked down the steps.

Janiece shut the door and ran to the bathroom. Her bladder was about to burst. While she washed her hands, she looked in the mirror and noticed how horrible she looked. Her hair had almost four inches of new growth, and her makeup didn't look anything like it did that morning when it was freshly applied.

Quickly, she put her hair up and started the shower. But first, she went over to her machine and hit the PLAY button to listen to her messages. There were none from her sister and not one from K.P., which was a disappointment. She turned on the music and went to take her shower.

After she showered, Janiece put on her SpongeBob pajama pants, with a yellow T-shirt and her thick socks, because for some reason, her feet always stayed cold. She mostly listened to the Smooth R&B station, but she flipped through and landed on the hip-hop station because she needed some Vi, Lil Wayne, Jay-Z, or T.I. since she was sad and didn't want to hear any love songs.

She grabbed her phone and redialed K.P.'s number, and when she got his voicemail, she didn't bother to waste her words on another hopeless, unanswered message to him. Instead, she threw her phone on the couch, cranked up the volume, and started dancing around her living room to Jay-Z's "On to the Next One" by herself. Then she pressed the MUTE button because she thought she heard the door. She stood still for a moment and listened to the knocking again. Finally, she went to answer it, and when she moved the curtain aside, she saw Isaiah. She had forgotten that quickly that he was bringing her a plate.

"Hey, here's that plate I promised you," he said when she opened the door.

"Thanks," she replied, reaching out for it, but he didn't give it to her. She sensed that maybe he wanted to come in or something because he wasn't handing over the plate.

"Cute pj's—SpongeBob is the man," he said, shifting the conversation to something other than the plate that he refused to give her.

"Yeah, he is quite the character, and these are my favorite. They are very comfortable," she added, giving him some conversation. That's what it seemed he wanted.

"Yeah, and they look comfy too," he said, still holding the plate hostage. "Grapes?" he asked, looking over her shoulder. Her kitchen was decorated with grapes because they were purple, like most of the décor in her condo.

"Yeah, grapes—purple happens to be my favorite color."

"Really? I like black myself, but I guess purple is cool since you're a female," he said, still not handing over the food.

"Would you like for me to take that for you?" she asked, nodding her head toward the plate. The aroma was driving her insane, and she wanted to get it so she could eat. She was instantly hungry as hell when she opened the door, allowing the smell of the grill to hit her nose again.

"Oh, I'm sorry. Here you go," he said, finally handing it to her. "You are just so beautiful. I forgot what I came over for," he said, and she knew he had to be the biggest liar she had ever met. She had her hair tied up in a wrap cap, and she wore no makeup, just gloss on her lips. She didn't get compliments that often, but to get one looking like a wrecked ship was a first.

"Come on, Isaiah, I know you've been over in the Middle East for a while, but beautiful?—you're pushing it. It's not the last call," she joked.

"No, you are beautiful, gorgeous. Nice, smooth complexion and the sexiest eyes I've had the pleasure of looking into in a long time," he said, sounding and looking genuine.

What's up with this cat? she thought to herself. *Is he trying to get some booty?* She'd heard about men coming back from military deployments. It's like a man coming home from jail, and they'll say or do anything to get it.

"Look, Isaiah, I appreciate the plate, and it was so nice to meet you. Hopefully, I'll see you around when you are sober. That way, you can be a li'l more honest," she said, letting him know that she wasn't falling for that mess.

"Look, Janiece, I'm not drunk. I know what I'm saying, and I don't have time to be out here playing with you. There are three other women here tonight that my sister, mom, and boy thought would be a good idea for me to meet. So getting with a woman is not my mission. I'm being honest. You are beautiful, as natural as you are right now, with the hair scarf and glossed lips. That is beautiful to me," he said, looking at her like he had just found a prize. She was shocked and flattered at the same time. No man had ever complimented her that way before.

"Oh, I'm sorry if I insulted you. I'm just not used to getting compliments like that, especially looking like this," she said honestly.

"Next time, just say thanks. Whenever you get a compliment, just say thank you because what you see is not always what other people see."

"You are right again. I didn't mean to—" she tried to say, but he stopped her.

"It's all good. You enjoy your food and have a good evening, Ms. Janiece," he said and headed down the steps.

"Thank you," she yelled to his back.

"No problem," he yelled over his shoulder without looking back. She shut the door and went over to the counter to see what was under the foil. Man, it was homemade mac and cheese, potato salad, baked beans, greens, and grilled chicken. In another small piece of foil was a slice of pound cake. The plate was still warm, so she grabbed a fork, went to the dining table, and dug in.

She ate and got full too quickly, which was good because she had enough left over for the next day. Then Janiece went back into the kitchen, and when she was about to put the foil back on the plate, she noticed that it was not a paper plate.

She thought to herself, another way to see him again, and she smiled. She had to catch herself from going there. "Girl, stop it," she said aloud to herself. She poured herself a glass of wine and went back into the living room, where she sat on the couch, grabbed the remote, and turned the music back on. She landed on the Smooth R&B station, sipped her wine, and reread a few magazines.

Before she knew it, it was ten after ten, and she looked for her phone. It had been two hours, eleven articles, and three glasses of wine since she last called K.P. She was so mad that he didn't at least text her to say one word.

She hopped off the couch, went into her room, and got dressed. She had to make a trip out to the south suburbs. She looked out the window, and the black Avalanche was still in her guest parking stall, but she didn't care. It wasn't like she needed it.

She grabbed her jacket, purse, and keys, then headed out the door. When she was locking the door, people were coming out of the condo across the way. They spoke as they were going down the steps. They were two girls and one guy. She proceeded to lock the door, and Isaiah came out next and went down the steps. When she got to the bottom, he talked to one of the girls who had just passed her. That made her a little jealous, but she went on like she hadn't known who Isaiah was.

She drove out to the south suburbs, pulled on his block, and just sat in her car for about ten minutes watching his house. His truck wasn't there, but his wife's car was. She redialed his phone because she figured if he weren't home, he'd answer, but he didn't. So she sat there and looked at their lovely house and his wife's nice Jaguar and thought about how Kimberly had all the things she didn't—including K.P.

She sat there crying and cussing him out. She talked shit about how much she hated him and how she wouldn't allow him to hurt her like that anymore. She damned him and yelled in her car until she was exhausted. Then she grabbed her phone and called him one more time, and again, he ignored her call, which made her want to go up to his door and ring the bell.

She wanted to tell his wife how her no-good-ass husband had been fucking her for the past five years and

that the bastard was so selfish that he was mad because she took too long having dinner with her sister . . .
but she didn't. She couldn't bring herself to get out of the
car. It would have been useless telling the wife because
she knew. She had to have a clue that he was messing
around, and she wasn't about to go anywhere.

Why would she? She had what she wanted—a big,
lovely house in a nice neighborhood, and she had a nice
ride. She wasn't going to let Janiece's words of truth
about her husband stop her from living the lifestyle she
had grown accustomed to. "What would be the point?"
Janiece asked herself.

So, she just sat there and noticed the clock. It was
twenty after twelve, and K.P.'s Escalade was still not
in the driveway. He wasn't with her, so he had to be
somewhere doing something. *Maybe he and the wife are
out,* she thought. Then again, his truck could have been
inside of their garage, but she was exhausted from trying
to figure it out.

She calmed herself down and dried her tears. Finally,
she started her engine and drove back to Ninety-Fifth.

Chapter Five

It looked like the party was over and everyone was gone, but the black Avalanche was still in her guest parking stall. She dragged herself up the steps and put the key into the storm door keyhole, and before she could put the key into the dead bolt, she heard the door behind her open. She thought to herself, *What is wrong with this dude?* She was not in the mood to talk. She just wanted to get inside and cry. She continued to unlock the door and tried to walk in, but, of course, he said something.

"Do you always make a lot of noise at this hour?" he asked.

"Noise? What are you talking about? All I'm doing is unlocking my door," she said with attitude.

"Oh, I'm sorry, Janiece. My ears are just sensitive, and I hear everything. I heard you coming up the steps," he explained.

"I'm sorry if I woke you coming up the steps. Next time, I'll tiptoe," she said, giving him more attitude.

"Janiece, are you okay?" he asked with concern.

"No, I'm not okay right now, but I'll be fine," she said, going into her place. He came out of his sister's condo and was at her door before she could shut it.

"Janiece, I'm a good listener if you wanna talk," he said through the storm door. Since the weather hadn't broken yet, she still had the screen in, so she couldn't close the door and pretend she didn't hear him. She wanted to talk and tell somebody how she felt, but she didn't want to talk to him. She didn't know him enough to be telling him her situation, especially about her married lover.

"No, thanks, Isaiah. I'll be fine," she said, trying to sound convincing.

"Are you sure?" he asked, and then she invited him in. She didn't want to talk about her problems, but she didn't want to be by herself either.

"Listen, I really don't want to talk about my situation. I'm too tired to rehash my problems," she said while taking off her jacket. She led him into the living room and offered him a seat. Then she went and put her pj's back on and came out and offered him some hot chocolate.

"Sure, I'd love some. I haven't had hot chocolate in a long time," he said with another flash of his pretty pearls.

His smile is so beautiful for a man, she thought. Almost as beautiful as K.P.'s. She put the kettle on the burner, pulled two mugs from the cabinet and two saucers, and grabbed the box of Swiss Miss out of the food cabinet. Afterward, she went back to the couch and chatted until the kettle whistled. Then she excused herself from the conversation to fix the hot chocolate.

"Would you like marshmallows?" she yelled from the kitchen.

"Sure, and a splash of milk if you have it," he requested.

"I sure do. That's exactly the way I like it," she said and returned to the living room with two perfect mugs of cocoa. She sat on the love seat so that she could look at him while they talked. First, he told her about his military career and how he only had one more year before getting out for good. Then he spoke about his dad's car dealership and how his dad wanted him to come back and be a part of the family business, which he was not interested in.

He was an electrical engineer, and that's the job he wanted to be in when he got out. He had his master's and went into the military as an officer and worked in that field. Working in the car business was his dad's dream for him, but not his.

He did most of the talking, and she asked many questions to keep the focus off her uninteresting life. She enjoyed hearing about his military experiences and the things in Iraq when he was deployed. They talked about his and his sister's childhood, which made her realize how Iyeshia could have a different car every week. After three a.m., he decided to go back to his sister's, and she walked him to the door. He paused.

"What do you have planned tomorrow night?"

"Huh? What do you mean?" she asked, sounding retarded.

"Tomorrow—evening—what—are—your—plans?—Do—you—have—something—going—on?" he asked again. This time he pronounced each word slowly as if he were talking to a deaf person, and they laughed.

"Oh, I'm sorry. You kinda threw me off for a minute. I don't have any plans for tomorrow evening. Come to think of it, I haven't had plans on a Saturday evening in a whole minute," she said, thinking out loud.

"I don't see why not. A gorgeous gal like you should have brothers lined up at the door," he teased.

"Man, please, I barely get a hello in the grocery store," she said.

"Well, that is certainly hard for me to believe," he said on a serious note. They both got quiet for a moment, and then he broke the silence after getting up his nerve.

"Well, Ms. Janiece, if you don't have any plans for tomorrow evening, would you like to go out with me?"

"You're asking me out? You're joking, right?" she asked with a smirk.

"No, I'm not joking, and yes, I'm asking you out," he said, waiting for her to answer, but she didn't right away.

"What is it . . .? Do you have a boyfriend, or are you seeing someone?"

Holding up her hands in surrender, she quickly stopped him. "No . . . not . . . no, I don't have a boyfriend . . . Look, never mind. I'd like to go out with you," she told him. Of course, K.P. wasn't her boyfriend, and she was still single and could go on a date if she wanted to. So she had made a promise not to go out with other guys. *Hell, he's married and has a life,* she thought.

"Okay, that's good. Can I have your number so that I can call you tomorrow?"

"Yeah, sure," she said and grabbed the notepad from the fridge. She wrote down her cell and home phone numbers. "Here you go," she said, handing him the piece of paper.

"What time would be good for you?" he asked.

"I dunno. Whatever time is good for you," she said, and she knew that would get them nowhere. "How about you call me tomorrow, and we'll decide then?"

"Okay, that sounds good," he said and reached for the doorknob. "Listen, thanks for the hot chocolate. It was good."

"Not a problem."

"And, Janiece, I am happy to see you smiling. Whatever was bothering you earlier, I hope it works out."

"It will. It's just gonna take some time."

"Well, again, it's been a pleasure, and I'll call you tomorrow," he said and touched her cheek. His touch was so soft it sent a small tsunami through her body. She knew then that it was definitely time to say good night.

"Okay, good night, Isaiah," she said, and he left. She shut the door and blew out the candles she had burning. After she crawled into bed, she snuggled under the covers.

She prayed and asked God to forgive her for the mistakes she had made and requested strength. She smiled at the thought of having a date on Saturday night with a fine man like Isaiah after five years. She imagined how great it would be and finally drifted off to sleep.

Chapter Six

When Janiece woke up, she felt good. She had a profound and good night's sleep, and she felt marvelous. She went to the bathroom, washed her face, and brushed her teeth. Afterward, she went into the kitchen and poured a glass of orange juice, and she couldn't resist looking out the window. The black Avalanche was gone, and her stall was back to being empty. Janiece never had company unless it was K.P., her sister, or Tia, so she was pretty used to seeing the stall empty. She looked over at the grape clock on the kitchen wall. It was 9:17 a.m., and *that* was a first for her. She never got up on a Saturday before noon.

She drank her OJ, turned on some music, and began dusting a little before running the vacuum. Her place was always clean. Nothing was out of place because she was meticulous about how it looked. She made her bed and then walked to the closet to go through her clothes to see what items could be returned to get some cash to get her hair and nails done for her date.

She was very low on cash, and her credit cards were not an option. She was trying to turn over a new lease on her finances to purchase her condo. It had been on the market for two years, and she wanted to be able to buy it, but she had to get her credit in order. She loved her building and where it was located. She just prayed to God every month that it wouldn't sell, and, so far, she had been blessed. All of her neighbors owned their units, so she was sure she'd be next.

She was getting nowhere on her search for merchandise to return. She not only needed a touchup, but she also needed her nails filled and her eyebrows done. And all she could come up with was maybe enough for a shampoo and style, and that wasn't going to cut it. She debated with herself and was dead set on not putting anything on her charge card, but she was starting to feel desperate.

She went to her computer and went online to check her account to see what items had cleared and what she had left, but she just couldn't afford to put money toward hair and nails. She hated the thought of using her charge card, and the only other option would be to call Janelle, and she really, really *didn't* want to do that.

But her date with Isaiah was so important to her, and after he had seen her looking a mess, she had to look good for their date. She was sad that she was in such a bind that she couldn't afford to get these things done. K.P. was supposed to give her the money on Tuesday to have everything taken care of, so catching an attitude with her was quite convenient for his wallet, but that's okay, she thought to herself.

Just when she was about to get upset about the situation, her phone rang. She got excited because she thought maybe she had talked K.P. up in her mind and she could get him to give her the money like he said he would, but when she looked at the caller ID, she noticed that it was a number she didn't recognize. So she started not to answer it, but she went ahead because it wasn't an 800 number.

"Hello," she said in a soft tone.

"Hello, beautiful," the voice on the other end said, a voice she was unfamiliar with.

"Hello," she repeated herself.

"Janiece," he said.

"Yes," she replied, still having a hard time catching the voice. She didn't get too many calls, and especially not from men.

"How are you?"

"I'm fine. Who is this?" she asked with a puzzled look on her face.

"Isaiah," he answered.

"Oh, hey," she said, changing her tone to a sexier one.

"Good morning. How did you sleep?"

"Like a rock," she said honestly. She had slept better than she had slept all week long.

"Good to hear."

"How are you?" she asked, taking a seat on her bed. She was delighted to hear from him and was surprised he was up so early.

"I'm great," he said, upbeat.

"I see you're up early."

"Yeah, I had to get out early to get me a phone, so you could have a way to reach me."

"Oh really?"

"Yes, and I guess my family too," he said with a grin.

"Yes, that would be a good thing. At least your mom can get a hold of you now," she joked.

"Yep, my mom's gon' be calling me," he joked back. "So, Ms. Janiece, have you thought about where you wanna go?"

"Well, not really. I'm just walking around wondering what to wear." She moved to her closet again, still trying to figure out what items she could return.

"I'm sure you'll come up with something fantastic."

"Well, I'm glad you have so much confidence in me," she smiled.

"To be honest, you looked good in your SpongeBob outfit," he said, and they laughed again.

"Hey, don't be making fun of my pj's."

"All right, all right. But I'm looking forward to seeing you, and I'm sure you'll be beautiful," he said, and she blushed. Now, more than ever, she *had* to get her hair and eyebrows done at least. She looked at her nails. She knew that she could buff them and get away on that part, and if worst came to worst, she could pluck her brows to clean them up.

"So what time are you picking me up?"

"Well, I have some ideas on where I wanna take you, so I'd say around six. Would that be cool?"

"Six? Wow, that's kinda early," she said. She figured about eight or nine.

"Well, I figured if we start early, we'd have time to do some things, but if that is too early—"

"No, six is fine. I'm glad I asked," she said. She was happy to talk to him, and she was eager to see him.

"Have you eaten?" he asked.

"No, why?"

"I'm going to be back at my sister's soon, and The Original House of Pancakes got some slamming food," he said, and Janiece smiled because that was her spot. She and her girlfriend Tia met there a lot before Tia and Rick fell so madly in love. Now she could barely get in a lunch with her girlfriend.

"Man, yes, that's one of my favorite spots," Janiece said excitedly. The name of the restaurant woke up her stomach.

"Are you dressed?"

"No, still in my pj's," she said. She was so mad her hair was in such a terrible state because she couldn't get dressed and ready to go in less than an hour. She needed to put the flat iron to her head.

"I'll tell you what. I can pick something up for you if that's okay?" he asked, hoping she'd say yes. He really couldn't wait to see her again. Six o'clock was over six hours away.

"You love to see a sista looking rough, don't you?"

"Man, come on, you look fine."

"If you say so, but you know a sista can't resist The Original House of Pancakes, so you will just have to look at the old monster Janiece one more time," she joked.

"It will be my pleasure," he said so sweetly that she smiled. She told him what she wanted, and he verified that she had his number, and then she hung up. By now, she was going out of her mind and was left with no choice but to call Janelle. Isaiah had seen the worst side of her, and she had to clean up for their date. Nervously, she dialed Janelle's number. Janelle answered on the third ring.

"Hello," she said, sounding half-asleep.

"Hey, Nellie, did I wake you?"

"Yes," she answered.

"I'm sorry. I can call you back later," she said, getting ready to hang up. She didn't want to ask her while she was half-asleep.

"No, sweetie, I'm good. Are you okay?" she asked, with concern, sounding exactly like their late mom.

"Yes, I'm fine."

"Are you sure?" she asked again, genuinely concerned about her little sister. She knew that Janiece had lots of things going on that she didn't share with her, and she knew that her sister kept a lot from her for the sake of not hearing her fuss so much.

"Yes, I'm good. How are you?"

"Good. Same ole, same ole," she replied.

"Look, Nellie, I know we had some words last weekend," she said nervously.

"Chile, please, don't worry about that. I know how stubborn and thickheaded you can be, just like Daddy, so I'm not even thinking about that."

"So you're not mad at me?"

"Jai, please. I can't stay mad at you. You're my baby sister. I just need to accept that you are a grown woman, and I can't keep treating you like a child, whether I agree or disagree with your lifestyle. It's none of my business."

"Oh really?" she said, surprised.

"Yes, really, so what's up?"

"Well, I hate to ask you this, and you know ordinarily, I wouldn't, but I need a huge favor," Janiece said fretfully. She never asked for anything, even if she were down to hot dogs and water. She just didn't borrow.

"What is it?"

"Well, Janelle, I promise I will pay you back," she said, and Janelle was OK with giving her anything she needed.

"How much do you need?" Janelle asked. Janiece knew she was glad to help with anything. There had been times when she offered to do things for her, but Janiece wouldn't take it. She'd have to give her significant birthday gifts to provide her with any type of monetary contributions. That way, she wouldn't refuse it. She'd try, but she'd have no choice.

"Well, first, I need it because I have a date."

"A date? Shit, I'm up now, and you are on some bullshit. When—what—who—how? Jai, answer me," she demanded.

"A guy I met last night."

"Get out. No way. I'm gonna kick your ass if you're lying. I'm on my way over there because I need to see your lying face," Janelle said in disbelief. She knew her sister, and Janiece knew she would not be easily convinced.

"Wait wait wait, Nellie. Let me tell you why I need the money," Janiece tried to say because she wanted to get the borrowing money part out of the way before Isaiah got there with their breakfast.

"Chile, who cares what you need the money for. You have a date. This's better than the Michael Jordan's comeback," she said, mimicking Isaiah Washington from the movie *Love Jones*, and they both laughed.

"Nellie, come on. He asked me out for tonight, and my hair is nappy, and I need my nails filled, and my eyebrows look like the Beastmaster. As rough as I look, can you believe he asked me out? So I got to get cleaned up better than this. I *will* pay you back, I promise," she explained like a little sister begging for candy.

"Chile, please, if it's for a date with a man other than that ugly-ass K.P., I'll get your hair, nails, feet, eyebrows, teeth, legs waxed—hell, I'll get you a new wardrobe. Give me an hour, and I'll pick you up. We're going to have a sisters' day out, my treat," she promised. She was more excited than Janiece. "And . . . I want to know every detail, blow by blow. Don't leave *one* thing out."

"Okay, but, Nellie, I'm really broke. I'm gonna need a few dollars for my purse too if you can. Momma always said we at least have to have cab fare," Janiece said. She was already pushing it with her hair and nails, but she knew she'd pay back every dime.

"Jai, don't worry. I gotcha. Whatever you need, I'll give it to you. Greg and I aren't hurting over here, and you know all you have to do is ask. You need to stop acting like Daddy, like you too good to ask for help."

"Thanks, Nellie, but I promise I'll pay you back—every cent."

"Janiece, stop it. You are *not* getting ready to put me in the poorhouse over something like this. Now, get ready, and I'll be over in about an hour," she said, and they hung up.

Janiece was glad she broke down and called her sister. She knew that she would do it, but she just had that pride, and it was hard for her to call and ask. But she was glad she did because now, she would be looking fantabulous for Isaiah.

She ran to the shower to be ready when her sister got there, but she forgot Isaiah was still coming. As soon as she stepped out of the shower, her phone rang. Then she heard knocking at the door.

She grabbed the phone, walked to the door, opened it, and talked into the phone, telling Isaiah to have a seat. After that, she quickly threw on some shorts and a T-shirt after she lotioned up with her Cotton Blossom from Bath and Body Works.

"Hey, the food smells good," she said as she walked into the kitchen. He had found his way around and was putting her food on a plate.

"No, *you* smell good," he said and smiled at her.

"Thank you. It's one of my favorites from BBW."

"BBW?" he asked with a confused look.

"Bath and Body Works."

"Oh, okay. It smells good," he said, and they went to the dining room table to eat. They made small talk and finished their breakfast. He had a mean appetite, that was for sure because he had a giant omelet, four hotcakes, six strips of bacon, four links, and a tall glass of OJ.

"I see you are not shy," she joked.

"I'ma grown-ass man," he kidded.

"So, where are we going this evening?"

"Someplace I'm sure you'll enjoy," he said and winked.

"Okay," she smiled. She didn't want to push. She just would wait. She cleared the table, and he yawned. "You tired?"

"Yes, a little. Still on Iraq time, so I'ma little thrown off," he said and yawned again.

"Well, my sister is on her way, and we're going out for a while. You should go get some sleep because I don't want you yawning on our date," she said, and they giggled. He enjoyed her smile, and she enjoyed his laughter. They couldn't help but look at each other. Janiece was so embarrassed about her eyebrows. She tried to avoid eye contact, but she couldn't resist looking at him.

They paused and were silent until Janiece heard her sister downstairs blowing her horn. She went to the window. Isaiah followed her into the kitchen because he was getting ready to go across the hall to sleep. She grabbed the phone off the wall and told her sister to give her five minutes. She noticed the black Avalanche again while looking out the window.

"Do you know who that truck belongs to?" she asked.

"The Avalanche—"

"Yeah, it's back in my guest parking stall."

"Oh, I'm sorry. My sister told me it should be cool for me to park there. I can move it," he said.

"No, no, it's fine. I was just curious who it belonged to."

"So I'll see you later?" he asked and stroked her cheek. She liked it when he touched her face. His touch was so tender. Even though she and K.P. had a healthy sexual relationship, the tenderness was gone, and she missed that.

"Yes," she said softly. "Six o'clock, right?"

"Right, and I will be on time. I only stay across the hall," he joked.

"I'll be ready," she said with a smile. She was getting excited in more ways than one, and she knew she had to calm down. He yawned again. She could see how tired he was, so she insisted he get some sleep. "Come on, go get some rest now," she urged him.

"Okay, but call me if you want to. You have my number, right?"

"Yes, but I want you to sleep because I don't want you tired later. Call me when you get up."

"Cool," he said and opened the door.

"See you later," she said and closed the door behind him. She ran and slipped on some clothes, grabbed a light jacket, her purse, and keys, and smiled as she locked her door. She looked over at Iyeshia's place and then floated down the steps.

Chapter Seven

When she got into the car, her sister immediately started drilling her. She wanted to know *every* detail, so Janiece gave her the rundown, blow by blow. They spent the whole afternoon together getting beautified. They both got their hair, eyebrows, nails, and toes done. After that, they ate lunch and shopped a little. Janelle ended up getting a few items for herself and Janiece, and she didn't hold back on the spending.

They made it back to Janiece's condo about a quarter to five, so Janiece had to rush up the stairs to shower and get ready. Her hair was done, which would cut down on her getting-ready time, and she was so relieved. Janelle poured them both a glass of wine and turned on the smooth jazz station while helping Janiece get ready.

"No, Jai, don't wear the black ones. Instead, wear the brown ones," she advised.

"You don't think that will be too much brown?" Janiece asked, holding up the brown boot next to her clothes.

"Yeah, you're right. That will definitely be taking the brown a step too far," Janelle said, and they both agreed. Janiece was happy, and she let it show. She walked around in her underwear, bobbing her head to the music, sipping on her wine, and smiling. Janelle looked at her. Her sister looked so much like their father that Janelle couldn't help but think about him.

She didn't want to ruin the moment, so she decided not to comment on their resemblance, because usually when they talked about their parents, they would end up crying. So, Janelle chose to bring up another topic to get her mind off their folks.

"I'm so happy to see you're getting all dolled up for a *single* man," she said and sipped her drink.

"Well, you never know. K.P. lied about being single when we first met," Janiece said, reminding her of how he had deceived her about his home situation. It took him four months to come clean.

"Well, now, you know better. If you find out this man is married or lying about being single, kick his ass to the curb. If I had known Mr. Paxton wasn't single, I definitely would not have allowed you to leave my housewarming with his fake ass," she said, and they slapped five.

Janiece polished off her drink and went into the bathroom to do her makeup because it was twenty minutes 'til six. Janelle stood in the doorway to keep her company while fixing her face and didn't like what she saw.

"Jai, what brand is that?"

"I dunno. I got it at Walgreen's up the street," she said, trying to read the label. It was old, and the words on the label had worn off.

"Hold on," Janelle said and went for her purse. She pulled out her makeup bag and began to take out her MAC, Lancôme, and Clinique products.

"Sit down. Let me introduce you to the *real* stuff," she said, and Janiece let the lid down on the toilet and sat. She was feeling kind of bad because this part she thought she had under control, but when she got up to look in the mirror, she realized she didn't, because she was looking better than she had looked in a long time.

She could tell that she really had on shadow and saw the different shades her sister had applied to her eyes. Her makeup always looked different in the compact, but it all looked like the same color once it was on. Her lips had that pretty frost look that she had seen on other women but never managed to achieve. She felt glamorous and stunning.

"See? I told you to stop buying that cheap mess at Walgreen's."

"Nellie, you know I can't afford to buy those expensive name brands you be wearing," Janiece said, frowning at her. She knew her money was too tight to be spending on expensive cosmetics.

"Yes, you can. Just put a few dollars to the side and buy one item at a time, and eventually, you'll have a complete makeup kit. Plus, it's quality, so it stays on longer, meaning you don't have to reapply it as often. Three tubes of this cheap stuff are one tube of this, so you *can* afford it," she said, and it made more sense.

"Well, I'll definitely keep that in mind," she said, pushing past her to put on her clothes. Her hair and makeup were done, and now she had about a good seven minutes to dress, apply perfume, and slip on some jewelry.

"Well, here, don't say I never gave you anything," Janelle said, handing Janiece her bag of makeup.

"No, Nellie, you've done way too much for me already. I can't take your makeup."

"Chile, please, you know I'm like Momma. Everything I buy, I buy two of them, and for every item, I have another one at home in that bag. So you'll be doing me a favor. Now, I can use the other ones before they're no good. You don't know how often I throw out unused cosmetics and fragrances because I have had them for over a year, and they are no good after so long," she told Janiece.

Janiece had no idea. She was still spraying perfume and using makeup that she had way longer, so she made a mental note to go through her things and get rid of the old stuff too.

"Yeah, well, you do have the Josephine Hawkins disease—buy two of everything. I'm so glad I didn't get it," Janiece said as she checked herself in the mirror. Then finally, she sat on the bed and put on her boots.

"Oh, before I forget," Janelle said and went into the bathroom and came back with her purse.

"Here you go," she said, handing her sister some money. It was folded, but she could see the number on the corner.

"What's this for?" she asked.

"You know, cab fare. You can never be too sure," she said and smiled.

"Thank you, Nellie. I appreciate everything you've done for me, and I can't wait 'til I'm able to treat you and be as generous to you as you have been to me," she said, hugging her. Her sister was the best, and she was glad to have her.

"Jai, you don't have to think twice about doing anything for me. Don't even think about paying me back. I did everything that a sister would do. I love you, and you can come to me for anything. If I have it, it's yours, so don't ever feel like you can't come to me. I'm your sister, and I know if the roles were reversed, you wouldn't hesitate to do it for me," she said, and she was right. Their sisterhood was strong. Janiece would give her the world if it were hers.

"Thank you, Nellie. I love you, and you have to know that I will—" she tried to say, but Janelle cut her off.

"No, you won't. Consider it a gift, and I don't want to hear another word about it," she said, sounding like their mom again, and Janiece knew she meant it. Also, Janiece tried to add something, but there was a knock at the door. "You want me to get that?" Janelle asked, smiling.

"Yes, and please, Nellie, *don't* embarrass me," she begged.

"Chile, please, I am not gon' embarrass you," she said and went to open the door. Janiece did her final checks in the mirror and decided to give Janelle a moment before entering the front. She fluffed her hair and checked her nose for monsters, then went into the living room where they were. Isaiah was looking fine as ever. He had a fresh haircut and shave, and his clothes were hanging on him as if he were a male model. If Janiece didn't know any better, she'd say he had gotten a facial because he was looking so fresh and fine.

"Hey," she said after checking him out. He was about to have a seat but immediately returned to a standing position when he saw her.

"Hey, yourself, beautiful," he said, taking a good look at her. His eyes gave her a look of approval, and she was pleased with his reaction because she went through a lot of trouble that day to make sure she looked perfect. Janelle was smiling too because her sister looked incredible, and she was pleased with her date. She automatically pictured them as a couple.

"You can have a seat," Janiece told him because he was still standing and staring at her like she was a stranger.

"Thanks," he said and sat on the sofa.

"I see you've met my sister, Janelle?"

"Yeah, she frisked me at the door," he joked, and they all laughed.

"Honey . . . trust me, you got off easy. By the way, I need the make and model of your car, including plates, and, oh, I'm going to need your mom's maiden name," Janelle teased, and they laughed again. Janelle liked this guy, but she had wanted anyone to keep her sister away from the two-timer.

"Would you like something to drink?" Janiece asked. He had to be either thirsty or hungry because he looked at her like he wanted to devour her.

"No, no, thanks. I'm good."

"Well, I'll have a bottle of water," Janelle said, looking at Janiece like, *why didn't you ask me?*

"Okay, sure—Your Majesty," Janiece teased and went into the kitchen and got a bottle of water for her sister. When she came back, she didn't sit. She just stood because she was anxious to get going and be alone with Isaiah. Janelle noticed her standing and got the hint.

"Well, I guess I'll be going, so you guys can leave," she said, taking her jacket from the back of the chair. She dug around in her purse and got her keys. Janiece walked over to the hall closet to get her coat. When she had her purse and keys in hand, she was all set.

"You ready?" Isaiah asked Janiece, and she nodded. He got up from the couch, and they all left together. Janelle and Isaiah went down the steps while Janiece locked her door. They waited at the bottom for her, and when she reached the last step, they said their *nice-to-meet-yous*, and Janiece walked Janelle to her car.

"Giiirrrrlllll, he is *too* fine," Janelle said to her sister.

"I know, right? He's looking even better tonight, girl. I had no idea he could get any finer than he already was."

"You better call me first thing in the morning, you hear me? I want to know if he tastes as good as he looks," Janelle teased.

"Girl, stop it and get your nasty behind home. Call me as soon as you make it," Janiece said and waited for her sister to get in the car. Then she walked over to the truck, and Isaiah got out and walked around to open her door for her. He helped her in and closed the door. She smiled, and he went around and got into the driver's seat.

Chapter Eight

She looked over at him, and she couldn't resist complimenting him because he really looked good, and he smelled delicious.

"You look so handsome tonight, Mr. Isaiah."

"Why, thank you, Ms. Janiece. You look lovely yourself. I couldn't believe my eyes when I saw you. I mean, your hair, the makeup, the nice color on your skin—you look gorgeous. I had to do a double-take. I mean, you are a beautiful woman, but tonight, you look radiant," he said. He had been very attracted to her. Now he was even *more* attracted to her.

Isaiah thought she was gorgeous, and he liked healthy women. Her size fourteen frame was perfect. She had nice curves, and her thickness was in all the right places. Her high cheekbones and cocoa-brown skin were the perfect accents to her almond-shaped eyes. Her lips were not full but not too thin, and her teeth were bright and even, and he was in love with her smile.

She was shorter than the women he had dated, but at five feet four, she was perfect. Her hair was thick and shiny, and it looked longer than it had looked to him before. He figured she straightened it a bit more, which was why it hung a little past her shoulders. He imagined it wasn't a weave, and he wouldn't dare go there and ask her that, but he was almost 99 percent sure that it was all hers.

"Thank you," she said, that time taking his compliment with confidence. She was pleased that he was happy with her makeover. She knew that she wouldn't let him see her looking as bad as he had the night before. If she could help it, he wasn't going to see her *ever* look like that again. "So, where are we going?" she asked, curious to know how they were going to spend their night out.

"Well, I wanted to have dinner first and then go shoot some pool. After that, we'll be going to this little spot to hear some jazz. My sister got the tickets for me earlier when I tried to get some sleep. Do you listen to jazz?"

"Yes and no, to be honest, like I don't have any jazz CDs, but I listen to the jazz station on my music choice, so I don't love it, but I definitely like it."

"Well, it's better when you hear it live. My parents are jazz fanatics, so we grew up on it," he said and looked over at her like she was a plate of food. She felt his eyes on her and couldn't help but smile. She wanted him to feel comfortable, so she returned the look to let him know that she was feeling him too.

"So, you know a lot about jazz?"

"Man, yes, maybe more about jazz than hip-hop, but don't tell anybody," he said and smiled. His smile was so beautiful to her. She couldn't help but smile back.

"I won't tell. Your secret is safe with me," Janiece said and winked her eye. She couldn't stop smiling around him. She hadn't thought about K.P. at all that entire day, and no way was K.P. *anywhere* in her thoughts right now.

They rode downtown and ended up at Ruth's Chris, one of the best steak houses in the world, Isaiah thought.

Janiece wanted to go so many times, but she never had the pleasure of going, other than the one time her sister and her husband Greg had taken her. And that time she went, she didn't have steak, so being the best steak house in the world was something she could not confirm. Isaiah told her the steaks melted in your mouth, but she insisted on having chicken.

"Why don't you eat beef? I can understand pork, but beef too?"

"Well, it's not like I've never eaten it. It was just a few years ago, I decided to change my diet and eating habits, and beef was one of the things I decided to let go of," she explained and took a sip of her wine. The ambiance was so lovely, and she was feeling good.

"Apparently, you've never eaten a steak here."

"No, I'm afraid I haven't."

"That's one of the reasons why you still don't eat beef," he joked.

"Are the steaks that good?"

"Man, are they! I dreamt about their steaks when I was in Iraq, and you are the first person I can enjoy one with. So if you see me dancing while I'm eating it, don't be embarrassed. I'm just enjoying my steak," he joked.

"Damn, that good, huh?"

"Yep, but don't take my word. You gotta try it for yourself," he said, and that made her want to try one. Her mouth started to water. She wasn't sure if it was watering from the sound of the steak or because of Isaiah.

"Okay okay okay, I wanna try one. I want a steak. For the love of God, why did you bring me to this place?" she whined.

"Because it is so worth it," he said and smiled. He took a sip of his wine, and when the waiter came over, he ordered for both of them.

They hardly spoke while they ate. Janiece really enjoyed her steak. She didn't leave any on her plate.

After dinner, they left and went to G-CUE, a pool hall, and Janiece felt relaxed, although she had no pool skills. She just enjoyed being with Isaiah.

He was very patient, and they shared many moments of being very close together because he helped her with most of her shots. He smelled so good, and Janiece wanted him to be all up on her, so she took advantage and played the helpless role the entire time. They held hands in the truck, and she couldn't help but beam at him every time he looked over at her. She knew he was enjoying her as much as she was enjoying him. It was the way he looked at her. Once they got inside the jazz club, they found a table not too close to the stage.

They slid into a cozy, little, dimly lit booth, and every-thing was good . . . until Janiece's phone started vibrating in her purse. She thought it was her sister calling back again, being nosy, but when she saw it was K.P., her heart stopped. She ignored the first call and ordered a glass of wine. She talked to Isaiah, trying to forget the call, but her phone vibrated again. She excused herself to the ladies' room, but by the time she made it inside, she had missed his call. She debated whether she should call him back and decided not to.

Janiece went over to the mirror and touched up her lipstick, and her phone rang again. She resisted the urge to pick up, and at that time, K.P. left her a voicemail. She declined to listen to the message, but her nerves were jumping by then. She felt like she was out cheating and was on the verge of being caught. She tried to get it together before she returned to the table, but K.P. had started something, and she couldn't fall back into the mood with Isaiah.

When she got back to the table, she was glad that the show had already started. That way, she didn't have to talk. She slid into the booth and got close to Isaiah. Her purse was on the seat next to her, and every ten minutes, it was vibrating. That made her so uncomfortable, and she was nervous.

When the show was over, she looked at her phone. It had nine missed calls, all from K.P. and ten text messages. What scared her was one call came from her condo, and she didn't know if K.P. would be there or not when she got home. She was so uneasy, and Isaiah picked up on it. When they got into the truck, he looked at her and could see the tenseness all over her face.

"What's wrong?" he asked.

"Nothing. I'm fine," she said, lying through her teeth, and he knew it.

"Are you sure? Did that phone call upset you?"

"No, why would you say that?"

"Because everything was going good 'til you got the phone call. You came back from the restroom, and it's like you can't even look at me."

"Well, the call just surprised me a little, but I'm fine," she said, giving him a weak smile. She was worried as hell, and he knew that something wasn't right, but he didn't push.

He started the truck and headed back to Janiece's place. They didn't talk much, and all the smiles and eye contact were gone. He wondered what was wrong, and she wondered if she would go home to hell. She wanted to tell Isaiah what was going on, but she felt it was too soon to give him details on her situation.

Janiece felt bad that K.P. had that type of power. She knew she had to make some decisions and make them quickly. She knew for sure that she had to get her key back, especially if she planned on getting to know Isaiah.

When they got on her street, she was relieved not to see the Escalade, but she still couldn't let Isaiah come up because it wasn't a guarantee that K.P. wouldn't be back. He had been known to creep up in her bed some nights as late as midnight, and she didn't want that to happen, so she struck up a conversation in the truck to avoid him going up.

"I really had a good time, and the jazz was awesome," she said as soon as he turned off the ignition.

"I'm glad you had a good time," he said, not giving her any eye contact, and she didn't like that. She knew she deserved it, but she still didn't like it. She felt more relaxed to see K.P. wasn't at her place, so her mood shifted slightly, but she still knew Isaiah going into her place would not be good until she spoke to Kerry.

"Isaiah, I'm sorry if you feel like my mood shifted or changed after the call, and it may have, and I apologize, but trust me, it's not you. I had a good time with you. It's just . . . there are some things—" she tried to explain but couldn't put into words the way she wanted to say them.

"Things like what, Janiece? You have to be honest with me. Whatever it is, just tell me. I don't want to start out on the wrong foot."

"I'm telling you the truth. It's just so complicated—and I . . ." she said, pausing again. "It's just not that simple, and I have some unfinished business that I have to handle, but trust me, Isaiah, it is not you."

"Okay, I see," he said and nodded his head. He was not for any games, and he was sincerely interested in her, but his time was short, and if he didn't have a chance with her, he didn't want to waste any of it.

"Look, I knew last night when you were upset that maybe you had something going on. But I'm interested in you, and if there is no chance for us to get to know each other, I'd like to know now because I don't have long before I have to leave," he said, and that confused her.

"Go where?"

"Back to Texas, Fort Hood," he said like she knew what he was talking about.

"When-when are you going back to Texas?"

"In about four weeks. I'm on leave, and I told you I had a year left. Well, not even a year. It's about ten months.

So I'll be out next July, but I should be back here next June."

"Yeah, you told me that you had a year left, but I thought you would be staying here in Chicago."

"No, I have to finish in Texas, but it's not that long. It'll fly by," he said like a year was a week or two. That changed everything, Janiece thought to herself. She wasn't interested in a long-distance thing; she was lonely enough with the married man that only lived in Lansing.

"Well, I didn't know that," she said disappointedly.

"So . . . Is my going back to Texas a problem for you?"

"I'm afraid it is," she said, in a low voice, holding her head down. He opened his door, got out, then came around and opened her door and helped her out.

"Thanks for the date. I had a good time," she said and walked away. They both knew that was the first and last date, and they both were discontented about that. He waited for her to get upstairs and inside before he drove away. She wondered where he was going and why he didn't go up to his sister's place, but she couldn't dwell on that.

When she sat to take off her boots, she noticed a massive bouquet of roses sitting on her coffee table. She counted them twice because she couldn't believe there were three dozen of them. Then she snatched the card from the clip and sat on the couch to read it after taking a deep breath.

I'm sorry, baby. You know, sometimes I can be a jerk. Please forgive me. I love you.

K.P.

She was so confused and didn't know what she would do. She loved K.P., but she now liked Isaiah. She couldn't get what she needed from K.P., but Isaiah would be leaving. She was ready to move on, but she was scared. She wanted Isaiah not to be leaving, but that was impossible.

She wanted K.P. not to be married, but that wasn't the case, so she was in a state of confusion on what her next move would be.

She got up and went into the bathroom to wash her face and tie up her hair. She thought about K.P. but not as much as she thought about Isaiah. After putting on a nightgown, Janiece crawled into bed. She thought about the evening she had with Isaiah, and a smile lit up her face because she enjoyed him so much.

She wanted to call him and tell him to come back, and for a split second, she didn't care if K.P. came back. She would just have to put the chain on the door. She told herself it was no big deal that Isaiah was going back to Texas, but truthfully, it *was* a big deal because she liked him. She closed her eyes and prayed for guidance. Then she asked God what she should do. She knew the obvious answer about K.P., but Isaiah was a tough one. She reminisced about their date and fell asleep before she could stop smiling.

Chapter Nine

The following day, the ringing phone woke her. She tried to tune it out and continue sleeping, but whoever it was hung up and called again. She turned over and looked at the clock. Five after nine. This person evidently didn't know that it was a Sunday morning, and it was just plain wrong to call a person before noon, she thought to herself. She grabbed the phone and looked at the caller ID, and, of course, it was Janelle calling for last night's juice. So Janiece hit the TALK button before it could go to the answering machine.

"Hey, girl," she said, yawning.

"Hey, girly girl, how'd it go last night?" Janelle asked, and Janiece could hear the smile in her voice.

"Funny you should call me this early for that information."

"Oh, is he still there? My bad, girl. I underestimated you. I'll call you later," she said, getting ready to hang up.

"No, he's not here, Nellie. I wish he were, though. But it didn't go that well," she said, getting up and going to the bathroom.

"Why? What happened? He seemed like the perfect gentleman."

"K.P. is what happened."

"K.P. . . . What happened? What did that asshole do? Did he step to Isaiah or something? That greedy mother—" she tried to say, but Janiece stopped her.

"No, no. Nothing like that."

"Well, what happened? You didn't run into him, did you?"

"No, I didn't run into him, but I let him ruin my date, or should I say, he is ruining my life," she complained and washed her hands. Then Janiece walked into the kitchen and poured a glass of juice. She peeped through the curtains, but the Avalanche was nowhere in sight.

"Jai, what happened?"

"Well, the date was going fine. I was having a good time. I even ate steak, you hear me? Then we got to the jazz club, and K.P. started blowing up my phone, which distracted me. I couldn't settle back into my date, and when I saw he was trying to call me from my condo, I really freaked out because I didn't know what to expect when I got home, so just imagine how panicky I was."

"Hold on. Let's get back to the fact that you ate steak. Now, if you ate steak, you must *really* like this guy."

"It doesn't matter because he's going back to Texas soon. Plus, I don't think we'll be going out again."

"Going back to Texas? I thought he was getting out of the military."

"Yes, in a year, but he has to finish in Texas."

"Texas is not far, girl. You can visit him in Texas. One year will go by before you know it, Jai," she said, trying to be encouraging. She wanted her sister to try anything—except continue to see K.P.'s, sorry ass. "I know you like him, and I can tell he likes you."

"Well, maybe he did in the beginning, but I don't think I'll be hearing from him after the way I behaved last night."

"So why don't you call him? It couldn't have gone that bad, Janiece."

"Nellie, when I got that call from K.P. I froze. I mean, I tensed up so bad, like I was out cheating, and I couldn't relax after that. I know Isaiah thinks I'm up to no good, and he's not the kinda guy that I want to lead on. I have to kill things with K.P. first."

"Jai, don't even try it. You're making excuses. You'll *never* be done with K.P. if you take that route. You have to allow someone else to occupy your time, so you can start to get over K.P., so don't play me, and don't play yourself."

"So if I call Isaiah, what do I say?"

"I don't know. Ask him out or over for dinner. You can cook. Just make up with him and ask him to allow you time to get to know him before he goes, and who knows."

"You think he'd be okay with that?"

"Why wouldn't he? You don't have to rush into anything. Just hang out with him, keep in touch when he leaves, and if something comes out of it, you'll see him when he comes back," she said, and it made sense. But Janiece didn't want to get close to him, though, because she knew she would end up falling for Isaiah, and when he left, she would miss him too much.

"Yeah, you're right. I'll call him. Because yesterday, I didn't give any thought to K.P. when I was with Isaiah, and that felt good for a change. Then I come back, and I got roses on my coffee table," she said and leaned in to smell them.

"Oh, and another thing . . . change your locks," Janelle advised.

"Slow down. Let me take one step at a time," she said, reminding Janelle that it wasn't going to be an automatic change.

"Well, if you don't change the locks, you're going to always worry about him popping in on you or being at your place when you and that fine-ass Isaiah come in from a romantic dinner. Or when Isaiah may want to stay late to massage places that you need to be massaged . . ." she teased.

"All right, I get your point. I'll get my key back."

"No, damn that—change your locks. Do you think he's just going to hand over the key?"

"Yes, I do," she said, fooling herself. Deep down, she knew it wouldn't go that smooth, but it was worth a shot. Plus, seeing K.P. face-to-face and ending things would be the best for closure.

"Whatever. As I can see, you still live in Jai-land, the land of the nutcases," she said in jest.

"See, there you go, minding *my* business again."

"I'm only suggesting. Now go, get off the phone with me, call Isaiah, and invite him for dinner and make something slamming."

"Okay, I'll call him, and if he refuses to talk to me?"

"Hey, well, that's his loss."

"Okay, I'll call you later."

"Okay, babe, good luck."

"Thanks. Bye, now."

"Bye," she said, and they hung up.

Janiece scrolled through her caller ID to find Isaiah's number. She called him, and it went to voicemail. She didn't leave a message. She just decided to try him a little later. She went back to bed but couldn't fall asleep. She got up and put a movie in the DVD player to watch. After two of her favorite movies and a shower, she called Isaiah again, and still, he let her call go to voicemail. She declined to leave him a message again and decided to order some Chinese food from her favorite spot a few blocks down the street from her place.

She usually drove down, but she decided to walk since it was a nice day. She was looking radiant again in case she ran into Isaiah. Then she slowly walked back, ignoring all the honks and guys trying to holla at her on the street. She had only one man on her mind, and she was disappointed to not see his truck outside of their building when she got back.

Janiece went inside, put her food on the counter, and decided she'd go over to his sister's place. But, first, she went into the bathroom to comb her hair and reapply her lip gloss.

She was a little mad that Isaiah didn't bother to call or say anything else to her. She knew the night before had gone badly, but she thought he liked her. When she got to the door to go across the hall, her phone rang. She was relieved and thought finally he called her back, but it was K.P. That was odd and shocking for a Sunday afternoon because that was his so-called family day.

She paused for a moment because she wasn't thrilled like she usually was to talk to him. He was not occupying her thoughts, at least not the past couple of days. She wasn't missing him in the worst way like before. He wasn't the HNIC anymore, and one date made her realize she was beautiful and important. That was one reason she didn't want to answer the phone, but she did anyway.

"Hello," she said in a monotone voice.

"Damn, baby, what took you so long to answer the phone?" he asked cheerfully.

"Nothing. I couldn't find the cordless," she quickly lied.

"So, what's up with you? I haven't heard from you since—" he tried to say, but she cut him off.

"Since you left my house mad at me for taking too long at dinner with my sister and leaving me that funky-ass note," she said. She didn't appreciate what he had done.

"Well, I was pretty pissed off, but now, I realize that I should not have acted that way. Did you get my note and the roses?"

"Yes, I got your roses and sorry-ass apology card," she barked. She hated when he just acted like a simple "sorry" would make it all better.

"What's wrong, Jai? I tried to call you last night, but you didn't pick up. I figured you were out with Janelle, so I came to apologize to you in person. I waited for you, and I got there about seven. After eleven, you know I got pissed when you didn't answer the phone, and I called you a million times. So where were you, Jai?"

"That's none of your business," she said before she could stop herself.

"None of my business? What do you mean none of my business? I'ma be there in a minute," he said and hung up. She tried to call him right back to tell him she was on her way out, but he was already pulling into the parking lot. *Damn damn damn* is what she thought when she saw his truck pull into the parking stall.

She opened the door just in case Isaiah came up. She didn't want him to see K.P. using a key. She stood in the kitchen waiting for him. He was taking an awfully long time, so she looked out the window. He was on the phone. Probably lying to his wife again, she thought.

He finally got out of the truck, and as soon as he started up the steps, her phone rang. It was Isaiah. She wanted to pick up so bad, but K.P. walked in the door. She quickly walked over to her answering machine and turned down the volume in case he left her a message. She was disappointed that she couldn't talk to Isaiah because that was who she had been impatiently waiting for to call her.

"Where were you?" K.P. asked first. She didn't answer. She looked at him, rolled her eyes, and walked away. He followed behind her into the living room. "Who were you with last night, Jai?"

"What are you talking about?" she asked, pretending to be clueless.

"Don't play games with me, Janiece. Who were you with that you couldn't answer your damn phone?" he snapped. "Now, tell me what's going on with you. Where were you last night?" he yelled.

"I was out," she snapped back.

"With whom . . . Your hair's all fixed, and you're looking like a superstar for some new cat, but when I'm around, you act as if you need me to give you money to fix your hair and nails. So what? Some other dude got your hair fixed and got you looking and smelling all good?" he asked, and he was angry as hell.

"No, I don't have a man doing nothing for me. Why are you so worried about how I got my hair and nails done? You didn't care on Tuesday when you were too busy being an asshole to get it done for me. You were so mad at me for nothing, K.P., and you disregarded the fact that you promised to give me money to get my stuff taken care of. I called you a million times last week, and you just ignored me, and now you wanna come up in here and question *me* about whom, what, and where? Man, please . . . gon' with that," Janiece said with attitude. She was tired of him treating her like she was a doormat. It was bad enough she played second fiddle to his wife and kids.

"Jai, you betta not be fucking around on me. I swear to God if—" he said, but she abruptly cut him off again.

"You swear to God *what*? And don't be swearing to God in *my* house," Janiece said, getting up off the couch. She wanted to get in his face. She wanted things to get ugly, so she could get her key back and send him on his way.

"Jai," he said, calming himself. "Look, I know I didn't have to go to the extreme with you last week, and I'm sorry, but please don't go throwing away what we have. Come on, babe, we can work this out," he said, moving closer to her, and that was definitely a bad idea. She was mad but not over him, and he had a way with her.

"Stop it, K.P.! It's not gonna be that easy this time," she said, putting up her guard. She had to fight him with force because he was slick, smooth, fine, and the man she was still in love with. She wanted to get to know Isaiah,

but her feelings for K.P. were not yet gone. She was just
angry and tired of the way things were between them.

"So what are you saying, Jai? Come on, babe, I'm sorry.
Don't make this bigger than what it is. I missed you," he
said, touching her arms. His touch was gentle, and she
missed him too.

"Look, K.P., I know you said you were sorry, and I do
accept your apology, but I'm tired of going through the
motions with you. You have so much control and power
over this relationship. Not to mention you abuse your
power, and I'm tired of it."

"What do you mean, Jai? I don't mistreat you."

"Yes, you do, K.P.," she said, getting in his face and
putting her hands on her ample hips. She wanted to put
a finger in his arrogant face, but she restrained herself.
"You come and go as you please, and *I* have restrictions.
You call and expect me to answer. If I don't, all hell
breaks loose, but if you don't pick up, I'm just supposed
to understand. You get mad or upset and go away for a
few days and just leave me out there, and then when you
feel good and when it's convenient for you, you come
around.

"I'm getting fed up with that. Like last week, even
though you knew I was out with Janelle, you still got
pissed off. Went off and didn't say anything to me for a
week. Damn how Janiece felt all week. Now you're calm
and can stand to be around me again."

"I'm sorry, Jai, and I know that was messed up. I am
sorry for being an asshole to you, Jai. My temper gets in
the way, and I'm sorry. Just know I love you, and I'm not
perfect. I fucked up, okay? That wasn't cool, and yes, I
was the one who promised to take care of your hair, and
I should have done what I was supposed to do," he said.
He pulled out his wallet and took $300 from it. "Here,
baby. Here's the money for your hair and stuff and for
whatever else you need," he said.

"No, I don't want shit from you." She refuted with her arms crossed tightly across her breasts. She didn't take it, so he put it on the coffee table. She rolled her eyes at him and tried to walk away, but he grabbed her arm.

"Baby, please don't be like this. You know what it is. You know how I feel about you, bighead. Don't make this hard for me. I'll do better. Believe me, I'm fucking trying, and I'd give you anything, you know this. I love you. I love you, and I can't stand it when you are hurt, upset, or mad at me. Please, Jai, just let me show you that you mean everything to me. My situation is fucked. Trust, I know, but you know my heart beats for you," he said tenderly.

She was touched by his attempt to make things right, and she stood there and let him charm her, and before long, he was kissing her passionately and touching her body. Finally, she allowed him to retake her body. They ended up in bed, and she gave him what he wanted, and he gave her what she thought she needed. She wished that she and K.P. could have been that perfect couple, but there was nothing perfect about their relationship. Now, there was no way she could get up the courage to ask for her key.

After their lovemaking session, he was sleeping while she lay awake in the dark. She thought about her food on the counter and got up to fix herself a plate. She put the plate in the microwave, peeped out of the window, and saw the Avalanche parked on the street. That made her stomach jump. How long had he been next door? she wondered. Damn. She knew he saw K.P.'s truck and must have figured out that she was seeing someone.

She opened the fridge and thought about how she would tell K.P. to leave so she could at least call Isaiah, but she didn't have to because he suddenly walked into the kitchen fully dressed. Although she wanted to kick him out, she instantly got an attitude because reality kicked in. Sex and then he had to bounce, which she hated.

"I see you gotta go," she said while rinsing a wineglass. She didn't look at him because she knew it would cause her to address the hit-and-run routine again, and she simply didn't want to go there.

"Yeah, I wasn't supposed to be out this long," he said and walked over to embrace her from behind.

"Jai, things are going to be different—"

"Different *how?*" she interrupted with attitude. She had heard it all before, and that was the last thing she wanted him to say.

"Things are going to change—"

"Change *when?*" she snapped, cutting him off again. She knew that change was coming soon for her. She knew she had to leave him alone soon. That was a change she was sure would happen.

"Look, baby, I love you. Please don't do this, Jai. I don't want to leave you upset," he said and turned her to face him. "Please, baby, give me a smile."

She gave him a fake smile and thought that she would definitely have to move on. At least if she were with Isaiah right now, he wouldn't have to run off and go home to his wife. "Do you love me, Jai?" he asked.

"Yes," she finally whispered.

"Don't worry, babe. Things are gonna be different soon. I promise you. You won't have to be fighting for my time anymore," he said, and she looked puzzled. What did he mean by those words? What was he trying to say? Were he and Kimberly having problems? She wondered because those words never drip from his lips.

"Just give me some time, babe, and you'll see. Please don't go and start trying to replace me. You're a beautiful woman, Jai, and I want you for me, and if I have to give up everything to have you—I will," he said and kissed her passionately. She was so mesmerized by the words he spoke that she didn't ask another question.

She just let him leave. She stood and watched him from the window get into his truck. Once he closed the door and pulled out of the stall, she bounced back to reality and realized he was jealous. He knew she was getting some attention elsewhere. He wasn't slick, she thought, then went into the bathroom to take a shower.

She was getting ready to get in when her phone went off. It was a text from K.P. saying, I love you. She just tossed her phone on the bed and went to shower. She tried to call Isaiah when she came out, but he didn't pick up. So finally, she left him a message, asking him to call her. After that, she heated her food, and by ten thirty, he still hadn't called back, so she went to bed.

Chapter Ten

The next day, she went to work and still hadn't heard anything from Isaiah, but K.P. certainly made it clear that he wouldn't let Isaiah have an easy win. He sent Janiece flowers and made a surprise visit to her office to take her to lunch. Then after calling at least five times that afternoon, he went that extra mile and picked her up from work. This was madness, Janiece thought to herself when he told her he was downstairs waiting for her. She snatched up her handbag, phone, and computer bag, furious that he thought that shit was just okay. She was all set to tell his ass the fuck off, but when she got off the elevator, he was standing there at the information desk like a model fresh outta *Jet* magazine.

She noticed his wedding ring wasn't on his finger, and she exhaled because that would have definitely embarrassed her with her coworkers. They heard the name K.P. a million times, and she had tons of pictures of him in her office, But they never had the pleasure of meeting him in five years. They had no clue she was seeing a married man. So taking off his ring was a brilliant decision, Janiece thought when she approached him. Since she stopped walking, her coworkers paused in their tracks too.

They had ridden down on the elevator simultaneously, and this was Janiece's opportunity to put all of the office jokes about K.P to rest. He was standing in the lobby looking fine as hell. He wore a suit that hung on him like

a tailor-made masterpiece. It was name brand, Janiece
was sure, but she had no clue who the designer was.

The closer they got to him, the more pleasing he
looked. She was proud that he was tall and dark and, as
always, well-groomed. Whether he was in sweats, jeans,
or a sharp suit, he looked good. She was anxious to introduce her nosy-ass coworkers, who always want to think a
sister is lying about her fine-ass man. The mortgage bro-
ker that she had bragged about finally was real, and her
face was glowing when she introduced him to everyone.

She had asked him to company picnics and parties,
and he'd always declined in fear that one of his clients
or someone who knew him or Kimberly would be there,
so this was the first time she had an opportunity to let
anyone from her office meet him. They chatted and
made small talk while the ladies checked him out. They
all flirted, and it didn't bother Janiece because she knew
that K.P. was a stud. She was flattered that he was getting
the type of attention that they were giving him.

Two of the ladies knew how far to go, and they said
their *nice-to-meet-you*s and bounced, but Shawnee
Williams acted like she didn't know how to stop running
her big mouth. All the eye batting and fake giggles made
Janiece want to slap the taste right out of her mouth. She
was flinging her fake-ass weave and batting her fake-ass
lashes like she was Beyoncé or somebody. Janiece kept
her cool, though, and when Shawnee asked K.P. for a
business card, he politely told her that he didn't have any
on hand and that contact with him should go through
Janiece.

Then he grabbed Janiece by the hand, and after taking
one last peep at Shawnee's big tits, he told her that they
had to run because of a dinner reservation. Shawnee's
jaw almost dropped. He kissed Janiece on the cheek,
asked if she was all set, and they walked out of the
revolving doors.

Shawnee was standing in disbelief, thinking to herself how fat-ass Janiece Hawkins could catch such a big fish. She quickly readjusted herself and ran to the ladies' room just to make sure she didn't have a monster in her nose because it wasn't often a man didn't notice her. Even if he was with his woman, she knew that she could turn heads.

Janiece walked hand in hand with K.P. up the block to his truck. She was glowing and felt more special that day than any day ever. She had pictures of her and K.P. on her desk, but the girls on her floor still thought she was making him up. They would always say, "Damn, girl, who is this fine-ass brotha?" while they examined one of the photos on her desk, and when she'd say her man, of course, she'd get the look of disbelief. Now, she knew tomorrow she would be the office chatter's topic, that the guy in the pictures was a real guy, and he looked as good in real life as he did in the photos.

They got in his truck and went to Lawry's Prime Rib restaurant for dinner. K.P. was outdoing himself because going out to dinner, let alone to a nice restaurant, was something that had never happened. Not only a lunch date but dinner too. She was in awe. Although she was having a good time, the thoughts of Isaiah still invaded her mind. She had her phone on vibrate to keep the peace between her and K.P., but she checked it every five minutes to see if he called.

By the time they made it back to her condo, there still hadn't been one call from Isaiah, which disappointed her. While she was with K.P., she was hoping Isaiah would at least call so that she would know that he was thinking of her, but he failed to do that. It was getting late that Monday evening, and she wondered how K.P. was managing to be out still. She didn't ask. She just went along with it and tried to enjoy him because she knew it would not happen again, not real soon anyway.

She went into her kitchen and peeped through her window curtains to see if Isaiah's truck was outside, but the Avalanche was nowhere in sight. Finally, she went into the bedroom. K.P. was sleeping peacefully, so she got her phone from her bag. It was after ten, and she wanted to call Isaiah while K.P. was in dreamland. She went into the bathroom and sat on the side of the tub. After scrolling through the numbers in her phonebook, she hit the TALK button when she landed on Isaiah's name, but the phone didn't ring. Instead, it went straight to his voicemail.

She wanted so badly to grab her sweats and go across the hall and ask Iyeshia where he was, but she realized it was too late. Plus, she had Mr. K.P. lying in her bed. She sat there for a moment and thought about Isaiah and the date they had. She missed him and desperately wanted to hear his voice. "What did I do?" she asked herself, thinking back to that night when she told him that him going back to Texas was a problem for her. "Isaiah, please call me," she said to herself and got up to go back to her bedroom. It was close to eleven by then, and she wondered, has this fool lost his damn mind? He must not know what time it was, so she shook him.

"K.P., baby, wake up. It's almost eleven," she told him, shaking his arm.

"Come here, beautiful," he whispered. He was looking at her with so much love. Janiece knew something was different, but what? *Why now?* she thought to herself.

"K.P., it's late. Shouldn't you be heading home?"

"No, this night is for you, and our time is important to me. Come here to me," he said and pulled her closer. He moved his hands down her back, caressing her skin so tenderly. He kissed her passionately and held her close. His kisses were seducing, and she couldn't control herself. She led his hand down to her breast and encouraged him to massage them. Her nipples were hard, and her clit was starting to throb. She wanted to resist him, but she had loved him for so long, she couldn't bring herself to stop him.

He removed her robe and took one of her hard nipples into his mouth. The heat of his breath and the wetness of his tongue made her spot tingle. She wanted his tongue all over her body. She lay back and allowed him to wander around her bare skin. He found his way to her particular area and blew on her trimmed hairs.

The sensation drove her insane, and she didn't know whether to enjoy him or push him away. She thought to herself that K.P. no longer deserved her body as he licked her like she was in love.

His tongue felt so good, and she was getting ready to climax—but the sudden ringing of K.P.'s phone knocked her out of her trance. K.P. jumped up like a grasshopper and made a mad dash to his phone. He looked at the caller ID and walked out of the room to take the call. That was definitely a first because he never was unable to talk in front of Janiece before.

She sat up in the bed and concentrated really hard on his voice. She made out some of what he was saying, but not all. She listened carefully and heard him say, "I'm going to be here for a while," and she continued to listen. "Look, I'll call you tomorrow. Kiss the kids for me, and don't call me anymore with any nonsense, Kimberly." Then he hung up. Janiece wondered what the deal was, but she and K.P. never, ever discussed his home business, and to ask him would cause a problem, and she wasn't in any type of mood to argue.

"I'm sorry, baby," he said when he came back into the room. He crawled back into bed with her and started kissing her like there was no pause in their moment.

She looked at him, but his eyes were shut while he went back to licking on her nipples. They were no longer erect, but it didn't take them long to wake up. They made love, and then K.P. rolled over to sleep. Janiece looked at the clock. It was after midnight. Maybe he's going to make one of his two a.m. exits, she thought. She grabbed her pillow and didn't bother to set the alarm for him.

She wasn't concerned about whether he got up. She stood up to blow out the scented candles that were burning. When she climbed back in bed, he cuddled up close to her and held her tight. It was too much for her, so she had to ask, "K.P. do you need me to set the alarm?"

"No, baby, I'm staying," he said, and she thought her ears were deceiving her.

"Staying? Staying what?" she asked like he was speaking French.

"I'm staying. I wanted it to be a surprise, baby. I'm staying all night tonight, tomorrow night, and the next night, and we'll see after that," he said.

Janiece was in a state of shock. She was exhausted and didn't even want to ask. Finally, she settled back into his arms and decided she'd wait until morning to ask questions. She closed her eyes and reminisced on her date with Isaiah again . . . how he fed her at dinner and how they held hands in the truck. She thought about his beautiful smile and wondered—how was she going to get rid of K.P.?

Chapter Eleven

The following day, K.P. went downstairs to his Escalade to retrieve his garment bag. He had a toothbrush and underwear at her condo, so he only had a nice suit and a pair of loafers to get from his truck. Meanwhile, Janiece walked around in a daze because she wasn't used to him being at her place in the morning, and it seemed like it took forever for her to get dressed. She arrived at work twenty minutes late because he insisted that she let him take her to breakfast. He promised he'd pick her up for lunch again that day, and she wasn't excited.

"Why, after all this time we've been together, he decides he wanna do all the things I wanted him to do when I start liking somebody else?" she asked herself as the elevator's doors shut. When she got up to her floor, another bouquet of fresh flowers was sitting on her desk, and she didn't smile or attempt to get excited this time. She knew they were from K.P. "Jealous bastard," she spoke out loud, and Shawnee came in on her words.

"Who?" she asked, being a nosy ass.

"Who what?"

"Who's jealous?" she inquired. Janiece thought she sounded like she wanted to make sure she wasn't talking about her.

"Why?" Janiece asked her. Janiece was no punk, and she spoke freely to them heifers up in her office. She learned a long time ago from her momma not to back down or show fear to anyone. "Don't give people an invitation to run all over you" is what her momma would say.

"Well-I-I-heard you say. Look, never mind," she said, stuttering. "What I came to ask you for is K.P.'s number because my brother is gonna be looking to buy a house soon, and I'm sure he could help him-you-know," she tried to say with a straight face. Janiece looked at her with the *bitch, please* look, but she didn't care. If Shawnee wanted to hit on K.P., she could do what she wanted. K.P. wasn't her man. He was Kimberly's man. So Janiece didn't look up or say a word. She just wrote down his office number and handed it to her. And Shawnee was a little surprised.

"Okay, that was easy," she said with a phony smile. She looked at the number like she had to memorize the digits just in case Janiece asked for it back.

"I'll let him know your brother will be calling him when he picks me up for lunch today," Janiece said with a smirk.

"Huh? What?" she replied as if she had forgotten about the lie she had just told about her brother.

"I'll let Kerry know that your brother will be calling him," Janiece said, refreshing the lying tramp's memory.

"Oh, oh, yeah, you do that. Thanks again." She turned to walk out, tossing her tacky-ass weave over her shoulder. She always reminded Janiece of Hottie from *Flavor of Love*. Janiece laughed and shook her head. Then she sat down and dove into work. Before she knew it, K.P. had called and said he was downstairs waiting to take her to lunch.

She grabbed her purse and phone and headed for the elevators. But first, she glanced at her phonebook just to look at Isaiah's name and wondered why he still was refusing to call her.

She spent the next two days with K.P. On Friday, before leaving the office, her phone rang. When she saw that the number was Private, she said, "Nope. If you gotta block yo' number, you don't want to talk to me."

She got to the bottom floor and hated that she had to take the train. It felt good for the last four days to get picked up and taken to dinner and not have to get on the metro. Now, she started up the street to the station. Once she got her seat, she pulled out her book and flipped through to where she had left off. She usually listened to her headphones too, but the book was so good she had to focus on just reading it.

As she got into her book, her phone rang again, and the number was still blocked, so she stuck it back into her bag, thinking maybe the person would leave a message, but that didn't happen.

Once she made it home, she climbed the steps to her building, and as she was going in, Iyeshia was coming out.

"Hey, neighbor," Iyeshia said, saying hello first for the very first time.

"Hey, Iyeshia, how's it going?" Janiece asked with a pleasant smile.

"It's going," she said as she locked her storm door. Janiece didn't want to ask, but she couldn't help herself. "Hey, Iyeshia," she yelled as she was going down the steps.

"Yes?" she said, turning back to her with a smile.

"How's Isaiah?"

"He's good. He'll be back in town today, as a matter of fact. My mom and I are going to the airport. He and my dad will be home in about three hours," she said, looking at her watch.

"Oh? He was out of town?"

"Yeah, he and my dad went to Dallas for a game. You know, father/son stuff, no-girls-allowed type madness. They left last Sunday. He didn't tell you?"

"No, he didn't tell me. We kinda, you know . . . things just . . . you know," Janiece said, trying to explain.

"Well, let me say this. My brother is very selective when it comes to women, and he doesn't go out with just anybody, and I know you got a little something-something going on with the dude in the Escalade, but trust me, I stay outta folks' business, so I didn't say anything or get involved when he said he wanted to take you out. So if you do like my brother, please give him a fair chance and get to know him. He is definitely not like other guys.

"All my girlfriends been dying to get with him for a long time, and he is picky, so if my brother likes you, there's something great about you, but if you aren't ready for him, don't even play with him because he is too good of a guy," she said, putting Janiece in her place. Janiece was shocked even to hear her say that many words to her. They barely ever spoke.

"Thanks for the heads-up, and trust me, that Escalade is not gonna be the cause of me not getting to know your brother, okay?" she said with a smile.

"You like him, don't you?" Iyeshia asked Janiece, and she smiled.

"Yes, and since I met him, I can't think of anything else."

"Well, let me assure you, he's waiting for you to square away whatever it is, so he can genuinely get to know you. My brother doesn't say much or tell his business, so I don't know too much, but I know he likes you, and my advice to you is to call him at 9:30 tonight. We should be leaving the airport by then," she said and gave Janiece a wink. She smiled and told Janiece she'd holler at her later and left.

Janiece's phone was blowing up with the private number. She tried to avoid it as long as possible, but she finally answered it. Since she knew Isaiah had gone out of town, maybe it was him, she thought. It was only ten after eight, so perhaps Isaiah was at an airport or something. She didn't know, so she just answered this time.

"Hello," she said, sounding a little sexy just in case it was him.

"Well, hello, Ms. Janiece," a female voice replied. Janiece didn't recognize her voice.

"Hello, who is this?" she asked, confused.

"Oh, bitch, wouldn't you like to know?" the female said with much attitude.

"Look, who is this?" Janiece demanded again.

"Ain't this a bitch? You trying to get tough, you stankin' ho?" she spat.

"Well, fine," she said and hung up, but before she could put the phone down, it rang again. This time she didn't answer. Instead, she went over to the window and looked out. Who in the hell was that crazy-ass woman calling her? she wondered.

Janiece sat on the sofa and looked at the clock. It was almost nine, and all she wanted to do was talk to Isaiah. K.P. hadn't called her since lunch earlier that day, and she knew if she called him, he'd have a lame excuse, so she didn't bother. She calmed herself because whoever "Crazy" was, she had stopped calling.

She went into the kitchen and poured a glass of wine, then sat on the sofa and kept checking the time. Finally, it was five after nine, so she went to shower to kill some time. After she lotioned up and got fresh, she went back into the living room. She was so excited because it was a minute before nine thirty, and just as she grabbed her phone to call Isaiah, the phone rang again. The private crazy bitch was calling once more. She decided she wasn't going to back down. Isaiah was coming home, and she didn't want that bullshit happening all night.

"Hello," she said in an aggravated tone.

"Look, bitch, don't hang up."

"No, *you* look, bitch. I don't know who you are or what your so-called problem is, but you need to quit calling my phone," Janiece demanded.

"No, bitch, *you* need to quit fucking my husband," she spat out, and Janiece instantly knew who the perpetrator was.

"Kimberly?" she asked in shock.

"Yes, bitch, this is Kimberly—unless my husband isn't the only married man you fucking."

"How'd you get my number?"

"Duh, bitch, your number is all over my phone bill. Did you think I'd never contact you?" she asked as if Janiece owed her an answer. "Listen, I was okay with your ass, and shit was fine 'til you got K.P. talking about leaving me and shit. Don't you know I got two damn children? It's bad enough you fucking him, but you trying to take him too?"

"Look, Kimberly, I don't *want* your husband. I have never tried to take him. I'm not your problem. K.P. is your problem, so that is who you need to be having this conversation with. I suggest you talk to him."

"Look, you homewrecker, tell K.P. it's over and send him home to his family. If you don't, I'm warning you, there will be hell to pay," she threatened, and Janiece laughed in derision. Of course, she would be delighted to tell him that it's over. That wouldn't bother her one bit, but this crazy woman didn't realize that all she could be doing was making matters worse. Just the fact of her making threats made Janiece feel empowered. Shit, if you gotta be begging women to stay away from your man, you got issues, and if Janiece weren't so crazy about Isaiah, she'd go against the grain just to fuck with Kimberly.

"Listen, Kimberly, don't call me with your threats and promises. I don't have any control over K.P. He's a man, and trust me, sweetie, he's gonna do what he wanna do, but I can assure you I don't want him, so don't call my phone ever again," she said and hung up. Then she scrolled through her phone, found Isaiah's number, and dialed it from her house phone. When it started ringing, she powered off her cell phone.

"Hello," he answered on the second ring.

"Hey, how are you?" she smiled from ear to ear. She wasn't sure if he wanted to talk to her, but she *definitely* wanted to talk to him.

"Hey, can I call you back? I'm getting my luggage right now. I'll call you in a few moments," he said and hung up. She was looking at her phone for a moment, wondering if that was a brush-off.

Next, she dialed K.P.'s to tell him that "Crazy" had called, but his phone went straight to voicemail. "Oh great," she said to herself and went into the kitchen to get another glass of wine. A moment later, the phone rang, and she almost broke her ankle trying to get back over to the couch where she had left it. She took a deep breath and then picked up.

"Hello," she said softly.

"Hello, to you, Ms. Janiece. How goes it?" Isaiah asked, and she could tell he was excited to talk to her.

"It's going well. How was your trip?"

"It was cool. Got to hang out with my pops. We kicked it, and it was good."

"Did you think about me while you were away?" she asked, hoping he'd say yes.

"Why? Did you think about me?"

"I asked you first," she said.

"Well then, I'd have to answer yes," he said, and she could hear the smile in his voice. "How about *you?* Did *you* think of me?"

"Yes, constantly," she smiled and was honest.

"Well, I'd say that's a good thing."

"Yes, it is," she replied, unable to get the smile off her face.

"Look, I don't know if you have plans tonight, but I'd really like it if I could see you," he said.

"You don't have to ask."

"Well, let's see, I'm with my sister now. She and my mom both drove, so I'll be around your way soon. I just need to shower and change. Can I knock on your door tonight?"

"Yes, you can knock on my door."

"Cool, I'll see you soon."

"Okay, bye," she said and then called Janelle.

"Giiiirrrrllll, he's coming over," Janiece screamed into the phone when Janelle answered.

"Who, girl? Who's coming over?"

"Isaiah," she said like Janelle should have known.

"I thought you said you gave up on him, and you were just going to let it go."

"Yeah, that was earlier, but I was wrong, way wrong."

"Okay, what made you change your mind?" Janelle asked before taking a bite of her Maxwell Polish.

"Well, I ran into Iyeshia."

"Who is Iyeshia?" she asked, chewing in Janiece's ear.

"His sister, and what in the hell are you smacking on?"

"A Polish, girl. I stopped on Halstead before coming home."

"Oh, well, anyway, I saw Iyeshia, so I asked about him, and she told me that he went out of town on Sunday to go to a game in Dallas and that he would be coming back tonight."

"So, how did you end up talking to him? Did he call you?" she asked, continuing to enjoy her Polish and soggy fries.

"No, she told me to call him about 9:30, and I did, and now he's coming over," she squealed.

"Well, my sista, you know what time it is."

"No, what are you talking about, Nellie?" she asked, needing clarification.

"Time to get some 'act right' in your life and leave that ugly-ass K.P. alone. Damn what he told you this week about leaving his wife and kids. He's just trying to keep you hooked."

"Oh, funny you mention that. His crazy-ass wife called me."

"*What?* When and why? Well, I know why, but when? What did she say?"

"She called not too long ago, and he isn't lying about leaving her."

"What? How do you know that for sure?"

"Well, let me see, 'Bitch, stop fucking my husband, or else it's going be hell to pay. If he leaves my kids and me, you gon' regret it,' she said," mocking K.P.'s wife. "Now, I'm not a genius or anything, but I figured that one out."

"She said that?"

"Yeah, and then she had to nerve to tell me that it was okay when we were just fucking, but now that he wants to be with me, she has a problem. How twisted is that shit?" Janiece thought it was foolish of Kimberly to freely admit that she was okay with them messing around as long as he wasn't going anywhere.

"Damn," Janelle said in disbelief. "I'll be damn if I would allow Greg to have a woman on the side," she said with a light laugh. "You mean to tell me that this crazy chick is okay with him cheating on her as long as he doesn't leave her? I underestimated K.P. That Negro dick must be bronze—hell—gold. Is it that good, Jai?" she asked, cracking up at herself.

"Ha, ha, ha, funny, Janelle . . ." she said, not really seeing what was so funny.

"So what you gonna do?"

"What do you mean what am I gonna do?"

"Exactly what I said—what you gon' do, bitch?" she said, mimicking Mo'Nique from the movie *Two Can Play That Game*.

"Well, first of all, I don't want him; second, I'm not gon' tolerate this drama. It's not that serious."

"Yeah, right, Jai. You know damn well you're talking shit. You said all this BS last Saturday when you were getting ready to go out with Isaiah, and then what did you do? Spend the whole damn week with K.P."

"Well, I didn't know what the deal was with Isaiah, and plus, K.P. wouldn't take no for an answer."

"Yeah, whatever, li'l sis. You act like you forgot who you are talking to. You enjoyed his sorry ass, and you know it," she teased. Of course, she was just messing with Janiece.

"Maybe a little, but honestly, Nellie, and this is the truth. I thought about Isaiah the whole time. Even when we were making love, I imagined it was Isaiah," she confessed.

"Damn, Jai, I guess the K.P. ship is sailing. You *are* coming around, girl. I'm proud," she teased.

"Things are just so different now, Nellie. I used to eat, sleep, and breathe K.P., but now, I have to kinda force a thought in my mind about him. Isaiah is taking up all the space. All the stuff that we did this week was beautiful, but it should have been months or even years ago."

"So why haven't you told K.P. to get lost, Janiece?"

"Nellie, truthfully, I didn't want to hurt his feelings. He was just so happy and excited. He walked around like he had done this great justice for me. I was amazed but not happy. You know what I mean? He was doing everything in his power to make me smile, and it was fake, Nellie."

"Okay, but you know you are gon' have to tell him that it's over."

"Yes, I know," she groaned.

"And he is *not* gonna make it easy for you."

"I know."

"But you can't drag this out. You gon' have to do it soon, especially if K.P. has told his wife he's leaving. Hell, he may be popping up whenever now. I told your ass to change your locks."

"Yes, Nellie, you told me," she agreed. However, she wasn't in the mood to hear, "I told you so."

"Well, if you need me, call me, and don't let 'Crazy' call you no more. Change your number first thing in the morning," she said, sounding like their mom.

"I will, but look, let me go. I have to change. Isaiah will be here soon."

"Okay, but behave yourself, young lady."

"Oh, I will, trust me," she said with a naughty smile.

"Okay, call me tomorrow."

"K, bye," she said and hung up.

Chapter Twelve

Janiece went to turn on the music and fix her hair. She stood in the mirror, getting cute, and sang like Aretha while putting on a little makeup. She took off her sweats and put on a pair of tight jeans and her favorite Chicago Bears, Devin Hester T-shirt. She was so excited she couldn't sit down, so she walked around, wiping down surfaces and straightening things that were already straightened.

Then she went over to the mirror leaning against the living room wall and checked herself out. She admired her voluptuous body and thought she looked good in her jeans. She turned to the side, looked at her bottom, and wished she had a smaller butt. She figured she'd be in size twelve instead of a fourteen if she had a smaller ass. Finally, she examined her breasts and stomach, and she definitely agreed that she needed to incorporate some sit-ups into her daily routine.

She wasn't sagging anywhere, but she didn't want to get any bigger than that size. Her breasts could stand to be a cup size bigger, she thought, but if so, she probably wouldn't be able to still get away with some of her cute little halters in the summer. She only had a C-cup, but the girls were still perky.

Satisfied, she went back into the kitchen and peeped out of the window for the Avalanche again, but there was no sign of it, so to kill some time, she grabbed her book and read several chapters. When she looked up, an hour had gone by, and still, he had not knocked on the door.

She got up to brush her teeth again because she wanted her breath to be super fresh when he arrived. So she finished her hygiene, dried her mouth, and reapplied her lip gloss. Then she rinsed her hands under the water she had been running since she had started brushing her teeth. When she turned it off, she heard knocking at her door, so she sprang to answer it. Stopping at the door, she took a deep, calming breath.

Janiece opened the door with delight because he was definitely finer than the last time she saw him. She invited Isaiah in quickly, and he handed her a bottle of Riesling. She thanked him before putting it in the fridge. They stood in the kitchen, looking at each other awkwardly until he broke the silence.

"You're looking good tonight," he smiled with his eyes moving from her eyes down to her lips, collarbone, breasts, and then ample hips.

"No, *you're* looking real good tonight," she giggled, taking a step back to give him and his body and outfit a once-over.

"I can certainly say the same about you, Janiece," he said, still wearing his warm smile.

"Look, Isaiah, I know we got . . . off to a—"

"Wait, Jai. Before you say anything, I'd like to apologize," he said.

"For what?" she asked, wondering why he wanted to apologize. She was the one who messed up the date.

"Well, first, for coming on so strong and for not telling you the full story about going back to Texas for the rest of my time in the service. I was afraid if I hadda told you that I was just here on leave, you would think I was just looking for a fling, and you wouldn't have wanted to go out with me. I didn't want to risk you saying no, so that's why I didn't mention my going back to Texas," he explained.

"Well, I'm sorry too for not being honest and straight-up with you about my situation," she said, and he looked at her confused.

"Come on, let's have a seat, and I'll explain." She led him into the living room, then went back and grabbed an MGD from the fridge. She didn't know if he liked that brand, but that was her favorite for some reason. She sat on the love seat instead of the couch so that she could look at him without having to sit awkwardly.

Janiece started at the beginning. She told Isaiah the truth about K.P. and her up to before returning to Chicago from Dallas. She promised God that if she were blessed to find a great man who had the potential of being a part of her life, she would be honest with him.

Isaiah listened, and from what she could see, he wasn't passing judgment on her, which made her feel good. So she got up to get him another beer and poured herself a glass of the Riesling that Isaiah brought over for her. She then sat on the sofa beside him because she was done telling her horrible life choices.

"So . . . Are you still seeing him?" he asked.

"I have already decided that it's over, but I haven't told him yet," she said truthfully. She hadn't come to that conclusion until after the crazy wife called.

"Well, when do you plan on cutting this cat loose?" he asked and took a drink of his beer. "I definitely don't want to be in any drama either."

"I wanted to tell him tonight, but when I called him, I only got his voicemail. I can't deal with the drama, and the harassing phone call from Kimberly is something I never expected our relationship to come to."

"Kimberly? Who's Kimberly?" he asked because she didn't mention the fact of his wife calling and harassing her earlier that evening.

"His wife," she said dryly and took a sip of her wine.

Isaiah's eyes bulged. "His *wife* knows about you?"

"Yeah, and today, she confirmed that she's known for a while."

"Damn, what did she say?" he asked interestedly.

"Oh, so I see you *do* like drama," she said, laughing.

"Nah, I'm just curious," he replied, laughing with her.

"It doesn't matter because that's the last time I'll be bothered with that shit fo' sho'. I'm changing my phone number first thing in the morning."

"Damn, girl—that is, some drama. Now—enough about the married cat and his crazy wife. What's up with *us?*" he asked in a more serious tone.

"Well, I would like to ask you the same question."

"You know I'm feeling you, and you know I want to get to know you on a more personal level," he said, taking her free hand into his. He took her glass and set it down on the coffee table.

"Well, Isaiah, I want you to know that you are going back to Texas, and that concerns me."

"Listen, Janiece, I know you think of it as a bad thing, but I promise you that if you and I are together, that means we are together. I'm not the kinda man who needs to run around on my woman. Since the moment I saw you, I haven't been able to stop thinking about you," he said, looking at her with genuineness. She could feel the attraction that was going on between them, and she was dying for him to kiss her.

"Me too—I can't front or play games with you, Isaiah. I'm attracted to you in more ways than one," she said, looking at him like he would disappear if she blinked.

"Really?"

"Really," she said. "So what do we do now?" she asked. He moved closer to her and readjusted himself in front of her. Their faces were so close there was less than an inch between their lips. She wanted his lips to kiss hers, and he wanted, so badly, to kiss her.

"We go with the flow and take advantage of every moment we have together. We take our time and get to know each other and see how it goes," he said softly. His mouth was so close she could feel his warm breath and smell the mint of his toothpaste mixed with MGD.

"Then what—" she tried to ask, but before she knew it, he kissed her. She relaxed and let his tongue explore her mouth, allowing him to suck on her bottom lip. His kiss tasted so good, and she thought to herself that he had to be a passionate lover by the way he grabbed the back of her head. His kiss was so sweet and soft, and she knew he had no intention of stopping. He wanted to taste her everything. Janiece's nipples began to harden, and she knew she was done.

She told herself if he tried, he would definitely get some for sure. They both thought of making love and teasing each other. Janiece was so anxious—she decided to help him out by moving one of his hands down to her breast. He grabbed her breast, massaged it gently, and pinched her nipple through her T-shirt. Then he pushed his weight on her, causing her to lie back a little. They broke from their passionate kiss long enough for him to remove her T-shirt. After that, he sat back a little to get a good look at her white-laced bra. They both smiled.

"You sure you wanna do this?" he asked.

"Yes," she whispered and climbed on top of him. They kissed again, and he grabbed her ass and gently squeezed it. Her ass was plump and was a pleasure to his hands as he palmed it. He licked her neck, and she leaned back a little, giving way to her cleavage. Her eyes were closed, and she held the back of his head. She was happy that she was no longer merely imagining his lips kissing her body. He was really there. She reached behind her back to unsnap her bra to expose her erect nipples, but her phone chose that moment to ring, jerking both of them out of their moment, and they both laughed nervously.

"You gon' get that?" he asked.

"No, I don't wanna move from this spot."

"Okay, then, don't get it," he said, and they started kissing again. They were getting back into the mood when the phone rang again.

"You *got* to be kidding me," she said, looking around for the cordless phone. By the time she located it, it had stopped ringing. She snapped her bra back, went over to the phone, and looked at the caller ID. It was the one person she feared it would be. The one person she didn't want to hear from that night: K.P. She became terrified when she saw his name because he still had a key. Before she could put the phone down, it rang again in her hand. She knew she had to answer it and handle her business.

"Hello," she said, giving Isaiah the give-me-a-minute signal. Then she walked toward her room.

"Who in the fuck is in my parking space, Jai?"

"What?"

"I'm downstairs, and some nigga's Avalanche is in my spot, Jai."

"K.P., you don't *have* a spot. That spot is for my guests, and I have a guest."

"Who, Jai . . .?"

"No need to make a scene, so let me call you tomorrow."

"Tomorrow? Are you planning on letting him stay the night?"

"Maybe—that is *not* your business, K.P.," she snapped.

"Jai, what the fuck is up? Tell me what's going on."

"K.P., please, let me call you later," she begged.

"You know what? I'm on my way up," he said, scaring the shit out of her.

"No, K.P. Come on, you have to respect my place. I can't walk up in your crib whenever," she reminded him.

"Well, you need to come down then."

"No, I will not, and you need to get a grip."

"Jai . . . Who is this dude? You've been acting distant all week. I can tell something is up with you because it's like you are not yourself," he said, and she knew he was telling the truth. Even if he was really leaving Kimberly to be with her, it was great . . . but too late.

"Look, K.P., I gotta go."

"Jai, baby, please don't hang up. Come down and at least talk to me for a moment. I know I've been an asshole, but, baby, please, tell me I'm not too late," he begged, and it penetrated her heart. She didn't want to be cruel to K.P. or hurt him.

She was just tired of the drama. Even if they got together, she had to deal with Kimberly's crazy ass, and she didn't have the strength to deal with the amount of stress that woman would bring to her life.

"Jai, baby, are you still there?" he asked because she didn't say anything. She was trying to fight the tears.

"Yes, I'm here," she said softly.

"Baby, please, tell me I'm not too late. I want to make you happy. You deserve to be happy, baby. So please give me a chance. Tell me I'm not too late, baby, please," he begged.

"I don't know, K.P. I'm tired of coming in second."

"Jai, I'm trying to change for you, and I can't make that happen overnight. It's gonna take some time, Jai. Do you hear me? I love you, and I have loved you for a long time. It is so much more than just getting up and walking out the door. I'm ready to be who you want me to be. I just needed time," he pleaded, and she had to hurry off the phone because if she kept talking, she would allow him to make her feel bad. She did love K.P., but things were no longer the same.

"Listen, K.P., I promise you that I'll call you tomorrow because I can't deal with us right now. We have too much to talk about, too much to cover right now, so please, let me call you tomorrow."

"Do you love me—"

"K.P., please—"

"Yes or no . . . I'm going to go out of my mind if you don't tell me you love me."

"Yes, K.P., I do, but things just aren't that simple anymore. Now, please, K.P., I don't wanna hang up on you, but I need to go," she pleaded.

"I love you."

"I know. Bye, K.P.," she said and hung up. Janiece sat on the bed and blew out a deep breath. She grabbed a Kleenex from the nightstand and went over to the mirror to pat her face. She was nervous about going back out to the living room. She fluffed her hair, got her lip gloss from her purse, and applied a fresh coat. She smiled when she realized she was in her bra. She put the phone down on the charger and went back into the living room.

"Sorry about that," she said with a smile and sat down next to Isaiah on the sofa. She felt awkward at first, but he started to massage her shoulders.

"It's gonna be okay, Janiece."

"Are you sure?"

"Yeah . . . Take it one day at a time. I'm not pressuring you. Take your time, handle your business. As long as you want me around, I'll be around," he said, rubbing her back. He grabbed her shirt from the floor. "Here, put this on," he stated, handing it to her, and she looked at him with a look of confusion. She had hoped to pick up where they had left off.

"Janiece, I'm not here to complicate things. We don't have to move too fast. I'm a patient guy," he said and gave her a warm smile.

"Isaiah, what did I get myself into?" she asked, thinking about how hard it would be to end her relationship with K.P.

"Yeah, you have a lot to work out, that's fo' sho', but you have to do what makes you happy, not what makes other people happy. If you give in just to satisfy the other person's needs, you're not doing them a favor. People need to be loved and cared for by someone who wants to love and care for them. If we do it because of what they want, we only make matters worse because you make yourself miserable in the process. Eventually, you'll start to make them miserable. It's impossible to make someone happy when you're not happy," he told her, and she understood exactly what he meant.

She honestly didn't desire to be K.P.'s chick on the side any longer, and his sudden move to leave Kimberly to be with her wasn't what she wanted anymore. She wasn't sure if she could even trust him. Walking in Kimberly's shoes and going through what he had put Kimberly through for five years made her feel sick to the stomach. She didn't want all the things she thought she did, and she was so happy that God was giving her the strength she had prayed for. She put her shirt back on and rested on Isaiah's arm.

"Look, I'll be here for you. If you need to talk, I'm here," he said to her.

"Okay." They sat there in silence for a moment, and Janiece suddenly felt sad for K.P. If only he had come around before she met Isaiah, maybe things would have been different.

"Hey, have you eaten?" he asked, breaking their brief silence.

"Yeah, way earlier."

"How about we go downtown to Portillo's and grab some Italian beef sandwiches?"

"Ooh, those used to be my favorite," she said, thinking back to when beef was in her everyday lifestyle.

"Then how about it?"

"Isaiah, you know I don't eat beef."

"Janiece, don't even trip . . . This booty and these hips ain't gon' get no bigger with one sandwich," he said, wrapping his arm around her waist, grabbing hold of her hip.

"Isaiah, no, it's late. We shouldn't be eating that kinda stuff this late."

"Says who? Who came up with that idea?"

"All right, all right," she said, getting up from the sofa. "Let me get my gym shoes."

"*That's* what I'm talking about," he said and slapped her on her bottom. She liked that and hoped he would do it again.

"All right now," she smiled at him.

"What?"

"Don't start up in here," she said and walked away. She made sure she gave him a view of her bottom as she did her sexy walk to the hall closet. He smiled and thought about smacking her ass without her clothes and knew he had to shake it off. As bad as he wanted her, he knew he had to relax. He wasn't afraid of K.P., but the added drama wasn't something he was too enthused about. He just knew that he would spend his last three weeks romancing Janiece. He planned to make her his woman before returning to Fort Hood, Texas.

Chapter Thirteen

K.P. rode back to his house, wondering what was going on in Janiece's condo with her "guest." He had difficulty focusing on the road because his mind was on her. He'd planned a perfect life for them because she was the one he truly loved. She was the one he was struggling with the last two years of his life preparing for. Kimberly was just his legal wife.

He didn't love her, and Kimberly knew that. She had known that even before they got married. He thought he'd fall in love with her over time, but that never happened. It couldn't have happened since he had been in love with Janiece for the last five years. He was taken by her since the very first day he met her. He worked for her sister Janelle and her husband Greg on their loan package when they purchased their home. After they closed on their home, they invited him to their housewarming. He hardly ever wore his wedding ring, so there wasn't a question of whether he was married because he didn't bother to take Kimberly. He hardly invited her out with him to any social events.

When Greg introduced him to Janiece, he couldn't resist her smile. She barely wore makeup that day, and she looked so beautiful. She wore a pair of blue jeans that hugged her everything in the right way, he thought to himself when he watched her walk away. The red halter she had on exposed her cleavage, and her breasts sat perfectly in position without a bra for support. He admired her naturalness. Her skin was clear, free of blemishes. Her cocoa-brown complexion had a soft glow, and he was mesmerized by her.

He stalked her the entire evening until she finally agreed to go out with him. He was so interested in her that he was one of the last guests to leave, and he begged her to have coffee with him because he didn't want the night to end. Things were going smooth until the subject of *why can't we ever go over to your place* kept coming up. He put her off for about nine weeks until he couldn't hide it anymore. Finally, when he told her he was married, she was so upset, she broke it off. He hated telling her because he had such strong feelings for her in that short period, and hurting her wasn't his intent.

Neither was it his intent to fall in love with her. After she put him out and told him to get lost, he went into romance mode, proving to her that he couldn't stand not being with her. He wore her down by promising her he would leave Kimberly if their relationship lasted more than a year. Then one year turned into two, two turned into three, and three turned into four, then five, and five into where they were now.

She didn't believe him, but he hated going home to Kimberly. He was always so horny for Janiece because he wasn't touching Kimberly. He and Kimberly hadn't made love in almost a year. He knew she had some type of dick on the side, but she was too busy making him out to be the bad guy. She would never admit *her* dirt.

All she would do was threaten him and remind him that if it had not been for her, he'd still be on the bottom, trying to claw his way up to the top. In all truth, she was right, but at the same time, she knew what she was getting herself into. She wasn't innocent to the game. She was just too perfect in others' eyes that she didn't want to look bad under *any* circumstances. So, for the sake of them both, they pretended to be the most blissful couple that they weren't.

She had her image, and he had his career to worry about. When they first met, they were at an office party. He noticed her staring at him while he was talking to a group of men from the company. She made her way over to introduce herself. He thought she was an attractive woman, yes, but she wasn't his type.

Although she was fair-complexioned with gorgeous gray eyes, she had loads of makeup on her face. Kimberly had a head full of beautiful, wavy hair, and she looked high maintenance. He had just started, and he was not in a position to maintain a woman of her stature. She was high class, and since he had just graduated and only been with the company for two months, he was on the very bottom. K.P. was brilliant and had a promising career, but he knew that he wouldn't succeed overnight.

After chatting, he realized that the tailor-made look was on the outside, and she was down-to-earth. She was like a closet freak kind of chick, so they ended up back at his place. He had just moved there, so things were not impressive, but what the hell. She was the one who volunteered to come tuck him in. Not sure why he didn't just say no and not go there was beyond him. He already knew that it would be a one-night stand because no way could he afford her. He knew that when she followed his Toyota in her Mercedes two-seater Benz.

Little did he know she wanted what she wanted, and regardless of how poor, broke, or penniless he was, she would get him. The morning after, she asked him if he'd like to go to breakfast. It would be her treat, and he declined. The sex was cool, and he had no complaints except she was a bit robotic, but he had no intentions of hitting it again, so that didn't matter. When she asked him to go to dinner later, he gave a lame excuse about not being free. She got the hint.

When he walked her to the door and didn't ask for her number, she didn't say anything. She just clicked her heels and bounced. After a few days of being off for the holidays, he returned to work, not even thinking about the chick from the office he had hit a few nights before. When he got to his office, there was a note on his door to see Mr. Grayson as soon as he arrived.

Aw, shit, was his first thought. What happened? Did she get salty and try to give some sexual harassment story?

He went into his office first to get himself together. He tried to relax and think about what he would say but just decided to tell the truth. He didn't do anything wrong. The sex was consensual, so no worries. Then he headed for the elevator and started to get more nervous on each floor that the elevator climbed. For this to go all the way to the top, it *had* to be bad. No one in the building had ever met with Mr. Grayson. He was the HNIC of the company. Some of his coworkers said that they barely ever knew when he was in the building—*that's* how often they'd seen him.

Once the elevator opened, he stepped out, and a receptionist called him by name at the desk. He wondered how she knew his name since he'd never seen that woman before. He said hello.

"Come follow me. Mr. Grayson is anxiously waiting for you," she said as she led him down a marbled floor corridor. Finally, they arrived at the most enormous, most beautiful mahogany doors that he'd ever seen. She knocked and walked in. The office was lavishly decorated with leather and wood furniture. Mr. Grayson was on the phone, and the evil liar was sitting in one of the chairs in front of Mr. Grayson's desk.

"Have a seat," the receptionist told him. He sat in the chair on the right, less than three feet from Kimberly. He had no idea what she had gotten him into, but he knew that he would be jobless before the ten a.m. hour. The receptionist, dressed very professionally with nice legs, short hair, and dimples, went over to pour a glass of OJ. K.P. tried not to look at her, but she was a dime and definitely someone he'd have given his number to if she had been the one that went home with him after the office party.

She smiled, handed him the glass of OJ, and excused herself. He was so nervous and not sure what was going on. He didn't even look over at Kimberly, afraid he'd make matters worse. He sipped his orange juice and decided to remain silent until Mr. Grayson finished his call. He tried so hard not to look at Kimberly, but he could feel her gaze on him. He couldn't help but look back at her, and she smiled. Not an evil smile but a bright smile, and that terrified him even more. He smiled at her and quickly turned away. Finally, Mr. Grayson got off the phone. K.P. tried to stay calm, although he was nervous as hell.

"Well, Kerry Paxton," he said, opening up a file. He looked over a few things. "Yes, good, good," he said, nodding and reviewing what K.P. figured was his HR package. "So, you've been here with us two months now?" he asked, looking at K.P.

"Yes, sir. A little over two months now," he replied nervously.

"Two months and you are stirring up the place already, I see," he said. K.P. didn't respond. He didn't exactly know what to say without incriminating himself.

"I'm not sure exactly what you mean by that, sir," he said, thinking he needed to choose his words wisely.

"Well, I'm going to get right to the point of business. I spoke to Kimberly, and she brought some very interesting things to my attention. I'm glad we recognized it early, or you might have been overlooked, and we certainly wouldn't have wanted someone like you looked over," he said. K.P.'s heart was pounding so hard he thought it would jump through his shirt. "Do you like working for this company so far?" Mr. Grayson asked him.

"Yes, sir, I do," he replied, and Mr. Grayson put on his glasses and looked over several more papers in K.P.'s file.

By now, K.P. just wanted to come out with it and say, "Whatever she told you were all lies. I am *not* that type of person to risk my career or my life on a one-night stand," but he was glad he decided not to say that when heard what he thought at the time was music to his ears.

"Well, that is good to know, son. My daughter, Kimberly, told me that you are very bright and ambitious, and you've got the vision that we're looking for to make our company one of the largest companies in the industry."

His daughter! K.P. thought to himself. They were screwing more than talking about his career goals and ideas. Although he had plenty of them, he hadn't shared any with her. All they shared was a night of hot, butt-naked sex.

"Well, yes, sir, I have plenty of ideas that I think will bring in a lot more revenue, and I don't know what this means, but if you would like to hear some of my ideas, I'll be happy to present them to you."

"I'd love to, but first things first, Paxton. We've created a position here for you, and I want to make you an offer. Gail drew up this contract for you. You can look it over and get back with us by Wednesday," he said, handing him the contract.

K.P.'s eyes almost popped out of his head because of the number of zeros on the contract. He eventually knew he would be making that amount of money, but he never believed he would in the first year of his career. He didn't want to seem anxious, so he took the contract and agreed to let them know his answer in a few days. He left early that afternoon and called his friend Marcus, an attorney, to meet him at Nick's to look over the contract. He read over everything and said it was too good to be true.

"You know this woman is about to stalk you, right?" Marcus said and took a drink of his beer.

"No, man, she is too, too high class for a cat like me. As much money as she and her family have, she doesn't want shit with me," K.P. said and took his shot of scotch.

"Shiiiidddd—okay, dawg. If she is all that and you're just nobody, you wouldn't have this offer here," he said, pointing at the contract. "Now, if you sign it, you best believe you and that gal gon' be married."

And why did he say that? Once K.P. signed the contract and moved up to a higher floor, shit changed. Kimberly started coming by, bringing him lunch. She made sure every woman in the building knew he was *not* on the market. They started dating, and the next thing you know, they were picking out china for the wedding of the century.

The night before they exchanged vows, K.P. took her to the lake and told her that he cared for her and wanted her to be happy, but he didn't want to go through with it. He wasn't ready. She told him that she knew that he didn't love her the way she loved him, but she said he'd learn to love her in time. He tried to make her understand that he cared for her because he did, but she convinced him to go through with the wedding anyway.

That *wasn't* the greatest mistake of his life, only the first. The second mistake was when she got pregnant. They had both agreed to wait a year before having a baby, but she was pregnant after the first month of marriage. She swore to him that she had been taking her pills, but he knew she had lied. When their daughter was born, K.P. changed and decided that he wanted to be loyal and faithful to his family, and he started to see Kimberly as his wife *and* the mother of his child. He worked hard and tried to learn to love her. The following year, she got pregnant again, and his son made him feel like a man that needed to be an example.

He didn't want his son to go through what he had as he grew up with his mom but without his dad. He was living up to the responsibility—until he handled a mortgage package for a friend out on bereavement. That was the package for Gregory and Janelle Peoples. Had he never been invited to the housewarming, he wouldn't be sitting in his three-car garage dreading going inside his six-bedroom home.

He didn't want to face Kimberly or talk to her. She was acting out so bad now that he had asked for a divorce. He could no longer stand to be in the same room with her. She knew all along he had another woman. She confronted him several times about Janiece, and he told her repeatedly, "If you can't deal with it, you can go," but she loved him so much. So she just put up with it as long as he came home, kept his shit discreet, and didn't make any babies.

She didn't outright make him agree to those terms, but that is all she drilled in his head. So he came home, didn't display his other woman by taking her out all over town, and he and Janiece knew that making a baby would only complicate things. So he and Kimberly got along. When they were together, people thought they were the perfect family. He took care of his kids and helped her with them, but there was no affection, and when they went to bed, she stayed on her side, and he stayed on his. Every once in a blue moon, they'd have sex, and that was just what it was—sex—because she knew he didn't love her, and he knew he wouldn't ever learn to love her, not the way he loved Janiece.

Chapter Fourteen

K.P. walked into the kitchen from the attached garage. He could hear music playing from the basement, but he didn't bother to go downstairs. Instead, he just went upstairs to take a shower. He stopped by his daughter Kayla's room first to kiss her good night. She was sleeping so peacefully, so he kissed her very gently, ensuring he didn't wake her. Next, he went into the adjacent room and kissed his little boy, KJ. They were the only things that were right about his and Kimberly's relationship, and he was so sad that they had to suffer. He loved his kids and thanked God for blessing him with his two little miracles.

Silently, he went into the master bedroom and sat on the chaise to remove his shoes. His home was beautiful, with designer everything. He looked around and thought about how different the world would be for him with Janiece. She had exquisite taste, and he admired her style. He knew that he wanted to give her everything. He wanted her to enjoy the finer things in life. He knew she'd appreciate it, not be a spoiled, whining, tantrum-throwing baby like Kimberly.

Everything that they owned was expensive. Whatever he couldn't give her or get for her, she got it anyway from her daddy. Now, K.P. wasn't broke—nowhere near it—but he spent his money wisely. He didn't want to continually splurge so that when it was time he really needed his money, there would be some left. Since Kimberly had a wealthy family, she didn't understand "no," or "we can't afford it right now." When they got ready to buy their house, K.P. wanted to buy a starter home and later go for the gusto, but no, Little Miss Gotta Have It All wasn't going for that.

Once they were married, she stopped working, and K.P. was okay with that because he had a six-figure salary and many investments that he was turned on to by colleagues and his father-in-law. He grew up poor, and everything that he received, he was grateful for it. Then once they purchased their $750,000 first home, real-life kicked in for him. He was lucky, and he knew that he was blessed. He never wanted to make hasty moves and lose everything. That's why he took the last two years to get other things for himself to branch off from the Graysons and start on his own and be with Janiece.

He set things up so that his children would unquestionably go to college, and they had that house without any worry. He incorporated spousal support and all the matters of their debts, so when he left Kimberly and her dad's company behind, he'd land on his feet. With the help of Marcus, who was now the partner of a large firm in Chicago, the time had finally come for him to give Janiece what she wanted. He already had his eye on the location where he wanted to buy her a home, and it was only a matter of weeks for him to open his very own business.

Janiece didn't know any of his success, plans, or money. She knew he and his wife did well, but she didn't know how well. K.P. had always done things for Janiece and offered, so many times, to do way more, but she refused. Like when she wanted to buy her condo, he was willing to pull all the strings necessary or even give her the loan himself, but she refused his help. She rarely asked for anything, and it was always small when she did. He'd buy groceries, fill up her tank, leave her a few hundred dollars, but she didn't make him do any of that for her.

That's why he would take care of her. He would make sure she had any and everything she wanted, but how was he going to do that? Just when he got everything in order, she was trying to leave him.

Janiece was trying to end it all before it even started. K.P. held back his tears. He went into the master bath and turned on the shower. He grabbed the remote, turned on the built-in stereo system, and keyed in the code to play his station. Then he got in the shower and let the hot water pour over him. He closed his eyes and thought about Janiece, sat down, grabbed the liquid shower gel, and squeezed it onto his bath sponge. Wearily, he stood and began to lather up. He rinsed and repeated the same steps.

The water and steam felt so good he didn't get out right away. He stood with one hand holding the wall and the other on his dick. Janiece and her hard nipples came to his mind. Brian McKnight's "Do I Ever Cross Your Mind?" played on their audio system, and the speakers installed in their bathroom allowed him to listen to music while he showered. He stroked himself while he thought about making love to her. Startled, he jerked out of his daydream when he felt a touch from behind. It was Kimberly, and he was unpleasantly surprised.

"What the hell are you doing?" he spat at her.

"I should be asking you the same thing," she said with a smirk.

"Get out."

"Why? Can't I take a shower with you? You are *still* my husband, Kerry, and I want to enjoy any time that I'm able to spend with you before this is all over," she said.

"You *got* to be kidding me," he said, looking at her like she was crazy. He hadn't seen her body naked in a while, and it wasn't looking too bad. So he figured her personal training was worth every dime.

"Look, I don't want to be bothered with you right now, Kimberly, so go on and leave me alone."

"Well, it looks like big man, here, feels a little different," she said, touching his erection. His erection started because of Janiece, but looking at Kimberly's wet nipples from the shower made his dick stiffen even more.

"Stop that," he said, moving her hand.

"No," she said, touching him again. He didn't want her, but his dick did. He let her hand stay where it was and let her stroke him a bit. She moved closer while stroking it, allowing the head to rub against her stomach. His dick was in heaven, but his mind was in hell. As bad as he wanted to push her away, he needed what she gave him. He leaned back on the shower wall and let her massage him. The next thing that happened was her sitting down on the tiled shower seat and taking him inside of her mouth.

He groaned and grabbed her hair out of pure pleasure while he wondered whose dick she had been practicing on because her skills for giving head had greatly improved. She was taking all ten inches in like a pro, bobbing her head on him like she was glad to be of service to him. He started rubbing her back. His groans changed to moans as he enjoyed Kimberly taking him in and out of her mouth. Then, she stood up in front of him, and they just stared at each other.

"Did you like that, daddy?" she asked him seductively.

"Yes," he whispered.

"Do you want some more?"

"Yes," he answered before he could stop himself. She licked and sucked on his dick like she sorely missed doing that job for him. She slapped it on her cheek, which turned him on. She had never done anything like that before. Then she stood on the seat and put her breast in his face. He didn't hesitate to take one of her nipples into his mouth. He grabbed her right breast and sucked on it as if it were a piece of candy.

She grabbed his hand and put it in her spot, and he felt how wet her opening was. His dick throbbed with delight. He had never wanted to be inside of Kimberly that bad before. She was a petite woman, so she was easy to pick up. He lifted her off the seat by her ass, and she wrapped her legs around his waist. In seconds, he plunged his thick dick into her tunnel, and it was unbelievably tight. Only a couple of strokes brought him close to bursting, but he slowed down.

He turned and sat on the tiled seat and let her ride him. As good as she felt, he knew she had to have been fucking someone else because she had never ever been that good. She was always lazy and robotic, which was one of the things he didn't like. But, now, she was popping her pussy for him like a prized lover. He loved it so much he grabbed her head and began to kiss her passionately, something that he hadn't done in years.

"You like it, baby?" she asked in his ear while she rode him.

"Yes, baby, I like it," he responded as he enjoyed her wet pussy. He was in a trance, and whatever Kimberly had up her sleeve for them to make love, it damn sure worked.

"Is my pussy good to you, daddy?" she asked, whipping that shit on him like any needy woman would who was desperate to keep her man.

"Oh yes, baby, your pussy feels good," he said, with his eyes closed. He was getting ready to bust one in her 'til she asked, "Is my pussy better than Janiece's pussy, daddy?" and *that* woke him up and knocked him out of his trance. The hypnotic state was gone, and he snapped.

"What the fuck did you just ask me?" he said, looking at her like she was a dude on the street.

"I-I-I . . ." she stuttered. His dick went completely limp. His heart started to pound. Why did she have to mention Jai's name? he wondered. That pissed him off.

"Move."

"K.P., baby, I'm sorry. Please, honey, I shouldn't have said that. I don't know why I said that," she cried in a panic.

"No, Kim, move. Get off. You just *had* to go there. You can't leave well enough alone."

"K.P., please, I don't know why I said that. Don't let that ruin our moment, please, Kerry. I missed you so much. I want you so bad," she said, trying to kiss him, but he pushed her away. He pushed her to the side, stood up, turned off the water, and stepped out. Angry, he wrapped a towel around his waist and walked into the bedroom. Kimberly put on her robe and followed him into the suite.

"What do you want me to do?"

"Leave me alone. That's it—just leave me alone, Kim."

"I can't, Kerry. I love you, your kids need you, and you're dumping us off for some fat-ass, home-wrecking bitch that doesn't give a shit about you," she yelled. She was crying at that point. "I don't understand why, after all these years and two children, you still don't love me."

"You don't know shit about her, Kim. You don't know how she feels or how things are between us. All you know is I don't want you. And I'm *not* dumping my kids. I will always be there for them. I love them, Kim. It's *you* I don't love, and *that* is why you hate Janiece so much. Do you know how often she has told me to stay away from her and work things out with my wife?

"Do you know how many times she has told me that I was an asshole for treating you so badly, huh? But I fell in love with her, Kim. I've tried to love you. I have tried, I swear I have, and I don't want to hurt you, but you knew how things were when we got married. I did what you've asked. I tried, but it didn't work, so please, just give me the divorce, Kimberly, and find someone that's going to love you the way you need to be loved because, I'm sorry, it's not me."

"You didn't try; you started seeing that bitch three years after we got married. I've known since you and that tramp got together. You think I didn't know that you were with that bitch all the nights you were out late? I sat up many nights waiting for you to come home to me, but you were at your bitch's house."

"I did try, but you were so stuck on an image and what the fuck people gon' say that you walked around in this fantasyland like our shit was perfect. I blame myself for marrying you, and, yes, I was wrong for going through with it, but you knew too. Kimberly, I want you to be happy. I genuinely want you to be happy, but we are miserable with each other. Why do you want to continue to live like this?"

"Because I love you, Kerry. I have always loved you. I can't see myself with any other man but you. Kerry, please, don't end our marriage. If you want to stay with Janiece, continue to be with her. Just don't leave us, please. I can handle you and her. I've done it for this long. Just don't leave," she pleaded, and K.P. was in total disbelief.

"Kim, listen to you. I hear you when you say you love me, but you can't do this to yourself," he said, feeling bad for her. He knew that she loved him, and he understood her pain. He was in a similar boat because he wondered what was happening with the woman he loved and her new "guest."

"It's not the end of the world, Kim. You are a beautiful woman, you are smart, classy, and you have a lot of love to give. I know this will not be easy. I'm not cold to just leave you without support. I will always be here for my kids, but you and I have to be friends. Kim, we have to be mature and get along, so our kids can be all right."

"If I'm so great, tell me why you can't love me?" she said, with tears rolling down her cheeks. He walked over to her and held her tightly.

"I tried, Kimberly. I tried, baby. If I could make myself love you to keep you from hurting like this, I would in a heartbeat. I don't want you to be hurt. I want you to be happy. There's someone out there that will make you happy. I just can't."

"Kerry, what does she give you that I don't? What does she have that I don't?"

"It's not about that, Kim. There's nothing to compare. I can't tell you why I love her. I didn't plan for any of this to happen. The only thing I regret in all of this is hurting you. You are a good woman, and you have been so good to me. I don't hate you, and I don't want this to get ugly."

"She doesn't love you. She's just some gold-digging tramp that wants to get out of the ghetto. She'll never love you the way I do," she cried. "She's a homewrecker, and she must not have any children because if she did, she would stop and check herself," Kimberly barked.

K.P. knew that every word she spoke was out of anger and pain, so he let her vent. After spending the next few minutes saying all the negative things she could think to say about Janiece, she was exhausted. She sobbed, and he held her to let her cry. He no longer bothered to defend Janiece because even if he told her that Janiece had no clue about his money and never opened her mouth to ask him to leave her and the kids, Kimberly wouldn't believe him.

He just held her and let her sleep in his arms that night. He stayed awake, wondering what was going on down on Ninety-Fifth Street. Once he settled with the situation being out of control, he prayed for God to help Kimberly and give her the strength to move on. He prayed for direction and asked God to forgive him for leaving his wife. He asked God to allow him the chance to be a good husband to Janiece . . . better than how he had been to Kimberly. He prayed for God to send Kimberly a good man, let him be a good husband, and love her double the amount he loved Janiece.

Over the years he had with Kimberly, he knew she could be a good person when she wanted to be, and she deserved true happiness. But, his thoughts wandered, and he decided to get up early to go to the jewelers. He had to make a statement when he saw Janiece again, and he had to come with it if he wanted to keep her.

Chapter Fifteen

Saturday was an eventful day for Janiece. She was now finding herself thinking less of K.P. and more of Isaiah. The night before, she stayed up all night getting closer to Isaiah. After they got back to Chicago's South Side, they went to a park not far from Janiece's condo. They sat in the truck, ate their beef sandwiches, and decided to climb in the backseat to cuddle.

The moon was bright, and they enjoyed the breeze that came in through the cracked window. The more they talked, the more she realized she hadn't done much of anything in the past five years because she and K.P. had been homebound.

She just grew accustomed to the circumstances with K.P. and dealt with it. Every once in a blue moon, he'd get brave and take her out to dinner, but it's like they'd drive forever before he would pull in to a restaurant parking lot. One year for her birthday, she remembered that he took her to Las Vegas, which was the first—and last—time he had done something big for her. It was awesome because she got to be with him on the streets without worrying about running into a colleague or a client.

He was responsible for many homes and business owners' properties, and although Chicago is a huge city, he never wanted to risk being seen out with Janiece. He had his reasons, and Janiece always understood. So when they went to Las Vegas, she had the time of her life with him. They kissed in public, held hands, and walked arm in arm. She felt like he was her king, and she didn't want the trip to come to an end.

Once they were in the air, they started acting like new-lyweds. When the plane landed, they stood in the aisle waiting for the people in front of them to exit, damn near glued to each other. Just to walk through the airport hand in hand felt good to Janiece. She smiled the entire trip, and not once did they argue. Even when he had to step off to the side to call home and fill his wife with the business-trip-related lies, she didn't get an attitude. She had such a good time that she asked K.P. if they could just move and run away to live in Las Vegas. She remembered him saying, "Baby, Vegas is not Chicago. No city in the world can compare to our Chicago."

"In Chicago, we're not free. In Chicago, our love only exists in my condo," she said, not wanting to cry. She loved Vegas so much because she could love K.P. all over that city with no worries.

"Baby, our love is way bigger than Chicago, and if you want me to move you to Vegas, I will if that's what you want," he said sincerely because, at that moment, K.P. wanted Janiece to have everything she wanted. Still, Janiece sometimes felt like he was just saying what she wanted to hear, like telling her if she wanted him to take her to Vegas, he would.

She knew then that it was all his game to keep her hanging on. That Saturday was different, though. She wasn't going to keep hanging on. She would allow Isaiah to do all the things K.P. couldn't or wouldn't do. He was her mind's escape from the beguiling K.P. After spending just a little time with Isaiah and being able to go out freely, she felt that she turned into K.P.'s ass on the side—his booty call, because the last couple of years there weren't any dates, just him coming through and having his way with her.

Janiece got up and looked around her room for Isaiah. They had lain in her bed about five a.m. to get some sleep. But he was no longer there in bed with her, and the smell of food hit her nose. She looked over at the clock on her nightstand. It read 1:30 p.m. She couldn't believe she had slept so long. She got up and went to the bathroom because her bladder woke her up.

After washing her hands and brushing her teeth, she washed her face and brushed her hair slightly. It wasn't too bad, but she didn't want to go into the kitchen looking crazy. Satisfied, she walked into the kitchen and saw her new potential man preparing a meal. Now, *that* was something K.P. had *never* done. He was a terrible cook, so she prepared all their meals.

"Good afternoon," he said when she walked into the kitchen.

"Good afternoon to you. It sure smells good," she said, getting a glass from the cabinet.

"No, no, have a seat, Ms. Lady," Isaiah said, taking the glass from her hand. He led her back into the dining area and pulled out a chair. She didn't fight. She just allowed him to cater to her.

Her purse and keys were on the table, so she grabbed them to put them on the love seat that sat behind her, near her table. But first, she pulled her phone out to check it. There were nine missed calls, and all but two were from K.P. She remembered she needed to call Sprint to change her phone number, but she stuffed her phone into her purse, then Isaiah came with a champagne flute of orange juice.

"Thank you," she said, beaming.

"My pleasure . . . How did you sleep?" he asked and leaned over to kiss her. She smiled back at him and was pleased to see him cooking in her kitchen and serving her.

"I slept so well," she said. "Why didn't you wake me? It's after one."

"Well, you were sleeping so peacefully, so I ran out to the store and got some stuff to cook for you. And I remembered the pork situation, so I got turkey bacon and sausage. I think it's criminal to pass turkey off as sausage and bacon, but I'm gonna try it," he said, chuckling.

"You didn't have to go through all that trouble."

"It was no trouble at all, so get comfortable, and I'll be right back." He returned to the kitchen and fixed their plates. He had found his way around her kitchen, and Janiece was duly impressed. Since she was a good cook, she had all the right appliances, like a griddle, waffle iron, rice cooker, and deep fryer. He managed to locate the griddle and turned out perfect hotcakes.

He served fresh strawberries and cantaloupe. Janiece said grace and dug in. She enjoyed her breakfast, although it was almost two in the afternoon. Once they were done, he insisted she sit while he cleared the table. Now, Janiece, being meticulous about her house and cleanliness, couldn't control herself. She had to get her own kitchen back into her working condition.

By the time she finished cleaning the kitchen her way, Isaiah had dozed off on the sofa. Janiece watched him for a moment, and suddenly, he started jumping. Her smile faded when she saw him jerking. She wondered if she should wake him. The windows were open, allowing a nice fall breeze to come in, so she wondered why he was sweating. She walked closer to him and could hear him mumbling something, but she couldn't make out the language he was speaking. She was scared to wake him, but she shook his shoulder anyway. Instantly, Isaiah jumped and grabbed her arm like he was getting ready to rip it out of the socket. His eyes were red and strange when he looked at her.

"Isaiah, let go! You're hurting me," she said, for the third time, and he finally realized what she was saying and who she was, and he let go. She backed away quickly once she was released.

"Janiece, I'm sorry. I'm sorry," he said, immediately apologizing. She just looked at him, trying to understand what had happened. "Janiece, I'm so sorry. I didn't mean to hurt you." She was still standing on the other side of the room. "It's just the dreams . . . ever since I got back. I-I-I—just, sometimes have these dreams . . ." he said, and she started to relax. She walked over to him and sat beside him on the sofa.

"What dreams? What's going on?"

"Iraq . . . that place . . . that place was . . . some of the things . . . I know this will pass," he said, trying to brush it off.

"Like what? What . . . tell me," she asked curiously.

"No, baby, no. It's too much. You don't wanna know what went on in that place. The horrible things that I've seen—I couldn't tell you about that place. It's—" he said, not finishing, and she knew it may have been too much for her to handle.

"You were saying something that sounded funny, like another language."

"Yeah, I know how to speak the language, not a lot, so that's probably what you heard. My sister told me that too."

"Have you talked to somebody?"

"Yes, the army gives us this standard postwar exam and debriefing, but stuff like this just has to pass," he said, wiping the sweat from his forehead.

"But what if it doesn't?" she asked with concern.

"Don't worry, Janiece, it will." He tried to assure her, but the look in his eyes frightened her.

"You scared me, Isaiah. It's like you didn't know who I was for a moment."

"Baby, I'm sorry. That won't happen again. I promise . . . I promise. Believe me when I tell you I will never hurt you, okay? I've been there four times in my career, and this will pass. I promise. It always does," he told her and smiled at her. Janiece smiled back at him, but she was concerned. She advised him to go in her bedroom and lie down and get some more sleep, but he said he had to go over to his dad's lot for a while and that he would call her later. He asked her out again, and, of course, she agreed. He left, and she showered.

Afterward, she put on her comfy SpongeBob pants and a wife beater and went downstairs in the front to get her mail. She had a few bills and a card with no return address. She walked upstairs and went through a few of her statements first. After that, she ripped open the card and almost died when she read it.

She grabbed the phone and called Janelle. The card was too unbelievable to read over the phone, so Janelle came over. When she walked in, Janiece handed her the card that read "*Congratulations*" on the front. Janelle didn't see what the big deal was . . . until she opened it and read.

You funky fat bitch. All the hummers in the world won't make you the first lady of his life. I told you once, and I'm not telling you again. Stay the fuck away from my husband. Don't think because I live out in the 'burbs that I can't get grimy. Now, you broke-ass, desperate piece of shit ho, stay away from Kerry Paxton. Your dick-sucking days with my man are over. Tell him to leave you alone, and you stay away from him.

You ain't shit, and he doesn't want your two-cent ass. I shouldn't have to mention that I'm the one with the five-carat piece of art on my finger. I'm the one that made him who he is today, and if you think for one minute that I'm going to let a fat-ass, low-budget, cubicle-sharing, pencil-pushing, broke-ass, underpaid, man-stealing bitch like you take him away, guess again.

I knew about that trip you and Kerry took to Las Vegas. Yeah, didn't think I knew, huh? So y'all can't play me. Kerry is the one who's going to get played. This is like a game of blackjack. I'm sure you know how that game goes. I'm sure you played it when you were off in Las Vegas, sucking my husband's dick unauthorized. I hope you realize when it's time to leave the table. You've played for five years, and it's time for you to get your fat ass up from the table and cut your losses because I'll be damn if you are going to take my husband.

Take care and have a fabulous day, ho.

"Naw, nigga, naw . . . Where does this ho live? It's time to teach this bitch a lesson. She fucking with the wrong one," Janelle said, acting like she was hard in her Anne Taylor outfit, looking like she just stepped out of a *Home and Garden* magazine, all the while trying to act ghetto.

"No, Janelle, it ain't that serious. She ain't even worth the headache."

"Well, call K.P. He gon' have to do something about this psychotic bitch. This woman done sent a card to your house, Jai, meaning she *knows* where you live. So you may walk outside and catch a bullet one day."

"Chile, please, all she got is threats. But you're right. She knows where I live. So if she wanted some, she'd come to get some instead of sending this garbage in the mail," she said, taking the card and tossing it on the coffee table.

"Jai, you gon' tell me that you are *not* the least bit worried about this fool?"

"Nellie, if some woman was fucking Greg and you knew where she lived, what would *you* do?"

"Go and beat the snot outta that bitch."

"Exactly . . . If Kimberly was so tough, I'da ran into her. I've been with K.P. for five years, and trust me, she knew. She wrote it right here," she said, pointing it out in the card. "For five years, her ass ain't ever wanted to ring my bell and open up a can. Now, suddenly when K.P. says he's leaving, she wanna act up. She doesn't care about me fucking him. She just doesn't want anyone to know that he's leaving her snobbish ass for another woman. That woman is scared of being embarrassed— not by me."

"Well, I suppose that makes sense, but still, little sister, you have to watch out."

"I hear you, but I'm not afraid of her. If she were so tough, she'd have been in my mailbox and not that card." They both fell out laughing. Janiece wasn't worried so much, but she was a little concerned about her sanity.

She didn't know how far a woman like Kimberly would go to keep her man. She had to call K.P. to see what she was dealing with. He knew Kimberly better than she did. Her sister left, but not before Janiece promised to change her locks immediately because that crazy ho could have gotten her key from K.P.'s ring and made a copy—who knows.

Janelle also made her promise to allow her to install an alarm system. Janiece was a little hesitant about that. She didn't want to go getting all worried and afraid of her own home because some crazy-ass wife was out to stop her from taking her man. She knew that Kimberly was mostly talking. Once she got a hold of K.P., she made him agree to meet her to discuss the situation. She didn't want to meet him at her place, though, in case Isaiah came back, and K.P. was so desperate to see her that he agreed.

Chapter Sixteen

"Kimberly, why did you do this to yourself, baby?" he asked her. He was standing in her hospital room, nervous as hell. She had taken some sleeping pills, and his son called him when he was on his way to meet Janiece at a coffee shop not too far from her house.

"Mommy won't wake up," his son said on the phone. K.P. told him to shake her hard and call her name. "I am, Daddy, but she won't wake up," he said, crying.

"Where's Kayla?" he asked KJ, and he put her on the phone.

"Daddy, I've tried to wake Mommy, but she won't get up. I don't know what to do, Daddy. She won't wake up," she said hysterically. "Daddy, please come home," his daughter cried. Immediately, K.P. turned his truck around and headed south on the highway. He was in such a panic he forgot to call Janiece. When he got home, he dashed up the steps two at a time. Entering the master bedroom, he found his kids crying and still trying to wake up Kimberly. She was on the bed naked, and she was out.

He checked her pulse and was relieved to know she was still alive. He dialed 911 and continued to try to wake her. Quickly, he searched the room, looking for what she had taken, and found a prescription bottle with her name on it that he didn't even know she had.

"Oh no, Kim, baby. What did you do, sweetheart?" He continued to shake her and talk to her, trying to make her open her eyes. "Baby, please don't do this to us. The kids need you, baby. Now, open your eyes," but she didn't respond.

He sent the kids to their rooms and went and got her robe. Held her and cried until the ambulance arrived. Once they departed, he followed behind with the kids and called her parents to meet him at the hospital. He was praying, asking God to save her because he didn't want her to die. Why would she pull this type of stunt? Kimberly couldn't have loved him that much to do this to her children. They needed her more than she needed him. She loved her children. No way would she leave them like this, he thought to himself. Once they arrived at the hospital, Kimberly was rushed into the ER. K.P. and the kids were left in the waiting area.

"Is Mommy all right?" KJ asked him.

"She's going to be fine. Don't worry, son."

"Are you leaving us too, Daddy? Mommy said you don't want to be with us anymore. She said, Ms. Janine is going to take you away from us," Kayla said, getting Janiece's name wrong.

"No, baby, Daddy would never leave you guys. Don't worry your pretty little head about what Mommy said. Everything is going to be fine, I promise." He hoped he was right about that. He had no idea what would happen with Kimberly. He was scared himself of what would happen. He sat there holding his kids close, finally getting them to calm down, and then Kimberly's parents walked in with their housekeeper, Kami. After a quick update, Kimberly's mom suggested taking the kids home to her house.

The Graysons didn't ask any questions because they could see that K.P. was in no shape to answer anything. Besides, he was waiting to hear from the doctor. They sat there a few minutes in silence, and finally, the doctor came out to talk to them. He asked to speak with K.P.

because he was her husband, and her parents understood. The doctor said she was fine, but he would keep
her for several days to keep an eye on her. He told K.P.
that she had to meet with the mental health physician to
determine when she could return home.

"Can I go in to see her now?" he asked.

The doctor said yes, but only one at a time. So, Mr. and
Mrs. Grayson advised K.P. to go in first. He followed the
doctor and went in to see her. He sat in the chair by her
bed and looked at her pretty skin and tangled hair. She'd
probably die if she saw herself in the mirror because
she was always the jazzy, never-catch-me-on-a-bad-day
diva. Kimberly didn't go to the local grocery store without makeup. He smiled at her, looking so natural without
makeup and fake lashes. He closed his eyes for a few
moments, remembering her being pregnant and beautiful carrying his children. He thought about the holidays
and how she color-coordinated them for all of their holiday pictures. Although he hated it, she loved it. There
were moments in the beginning when he was giving his
marriage a genuine and honest effort where Kimberly
did make him laugh and even be happy. Yes, she was a
rich, spoiled-ass bitch, but she adored him and his children, and she had done a great job running their home.
She was an amazing mother, and those memories would
be the reason it was so hard to actually leave. Finally, he
opened his eyes to find Kimberly smiling a weak smile
back at him.

Instantly, it came back to him why they were there, so
he closed his eyes again. He wanted to ask her a million
questions, but he declined. Finally, he felt her moving
and opened his eyes to see her struggling to readjust
herself in the bed. He figured her stomach was sore, so he
gave her some assistance.

"I'm sorry," she whispered.

"No, baby, don't worry about it right now. Just rest."

"Are you leaving me here by myself?"

"No. I'm going to stay here with you 'til they let you come home."

"You're going to stay here with me?" she repeated, and the tears started rolling. He wiped them, but he was angry that she had gone that far to try to keep him from leaving.

"Kim, we're going to be all right. Don't worry, okay? I don't want you to worry. Your parents are here, and they want to visit with you too."

Shocked, she said, "You called my parents?" She questioned him in a panic.

"Yes, I was horrified. I wasn't sure what would happen to you. I *had* to call them."

"Did you tell them what I did?"

"No, I told them that you took the wrong pills by accident, so they don't know."

"Are you sure? I don't want them to know, K.P.," she cried.

"Kim, the doctor talked to me in private. He didn't talk to your parents. They don't know. Now, I'm going to get your mom because the doctor said only one at a time, okay?"

"Okay, but don't leave, K.P. Please, don't leave."

"Baby, I'm not leaving. I'll be right outside, and when they're finished, I'll come back in."

"All right," she said, and K.P. went out, so her mom could visit.

He went back out to the waiting room. Her dad didn't say much or ask a lot of questions, and K.P. was glad he didn't. He went to the nurse's station and filled out some papers for his wife to be admitted. His mind was all over the place, and he had so many questions for Kimberly. When her parents were finished, he walked them out.

Then he moved his car from where he was and parked where visitors were supposed to park. When he got ready to get out, he noticed the KBanks Jeweler's bag on the passenger-side floor and realized that Kayla must have put it on the floor when she got in the truck.

He took the black velvet box out of the bag and stuck it in the glove box. Before going back inside, he called Janiece to tell her what was happening, but she didn't answer. He left her a message that she needed to call him. He went back into the hospital and asked what room they put his wife in. He heard his phone alert that he had no signal. *That figures,* he thought to himself.

He got on the elevator. Why would Kimberly do something so crazy, like try to commit suicide? He had a mind to take custody of his children from her. He had vowed he'd never do that to her, but her suicide attempt changed everything.

He knew she was a good mother, but it was plain ole selfish of her just to decide to kill herself—unless she was trying to scare him, he thought. She was a spoiled brat who always wanted things her way, and he would not have been surprised if she faked it.

When he got to her room, he saw she wasn't in her bed and figured she was in the bathroom because the door was now closed. So when she came out, he helped her back into her bed. She held her hands against her abdomen and complained about her stomach being sore, and he wanted to say, "That's what you get for taking a bottle of sleeping pills," but he didn't.

"Why can't I go home?" she asked.

"Because the doctor wants to evaluate you in the morning."

"For what?" she snapped.

"For what? Kimberly, you tried to kill yourself. So why do you *think* they want to evaluate you?"

"Well, I'm fine. I just need a comb and my makeup bag and to get out of this hideous gown."

"Kim, what's wrong with you? You're acting like you didn't do anything. What you did or tried to do to yourself *is* a big deal. What were you thinking, and our babies were there, Kim," he said, angry and confused. He didn't want to stress her out, but he had to know.

"I don't know, okay," she yelled. "I just wanted to stop the pain. I just wanted the pain to go away. I wanted to sleep and wake up with all the pain gone. I feel like I'm losing my mind and my life, Kerry. I just want to make this work. I just want our marriage to work," she said and started to sob.

"And killing yourself would make our marriage work, Kim? Swallowing a bottle of pills was the answer? Kim, help me to understand. You could have been dead. Have you thought about *that?*"

"Would you even have cared, Kerry? That probably would have made you happy."

"Kim, stop making this about me. What about Kayla and KJ? Have you thought about *them?*"

"I have—have *you?*"

"Yes, I have!" he yelled and quickly caught himself. He was in a hospital. He didn't want to make things worse. The last thing he needed was some shrink to make him the bad guy.

"Look, Kim, I think about my kids all the time. I don't want to make them miserable by faking the funk. I don't want my unhappiness to trickle down on them. I won't be doing my kids a favor by staying where I'm not happy. Kayla and KJ will adjust, so don't think I don't think about my kids. You, on the other hand, didn't think of them today when you swallowed those damn pills. You were going to leave them to be without a mother."

"You're leaving them to be without a father for some tramp," she spat back at him.

"Stop it. I'm not going there with you, so let's just end this right now."

"Why, Kerry? Why can't you understand what you're putting me through?"

"Kim, what do you want me to do? Stay?"

"Yes," she said sadly.

"And then what? We walk around the house like we have been doing for the past year with no words, no time spent with each other, and no lovemaking? *That's* how you want it, Kimberly?" he asked, and she was quiet. She began to cry again, and that he hated. He hated to see Janiece cry, and he hated to see Kimberly cry because he remembered how his mom used to cry, trying to raise him by herself when he was younger. Seeing a woman cry was the worst thing for him.

"No, I just wanted you to love me. I just want my husband. No woman wants to let her husband just walk out the door and go to another woman. I can't help that my heart loves you, Kerry, but if you don't see any way that we can be together, then fine," she said, with the tears flowing.

She turned her body around and put her back to him. He knew she didn't mean that shit, so he didn't say another word. Instead, he grabbed the remote hanging on the side of her bed and turned on the television. Of course, they had a nice big private room, so the TV was quality. He reclined in the leather La-Z-Boy and flipped through the channels.

When he heard her whimpering, he didn't know what to say. So instead, he got up and went down the hall to get a coke and spotted the pay phones. Since he had no service on his phone, he tried Janiece again. When she didn't pick up her house phone, he dialed her cell, and she still didn't answer. So finally, he took his soda and went back into the room. Kimberly still had her back turned and was still sobbing. He rubbed her back, trying to comfort her and let her know that he did care that she was hurting, but he couldn't stay with her. He didn't love her, and he couldn't live another year like he had been living.

"Kim, baby, I'm so sorry. I never wanted to see you hurt. You gotta believe me. If there were another way, I would do it, but I promise you that I'm not deliberately trying to hurt you," he told her and was thankful and surprised that she didn't respond. He sat back on the recliner and flipped through the stations again.

After an hour, Kimberly was sleeping. He called her parents from the phone in the room to check on the kids, and then he walked back down the hall and tried calling Janiece again. She didn't answer. He was tempted to go by her place, but he didn't want Kimberly to wake up and find him missing. So finally, he called it a night and walked back to the room. He was relieved that Kim was still asleep when he got there. He looked at her caramel skin and high cheekbones. Her hair was nice and wavy. He never could understand why she was addicted to weaves.

He was attracted to her when they first met because she was a beautiful woman, but that attraction faded the more he got to know her. He looked at the little light freckles on her nose and smiled because his daughter Kayla had them too, just like her momma. He wished he could have fallen head over heels in love with Kimberly like he had fallen for Janiece. He wished he could turn back the hands of time and not have married Kimberly. He wished he would not have listened to her tell him that he'd grow to love her that night before their wedding.

Had he called it off, he would not be in the situation where he was now, ripping her heart apart. He thought he loved her some days, but he knew that wasn't true because the way he loved Janiece wasn't this day or that day; it was every day. He knew he was in love with Janiece when they went to Vegas. He didn't want to get on the plane to come back. He remembered that scene from *Harlem Nights,* when Sunshine made that catcall home and said, *"Put your momma on the phone. Look, I ain't never coming home no more; take it easy,"* and hung up. He wanted to do that, but he couldn't do that to his kids.

He decided then that he needed to make some changes, but to keep Kimberly off his back and keep the peace until the time was right, he tried to act normal, or at least as normal as he could, given their situation. He didn't want it to come to this bullshit that he was going through with the fighting, the drama, and now, the suicide attempt. All he could think about was how he would get custody of his kids. He didn't trust Kimberly anymore after that suicide stunt. He couldn't wait to call Marcus and tell him what that nutcase did this time. He knew Marcus had a solid case to get him custody of his kids.

K.P. tossed and turned in the chair, and the leather wasn't quiet. He was used to sleeping in his bed or the nice, comfy bed he had bought for Janiece a couple of years back. She always complained about having backaches, and he kept telling her it was her mattress. She denied it and said her mattress wasn't bad, but he knew that was her way of saying she couldn't afford to buy a new mattress set. So he went to the furniture store and had them deliver her a brand-new mattress. Later, she expressed how she was in shock. They set up and hauled that old back-aching mattress she had away, and she hasn't had a backache since, and neither had he.

"Come on, lie here with me," Kimberly offered him in a low, scratchy voice.

"Naw, I'm good," he said, refusing to get in bed with her.

"No, you're not. There's enough room for you." She pulled back the blanket for him to get in. Since her room was private, the bed was larger than the normal twin-sized ones.

"No, no, you rest. I'm fine over here."

"Look, I can't rest with all of that noise you're making on that leather."

He didn't argue anymore. He got up, and she slid over a little. She didn't have to because she was a tiny woman. She didn't take up much bed at all.

The first thing he thought about was Janiece when he closed his eyes. Was she in bed, lying next to another man? He would have liked to have been with Janiece, holding her close rather than lying next to the unstable one. He hoped Kimberly didn't have a shank under her pillow. He prayed and asked God to protect him from the evil one lying next to him, and soon, he fell asleep.

Chapter Seventeen

Janiece held Isaiah's hand tighter after putting her phone back into her purse. He looked over at her, and his warm smile made her relax and not let the thoughts of K.P. and his crazy wife ruin her evening. When she got back to her place earlier that afternoon, she saw a silver Chrysler 300 in her guest stall. She was a little nervous now since "Crazy" knew where she lived. She didn't want to come home and have her psycho ass jumped out of nowhere with a blade or something, so when she got out of her car, she looked around carefully and watched her back going up the steps.

She was relieved when she found out the car was another vehicle that Isaiah had gotten from his dad's dealership. This was beginning to be too much for Janiece, and this stress was unwanted. She wanted to give K.P. back to Kimberly and stop the harassment. She was so furious about K.P. not showing up to meet her at the coffee house that she grabbed a trash bag from the kitchen and cleaned out his drawers. She was doing fine putting his stuff in the bag until she came across the photo envelope with pictures from the trip to Las Vegas.

She stopped and sat on the bed, looked at them, and thought about how much fun it was and what a good time she had with him. She fought back the tears as she thumbed through the memories. She wanted to live like they did when they were in Vegas. They didn't stay in one of the hotels. Instead, K.P. rented a vacation home, so they had a backyard with a giant barbecue grill and a pool with a hot tub. A colossal whirlpool tub was in the master bedroom, and Janiece was amazed when she saw it. She knew it had to cost a fortune, but she didn't dare ask.

They rented a car and went to the store to get groceries. They didn't cook because they were so used to being indoors in Chicago. Janiece prepared breakfast, but for lunch, they ate out. And for dinner, they ate out too. Only one night did they take advantage of cooking, and they grilled outside and ate on the patio.

It was so lovely to go out in public and be able to hold hands and kiss. K.P. displayed so much public affection it made her feel like a teenager. He showered her with kisses and held her close to him the entire trip.

Everywhere they went, people knew that they were a couple, which made Janiece smile the whole time. They made love every morning, in the afternoon, and every night. They took long baths together and enjoyed the seven days and six nights in their own little world. That was the only time she had him all night in their five-year relationship. You couldn't pay him to take that chance in Chicago back then.

Janiece wanted to go on another trip, but it never happened. She begged him to take her to Vegas again, and he'd always say, "Soon, not now. Be patient." "Be patient," she said out loud and laughed. She stuffed the pictures back into the envelope and stuck them into her nightstand drawer. Finished, she walked over to her closet and picked out a pair of jeans that she didn't have to iron. Next, she pulled the Rubbermaid storage container from under her bed and took a sweater out of it. The weather was starting to get a lot cooler. The first of October was rolling around again, and Old Man Winter was packing his bags to get ready to visit Chicago.

Janiece hopped in the shower to do a quick wash because she had bathed before meeting K.P., but she knew she wanted to invite Isaiah up after their date, and you can never be too fresh. So she got out and wrapped a towel around her, decided to do her makeup first, and after that, she'd lotion up when her skin dried a little more.

She combed her hair down from her molded wrap to see if she had to flat iron it and was happy to find that she didn't have to. Her relaxed hair was still fresh, and it looked beautiful. She wrapped it back up and put her wrap cap back on. Finally, she lotioned up and then dressed. After putting on her jewelry, she went back to do her hair. Applying her lipstick was the finishing touch. She wiped down and straightened things to make her company friendly. At that point, her phone rang. She looked at the caller ID and noticed it was a 708 number, but she didn't recognize it, so she didn't pick up.

A few moments later, the same number came on her phone, and she thought whoever it was had to leave her a message. She looked at the clock and checked her voicemail because that person did leave a message. When she heard K.P.'s voice, she was tempted to hang up, but she didn't because she was curious why he was calling from a different number than his usual number. It wasn't his house number unless they had gotten that number changed because she knew it.

She hit the SEND button to call the number back but got a busy tone. She tried calling his phone, and it went straight to voicemail. She didn't leave a message. Instead, she just hung up. She would call the other number back again, but suddenly, someone knocked on the door, and she knew it was Isaiah. He was looking so good that she wanted to skip their plans to go out and just do him.

"Hey, handsome," she said and kissed him.

"Hey, yourself, gorgeous. Are you ready?"

"Yes. Let me get my jacket and my purse." She went to the hall closet and grabbed her jacket. Then she picked up her keys and her purse, and they headed out the door.

"This is a nice ride," she said, complimenting the Chrysler.

"Thanks. I wanted to try something different," he remarked, opening the door for her.

"I wish I had the hookup to drive a different car every other week."

"Stick with me, kid. Who knows." He smiled, and they rode out.

They hopped on the Dan Ryan and headed downtown. Isaiah looked at her like she was a piece of steak, and she gave him the same stare. First, they went to Houston's to dine. They were having a good time talking and laughing. He was telling her army jokes, and she was cracking up at the table. She enjoyed him so much and thought he was a great guy she could see herself with for a long time.

She was laughing at something Isaiah said and happened to look over and saw Shawnee Williams from work. Janiece tried to turn fast to avoid eye contact, but it was too late. She stopped laughing when she saw Shawnee, the nosy one, get up, and she knew she was headed over to say hello. And indeed, Shawnee strutted over and paused when she realized it wasn't K.P. that Janiece was out with.

"Hey, girl, what's going on?" she said, sounding so lively and bubbly.

"Hello, Shawnee, this is Isaiah Lawton. Isaiah, meet Shawnee Williams. We work together."

"Hi, Isaiah, it's so nice to meet you," she said, extending her hand, and they shook for what seemed like an eternity. Since Shawnee assumed Janiece was in love with K.P., she thought maybe this man was someone she could hook up with.

"So, Janiece, I didn't know you had a brother this fine."

"I said Lawton, not Hawkins, and I only have a sister, and you know that. So Isaiah isn't my brother, Shawnee," Janiece said, looking at her like she was slow.

"Oh yeah, that's right. Janelle, right?" Shawnee said, not taking her eyes off Isaiah.

"Yeah, right."

"Well, who is this handsome man?" she asked, smiling and being her natural flirty self. Every time Janiece saw her, she would think of Hottie from *Flavor of Love*.

"He's my date."

"Oh really? My bad," she said, looking at Janiece like *this ain't K.P.* "Well, you and your date have a good evening, and tell Mr. Paxton I'll be calling him soon about that mortgage."

"Will do," Janiece said as Shawnee trotted back to her table. Her clothes were always a size too small, and Janiece wondered what her hair looked like under all that weave. She had been working with her for years and had no clue about what her hair really looked like . . . or even if she had any.

She mentioned K.P. on purpose, ole heifer. Janiece knew she had done that deliberately, but she didn't sweat it. They left and went to the movies, and while Isaiah was getting popcorn, Janiece was by herself in the theater. The film hadn't started, so she tried to call that 708 number again. It rang about ten times, and finally, someone picked up.

"Hello," said an unknown voice.

"Hello, someone called me from this number."

"Maybe so, but this is a pay phone," the woman told her.

"A pay phone? Where?"

"This phone is in the hospital."

"Which hospital, please, ma'am?"

"South Suburban," she replied.

"Okay, thank you," and she hung up. "South Suburban Hospital," she said out loud. "What's K.P. doing at the hospital?" She started to stress. What if he had been hurt or something happened to one of his kids? She tried his phone again, and it went straight to voicemail as before. She was about to get up, but Isaiah returned with the popcorn and soda.

As soon as the movie started, she relaxed a little. However, she was still thinking about K.P., and she hoped he was okay. After the movie, she went to the restroom and called again. That time, she left him a message. *"K.P., this is Jai. Please call me. I'm worried out of my mind. What happened? Are you or one of the kids hurt? Just call me,"* and she hung up. Her stomach was tied in knots, but she went back out like everything was good. When they got back to her condo, Janiece poured herself a glass of wine to calm her nerves.

"What's wrong?" Isaiah asked her.

"Nothing. I'm fine," she said and took a sip of her wine. She didn't make eye contact because she didn't want him to see her distress. She just needed a few more sips, and then she'd be better.

"Are you sure? You seem a little tense. Am I making you nervous?"

"Of course not, K.P. Why would I be nervous?"

"Well, if I were K.P., maybe I'd know the answer to that."

"I'm sorry, Isaiah. I don't know why I said that. That was totally an accident." He looked at her and knew something was up.

"Okay, Janiece, I need you to level with me. Are you really *ready* to move on?"

"Yes, yes, I want to move forward."

"Are you really ready to move forward?" he asked and allowed her time to think before she answered.

"Listen, Isaiah, K.P. and I had some wonderful times, and I loved him for a while. If you ask me if I'm ready, I honestly can't say yes, but being ready isn't always the case. I wanted something that wasn't for me for a long time, and now I know that if I keep waiting to be ready to change, it won't happen. I have to make that change, and then the change comes."

"Okay, I understand. You have to crawl before you walk, and I will work with you, Janiece, but I want you, and I don't know how much longer I can take being around you and not being able to have you."

"You want me?"

"Yes, that's a fact."

"What if I told you that I wanted you too?"

"Then I'd say I'm right here." He leaned over and kissed her. She put her glass down on the coffee table and turned her attention back to him. She wanted Isaiah, yes, but she thought about K.P in the back of her mind. She was silently praying to God that he was safe and well.

Now, Isaiah's hands were all over her body. His kisses were so sweet and good, but she kept thinking about K.P., and she felt like she was cheating on him again. She let Isaiah lift her sweater away from her body. She was wearing a camisole under it, without a bra. Before long, the camisole was off too.

Her hard nipples were exposed, and he rubbed and squeezed them just the way she liked. His hands were feeling so good she couldn't wait to have his wet mouth on them, so she pushed his head down to let him know where she wanted his mouth to reside. As he sucked on her nipples, her clit started to pulsate.

She could feel the moisture coming on. He licked and sucked on her nipples so well she couldn't hold back the *oohs* and the *aahs*. That encouraged him to suck even harder. She was becoming more and more turned on. Finally, she told Isaiah to hold on, and she stood up.

"Follow me," she said, and obediently, he followed
her into her bedroom. They immediately began kissing
when they got into her room. She helped him take off his
sweater, and he began to unbuckle his belt and unfasten
his jeans.

Janiece lit some candles and turned on the disc player.
Then she removed her jeans, and all she had on were her
pink-laced panties. He walked over to her and started
kissing her on her neck. "You are so sexy. You know that?"

"Yeah, I know," she said, and they softly laughed. He
wasn't expecting her to respond like that. "Hold on a
minute." She walked over to her nightstand and opened
it to get a condom. The pictures from Vegas were lying
on top of the condoms, which caused her to pause for a
moment.

But it was too late to stop now. She had to finish what
she had started. She just wanted that feeling of cheating
on K.P. to go away. So she handed Isaiah the plastic.

"Thanks, but I have this one covered," he said to her,
taking it from her hand.

"Well, you never know, right?"

"You're right; now, come here," he said, pulling her
close. He nibbled on her neck and teased her with his
tongue. His hand moved down south and felt her moist-
ness, and that made his erection stiffen harder. Next, he
slid her panties off and let them drop to the floor. She
stepped out of them and moved her right leg apart, allowing him more access to her wet tunnel. She moaned
while his fingers stroked her clit.

She made her way to his waiting dick, grabbed it, and
stroked it. It was not thick like she thought it would be,
but it was long. It curved at the tip, which made her pussy
jump for joy because that curve just had a way of pleasing
a sister. They made their way to the bed, and she eased
back and watched him roll the condom on what indeed
looked like twelve inches of solid steel.

She was used to K.P., who had a big, thick dick. It was only about nine or ten inches, but it always made her feel good. She was afraid that Isaiah would end up puncturing her uterus with his love tool. His body was cut and defined, and he looked sexy as hell to her putting on that condom. With that business taken care of, he climbed on top of her, and she spread her legs wide. She was ready to receive that beautiful piece of dick.

He kissed her deeply before dipping his dick into her by now, soaking-wet canal. His eyes lit up with excitement when he felt the walls of her insides. The cushion that surrounded him was giving him unbelievable pleasure. It was so wet that he could hear her juices popping as he stroked her. She moaned as he pumped her at a steady pace. "Oh, Janiece, baby, it's good," were the only words he could come up with.

He enjoyed the silky, soft massage her pussy gave his hard dick as he rode her thick thighs. He had to bury his face in her shoulder to concentrate on not exploding. He hadn't had sex since he had come home over six months ago on break. And before that, it was with a woman at Fort Hood that he dumped before going back to Iraq because she was a lying ho.

The first night he got back was nothing but drama. So after he tapped that ass, he told her to beat it. He hooked up with another chick right before he left that he thought he liked and thought he'd try to get to know, but when he got back to Iraq, she told the truth. She was married.

He kind of knew something was up because the night they hooked up, it was at her girl's house. Finding out she was married didn't come as a shock because most women around military bases lied anyway, especially when their husbands were deployed. This was fucked up because their husbands may not make it home, and they don't care. Those hoes just spend all their husbands' hard-earned money and give away the ass. That was why he hadn't found a wife yet.

Damn, he thought to himself, trying to hold back his nut. He slowed his movement, grabbed Janiece tightly, and told her to be still. She knew that was a man's way of saying, "Freeze, or I'll shoot," so she stopped her hip rolling. But it was feeling too good to her for him to stop. She didn't want it to be over just yet. He moved his attention back to her nipples, and the sensation for him to stroke her started to reactivate.

"Come on, baby, give me some more," she begged.

"Oh, you want more?"

"Yes," she whispered, letting out a deep breath. He forced his way back in. He'd come almost entirely out and slid back in, and *that* drove her insane. He pushed her legs up higher so that they were on his shoulders by now. She was so wet. The popping sounds were louder than the soft music that was playing. He had to take a look at her treasure box, so he eased back and opened her legs wide, so he could see himself going in and out of her.

He shouldn't have done that, though, because the sight of it made him pump harder and faster, and he shot his juices into the condom. He was mad at himself for not letting her get hers first, but the sight of her glistening opening was all he needed to send him off, and he was not happy with his six-minute session. "I'm sorry, baby," he said, apologizing.

"For what . . . ?"

"For . . . you know . . . if I could only have held on to it a little longer. It was just too good, baby."

"You don't have to apologize. We got all night."

"Oh, it's like that?"

"Yeah, mon, it tis like dat," she said, giving her Jamaican-girl impression.

"You gon' regret saying that."

"Oh yeah? *Make* me regret it," she teased. She wanted him to bring it again if he could bring it like that. He went into the bathroom and flushed the condom down the toilet. She was lying in her bed feeling a little guilty, but she straightened up when he came back into the room. She pulled the covers back, and he climbed into bed.

"Damn, girl, do you get wet like that all the time?"

"I guess. I never knew that wasn't normal," she lied. K.P. told her that she was like a water hose down there, and he loved that shit.

"No, that is extra good. I thought I was in a tunnel of silk."

"Ump, now, don't be blowing up my head."

"Naw, I'm just speaking the truth. I don't know how a man can get some of that and want someone else."

"Well, not all men are the same," she said, trying not to get started on how K.P. could leave her and continue to be with Kimberly. She knew deep down that K.P. loved her. And she didn't want anything bad said about him.

"Yeah, you're right, we're all different," he said and held her close in her candlelit room, and it reminded her of K.P. He had been the only man she had been within the past five years and the only man to climb into her bed. She looked over at the clock and smiled. At least this time, she didn't have to set her alarm for two a.m. Isaiah was able to stay all night, which she wanted. She rested on his chest, and he caressed her back as she rubbed the soft hairs on his stomach, admiring his long dick, which seemed to tap her on the hand.

"Oh, I see what time it is," she said.

"And you know it," he said, and once again, it was on.

Chapter Eighteen

The morning light hit her room, and the sun shined all over her face. He was sleeping like a log, so Janiece eased out of bed to go the bathroom. When she finished, she washed her hands and face, brushed her teeth, and pulled her hair back into a ponytail. It was messy and wild from the events the night before. She wished she had taken the time to tie it up, but since she didn't, she had to work with it later to get it back the way it was supposed to be. Quietly, she went into the kitchen and looked out the window.

Janiece took out her frying pan and a pot and started breakfast. It was close to noon, and the light was blinding. She cracked the kitchen window to let in some fresh air while she cooked. Then she popped in her Jill Scott CD and pulled her bedroom door closed so that she wouldn't wake Isaiah. While she mixed the pancake batter, she sang along to "So In Love With You." Next, she went into the fridge and pulled out onions, tomatoes, and green peppers for the omelets she would make.

She rocked to the music while dicing the veggies and slicing the cantaloupe. She also made herself a mimosa and frowned because she made it kind of intense. Janiece tried to get through at least thirty minutes of her morning without thinking about K.P. She wanted so badly not to think of him and just let him go, but he was always on her mind. She wanted to enjoy Isaiah and not let K.P. be a distraction, but she couldn't help but wonder how he was doing and what was going on with him.

He didn't show up the day before to meet her, and now the hospital thing was puzzling her. She grabbed the phone book and the phone, looked up the number, and called the hospital. She asked for Kerry Paxton, and the operator replied that no one was admitted by that name. She hung up but called right back and asked for Kerry Jr. or Kayla Paxton. The operator apologized and said she had no one by their names either. Janiece hung up and waited five minutes, then called back. That time, she asked, for Kimberly Paxton. The operator patched her through. When she heard Kimberly's voice, she hung up.

Once more, she called K.P.'s phone and only got the voicemail. So she figured he was with her and had his phone powered off. She was relieved when she found out it wasn't K.P. in the hospital, but it was crazy. She couldn't help but wonder what happened to "Crazy." Maybe she got run over by a bus, Janiece thought to herself and laughed out loud. That woman was an evil bitch, and maybe God decided to take her out. She laughed at her crazy thoughts and then asked God to forgive her for thinking such terrible things about that woman.

She didn't want to be like Kimberly's evil ass. She couldn't help but wonder what was wrong with her, though, that caused her to be hospitalized. She hoped it wasn't horrible. "Oh well," she said and went back to preparing breakfast. She was just about finished when Isaiah entered the kitchen.

"Good morning. It smells good in here."

"Morning to you, too, sleepyhead."

"Why didn't you wake me? I could have cooked for you."

"Naw, I can cook, plus you were sleeping so hard."

"Yeah, that bed of yours is very comfortable. That's an excellent mattress. I could sleep for days in that bed," he said, stretching, and it gave Janiece a weird feeling. K.P. had bought that mattress for her, and now she was letting another man enjoy it. She felt like crap.

"Yeah, it's the best." He made sure of that, she mumbled under her breath.

"Well, I'm gon' run across the hall and brush my teeth and wash my face. How much longer is it gonna be?"

"About five minutes, so hurry. I don't want the omelets to get cold."

"Okay, I'll be right back," he said and walked out the front door instead of the back because the front hallway was closed in. He didn't have on anything but his jeans and wife beater, and the air was cold. Janiece grabbed the phone and called Janelle while she was alone to talk.

"Girl, I gave him some," she smiled.

"Gave who what?"

"Isaiah, you nut. I gave him some last night."

"You're a liar," Janelle teased. She knew little Jai was too sprung on K.P. to be giving her goods away to another man. "K.P. gon' kick your ass."

"Yes, I did, and K.P. ain't gon' know."

"Girl, K.P. gonna know. He probably was twitching all night," she joked as they chuckled. "Was it good is what I wanna know," Janelle asked, itching to know the details.

"Girl, let me tell you, that shit was the bomb."

"That good? Aww, snap, there's a new sheriff in town."

"We'll see. Now, Janelle, how in the world can I have met a brother that is fine, intelligent, and got it going on in the bedroom, and I can't stop thinking about K.P.? What's wrong with me?"

"First, you know the answer to that. It's because you're still in love with him. It's early, Janiece. It's gonna take a minute or two to get over him."

"Yeah, I guess you're right. It hasn't been long since I declared I was leaving him alone."

"So when are you gonna tell him, little sis?"

"I wanted to tell him this weekend, but I haven't heard from him or seen him. Then his wife is in the hospital."

"How do you know that?" she asked, and Janiece filled her in briefly on what had transpired over the weekend with the pay phone and so forth. She talked for several more minutes, and then when she heard Isaiah come in the door, she quickly got off the phone. After she and Isaiah enjoyed their food, they got busy again.

After two sensational rounds, they got up, showered, dressed, and then Janiece went to her sister's. She tried K.P. again on her way and still got his voicemail. When she pulled up to Janelle's house, she used the garage door opener that Janelle had given her awhile back.

She didn't park inside the garage because Janelle's car and Greg's truck were already parked inside, but she went through the garage, walked into the house, and called out their names, but no one answered. So she went into the fridge and grabbed a bottle of water.

"Hello," she snapped again, and still, no one responded. She stood at the bottom of the steps and called out her sister's name, and by now, she was a little spooked when there was no reply. She knew they couldn't have been getting busy because she called Janelle to tell her she was on her way.

She walked away, went into the family room, and grabbed the remote to turn on the TV. However, before she hit the power button, she heard screaming and thumping, so she quickly hopped up from the couch to see what was wrong. She ran up the stairs calling her sister's name.

"In here," she heard Janelle's voice coming from the master bedroom. Janiece slowly pushed the door open and called out again. "In here, Jai, in the bathroom."

Janiece walked into the bathroom and found Greg leaning against the vanity, and Janelle was sitting on the tile frame around her garden tub.

"What's going on? I heard you scream."

"You wanna tell her, or should I?" Janelle asked Greg.

"Tell me what?"

"You're going to be an auntie!" Janelle exclaimed, holding up the pregnancy test stick. She was waving it in Janiece's face as if she had not pissed on it.

"No way," Janiece said and grabbed her arm to take a look at the stick and to keep her sister from waving that pissy thing in her face again.

"You're serious. Oh shit." She hugged Janelle, and they started screaming together. "I'm gonna be an auntie," she said again, and Greg stood aside, waiting for them to acknowledge that he had a part, however small, in it too. "Oh, congratulations, brother-in-law," Janiece said and hugged him as well. He said thanks and got out of their way.

"I'm going to head down and start dinner," he told Janelle and kissed her on the cheek. He smiled at her and hugged her tight. They were going to have their first baby, and you could see how happy they were. More than ever, Janiece wanted to have what they had one day.

Greg went downstairs, and Janiece stood and watched Janelle looking at her belly from the side in the mirror like she was expecting to see a baby bump already.

"A baby! I didn't know you were over here making babies, Ms. Janelle."

"Chile, I wasn't. Greg snuck me one night about six or seven weeks ago after we had come home from one of his coworker's parties. We both had been drinking, and we walked into the house attacking each other. The next morning, I realized what we had done it without my diaphragm, and we both decided to be careful from that night on. Since my period hadn't shown its ugly face in almost two weeks now, he decided to go out and get the test for me a little while before you called."

"So why didn't you tell me this morning when I called?"

"Because I wanted to be sure first, and now I'm sure, and you, my darling, are going to be an auntie," she smiled at the mirror and looked at her stomach like it would grow in a matter of minutes. "I'm gonna be so fat, I know I am."

"Girl, please . . . Your little bitty waist gon' pop back to its original form afterward. You got Daddy's genes. Me, on the other hand, take after Mom's big hip, thick thigh, brick house side," she said, and they cracked up.

"Jai, girl, please, all women are not meant to be small, and trust, I got Momma's genes in me too. Who knows how I'm gonna look once this bighead little boy pops out."

"Boy? You mean my *niece*. We ain't used to no boys. We don't know what to do for a boy."

"I know we don't, but Greg does, and I know he wants a son," she said and walked into her bedroom. Janiece followed and sat on the bench at the foot of the Queen Anne-posted bed. Janelle's entire house had that Victorian look, really princess-type of décor, which was beautiful for Janelle, but the opposite of Janiece's style.

"Well, I feel sorry for Greg because this baby is going to be a girl. All we know how to do is dress pretty and comb hair. We don't know about taking care of no boys."

"Well, whatever this baby is, I know we're going to spoil it rotten. And when I become an auntie, I'm gonna do the same thing."

"If that ever happens . . ."

"It will, Janiece. Just give it time."

"Yeah, whatever you say."

"Just wait, you'll see. The right man will come along, and you'll be married with a house full. You watch."

"Nellie, don't be mad, and I don't want to upset you or start no shit, but I want you to listen to me without getting mad."

"What is it?"

"I know you don't approve or respect my relationship with K.P., and I understand your reasons, but I want you to know I love him, Janelle, and I'm trying so hard *not* to love him, but it's not easy. It wasn't planned when I fell in love with K.P. I know I should have left him a long time ago, but I didn't. So I'm baffled right now, and I'm not sure what to do.

"I like Isaiah, and he's so much fun, and he's great, but I love K.P., and if he's finally leaving Kimberly and is going to divorce her, why can't I consider giving us a chance? Maybe things will work, and he will make me happy," she said and waited for Janelle to blow up and call her stupid and say horrible things about K.P., but she didn't. Instead, she blew out a breath and carefully chose her words before speaking.

"Look, Jai, you know K.P. better than I do, and I know that he may love you. You're an excellent person. You're bright, beautiful, and I can see why K.P. loves you, but all I ask is for you to be smart about it, Janiece.

"You are not some desperate old chick that is in the husband-stealing business. You are 27 with time to find Mr. Right. If he wants you, he has to come honest and correct. I think him cheating on Kimberly is a low and dirty thing, but I don't know what his marriage is like, and it is possible for him to love you and be faithful to you, although he didn't do that with her. Just don't allow him to continue to live on both sides of the fence. If it's you, demand it's only you—no back and forth between you two women.

"Don't continue to be his mistress. Tell him that you love him and you will be there when he has resolved his issues with his wife—and only then. If you are still in love and interested in being with K.P., that's the time to pursue the relationship. All that crap that his wife is doing—with the threats and the phone calls—you shouldn't have to deal with that type of mess.

"That's what I don't like about K.P. because I know you are a smart person, Janiece, and if you love him, I know he is worth loving. I just hate to see you let him treat you like you are less important."

"I understand everything that you're saying. I just want you to know that I can't guarantee that I won't give him another chance. My mind says move on, but my heart says otherwise."

"In a case like that, you have to be wise, just like your heart may want a pair of shoes or a cute purse, but if you have to pay the light bill first, your mind overrules that urge, and you do the right thing."

"I know, but love is much more complicated than buying yourself a cute purse."

"You can say that again," she said.

"Nellie, I just don't want you to be disappointed in me or look down on me because of my decisions where K.P. is concerned."

"Jai, listen, I will never look down on you. You have your own life to live. My main concern is your happiness, and if that turns out to be with K.P., or Isaiah, or whomever, as long as you're happy, I'm happy."

"And if it is K.P. I don't want you hating him and treating him like you've been treating him, like crap."

"Now, I can't promise you anything on that," she said, smirking. "But if you ever marry him, I will let the past be the past. Family is family, and if he turns out to be the father of my nieces and nephews, I'll have to be nice."

"Hold on, that is, *niece* or *nephew*. Keep in mind K.P. already has two with 'Crazy.' He doesn't make that much money." They giggled and talked a bit more about the future and the new baby. Soon, they got the calendar and calculated the month the new baby would come. They guessed it would be around June of next year. Janiece remembered that was when Isaiah would be returning to Chicago.

After that, they ate, and then Janiece headed back home. She tried calling K.P. and still didn't get him. Confused and lonely, she called Isaiah to see if he would be at his sister's, and he said he would and wanted to come over when she got in.

At first, she said no and told him she was a little tired, but after he bribed her with pralines and ice cream from Baskin-Robbins, she agreed to have a bit of late-night company. She definitely didn't want him to spend the night because she decided to ease up a little since she wasn't ready to pursue that relationship. She thought about how she had so many fantasies of her and K.P. getting married, moving to Las Vegas, and starting a family.

They always talked about moving there and how many children they'd have and everything they would do if circumstances and situations differed. Janiece never took any of what they spoke about seriously because she knew she'd set herself up for disappointment. There were no talks of him leaving Kimberly until a week or so ago. She wanted to believe that it was true, and he was earnest about leaving his wife, but she had a hard time trusting that.

Also, she didn't want to get all excited because leaving Kimberly wasn't a guarantee that he would be with her. so she was still in a state of what-ifs. What if he does this, or what if he does that? What if Isaiah wants this? What if he has someone back in Texas? What if she was moving too fast? What if she was using Isaiah? What if K.P. was serious about being with Janiece? What if his wife was really crazy and she had to watch her back? She didn't know what to do. Too many what-ifs. She was perplexed.

That night when she shut the door behind Isaiah after finally convincing him that she wanted to be alone to get some rest, she tried calling K.P. again. When she reached his voicemail, she didn't say a word. She just held the phone until she heard the automated system tell her there was no more time allowed for her message.

She hung up the phone and tried to go to sleep. After tossing for a while, she fell asleep with her sister Janelle and the pregnancy on her mind. She smiled at the idea of having a new baby in the family, and that helped her finally settle down.

Chapter Nineteen

Two days later, Kimberly was finally released from the hospital. They were on their way home in K.P.'s truck, and Kimberly wanted to stop for some food. Of course, K.P. didn't want to stop because now that she was no longer in the hospital, he was free to go. He wanted to see Janiece as soon as he possibly could.

The last three days were hell because he was stuck in the hospital with Kimberly, and when he was there, his phone had no service. He went home briefly to shower the day before, but he could hardly shower because Kimberly called him every three minutes, making sure he was coming right back.

To avoid any argument and the fact that Kimberly was still a little unstable, he hurried back to the hospital after only having a two-minute shower. She was a bit nutty, and he didn't want to do anything to make matters worse.

He tried calling Janiece on her phone on the way back, hoping he'd catch her, but he got her voicemail. So he called her work phone but figured she wasn't at her desk when he called.

The last three days went by slow as hell, and being with Kimberly was driving K.P. crazy. He had been by her side night and day. When they released her from the hospital, he felt like he had just been released from prison. Now, instead of just letting him take her home, she wanted to stop for food. There was plenty to eat at the house. She had only been in the hospital for three days. The food didn't spoil or disappear from their fridge.

"Kimberly, you just got out of the hospital. Don't you want to go home and shower and relax?"

"Kerry, I've been eating hospital food for three days, and trust me, it was horrible. I'd like to go and have a nice meal with some tasty seasonings."

"Kimberly, do you think your stomach is ready to digest spices and stuff? You just had your stomach pumped a couple of days ago. Why don't you let me take you home, you take a nice, long shower, and I'll fix you something?"

"No, K.P. So many restaurants are here. We can stop and get something to eat. I'm hungry," she whined.

"Fine," he said and pulled into the parking lot of Texas Roadhouse. He parked, and before they got out, she pulled down the visor to check her face. Then she opened the glove box looking for only God knows what, when he heard her yell, "What the fuck is this?"

"Give it to me," he said, reaching for the box.

"No, what is this?" she asked, shaking it in his face instead of opening it.

"It's none of your business," he said, trying to take the box. He didn't get it out of her hand, and she finally opened it. When she saw the diamond, she clutched her chest.

"You got her a fucking ring, K.P.? Our divorce ain't nowhere near final, and you buying rings and trying to propose?" she snapped.

"Kimberly, let me make something clear to you. When we get the divorce, what I do and whom I see is none of your business. I bought that ring, and to be honest, I'm not sure when I was gon' give it to her. Now, please, give me the ring."

"No," she said and closed the box in her hand. She was holding on to it like, *I dare you to try to take it.*

"Kim . . . Why are you so difficult? I'm so tired of dealing with you. *This* is why I hate to be around you because you are so evil and spoiled. If things are not Kimberly's way, then it's no way."

"You know what, you ungrateful son of a bitch? I'm done with your tired ass. You wouldn't have shit or even be shit if it weren't for what *I've* done for you."

"Kim, here we go again. You didn't make me into who I am. I've worked my ass off for your father and brought plenty of business and revenue to that company, so don't give me that shit. All you did was help me help your dad's company damn near triple in business since I've been there. I worked my ass off to have what we have. Every dime I've made, I *earned* it. So you can stop walking around thinking you made me.

"I've given you everything that I could afford to provide you with, but it's never enough. You are the one who always wants more and more and more. I'd love it if I could please you, Kim, but nothing I do is ever good enough.

"You always go running to your daddy when I say no to something. You can't settle for less than this or less than that. Even the ring I bought you wasn't good enough. You just had to upgrade, so what do you do? Run to your daddy. 'Daddy, I want five carats, and all he gave me was three.'

"I want a six-bedroom house, with four bathrooms. Four bedrooms and only two bathrooms will be too small. No, Kerry, we can't possibly buy that cheap old crib for our baby to sleep in. This more expensive one is better," he said, mimicking her. He was tired of trying to please her. He couldn't satisfy her. She always had to have a newer, bigger, more expensive name-brand something.

"That's why I love Janiece, and if you want to know the truth, she doesn't ask for anything, nor does she complain about anything I give her. She doesn't frown up her face if I provide her with something not made by Prada or Gucci. She's happy if I buy her half a carat or a twenty-inch television versus a giant plasma screen. One dozen roses are fine for her. She's never counted them in my face to make sure they were all there.

"You want the truth? Here it is. I feel as if there is nothing I can do to satisfy my wife. If I can't hand over the world, I am less than a man to you. If I can't compete with Kimberly's daddy, then what good am I? Every attempt I make to try to please you, you poke your lip out. Not once in our entire marriage have you just smiled and said, 'Thank you, baby, this is nice.' Whenever I have done anything for Janiece, her face lights up, and she appreciates the thought. What do you want me for, Kimberly? I don't understand why you want to hold on to me when I can't give any of what you want," he said, glad to finally tell the truth and say how he really felt.

"First of all, I can't help it if I want the best of everything. It's not my fault, K.P., that I feel like I should have the top of the line or the biggest or the most expensive. That's just who I am. Second, just because your low-class, broke-ass mistress will settle for the measly scraps you throw her is hardly a good enough reason for me to accept *that* as the reason why you want her more than you want me. I can't help it if her daddy didn't work hard and spoil her like my daddy spoiled me.

"That's *her* misfortune. I'm not going to apologize to you because my face doesn't light up at some of the things you give me, K.P., when I'm used to having it all and having the best, and I ain't gon' change. As long as I can get it, I'm going to get it. So if you're leaving me because you feel less than a man because you can't measure up to my daddy, hey," she said, with no regard to anything he had said. She was just a spoiled brat, and he felt at that moment that she didn't love him. She just didn't want to lose to Janiece.

She felt like she was better than Janiece. For K.P. to be leaving her for someone not of her caliber, Kimberly's biggest problem was not because she truly loved him. The outside appearance was everything, and in her circle, there was only wealth and riches. If word got out that K.P. left her for a regular ole poor girl like Janiece, she'd be the talk of the country club.

"Well, I guess we're clear because all you're saying is what you want and what you can get, so fine. We know that you can get and have everything that you want, so I guess you'll be totally fine. Continue to be that little spoiled, tactless brat that you have been, and everything for Kimberly will be just fine."

"Call me what you want. You can take this funky-little-ass ring," she said and threw it at him. "This bullshit is too small for my taste anyway. Now, take me home to my house, the house that I *deserve* to live in. I hope you and your fat, broke-ass, humble bitch live happily ever after in her little bitty-ass apartment on Ninety-Fifth Street," she spat and then quickly paused. He was sure she didn't mean to let those words slip out of her mouth. Revealing that she knew where Janiece lived definitely wasn't her intent, he thought as his right brow raised.

"So, what else do you know, Kimberly? You don't have to fake the funk now. How long have you known? What, you've been following me?"

"You've been fucking her for more than five years. Why does my knowing surprise you? And what does it matter how long I've known? The fact is I know."

"You know, you're right," he said and started the ignition. He pulled out of the parking space and drove home. He didn't say another word to her the entire ride. He pulled into their garage and got out without helping her out of the high seat. He put the ring he had bought for Janiece into his pocket, walked inside, and keyed in the code to turn off the alarm. Then he walked over to the cordless and grabbed it from the charger. He dialed his friend Marcus's phone.

"Hello," he answered.

"Hey, man, what's cracking? This is K.P."

"Yo, man, what's up?"

"Listen, I need a favor," he said, rubbing his temple.

"Yeah? Whatcha need?"

"A place to crash for a minute, you know, 'til my shit is square out there," he said, not caring what he said in front of Kimberly. There were no secrets now, except for his plans to relocate.

"Sure, man, no problem. I haven't been there in days. I've been at Tracy's. You know, that girl gon' be Mrs. Hannon?"

"Naw, man, didn't know she was working it like that," he said, and they snickered. "Well, I'll be by your office in a little while to get the key."

"I'll leave it with my assistant because I got court in about an hour."

"That's cool. I'll holla." He hung up the phone and walked by Kimberly as if she were invisible, then ran up the stairs with her on his heels.

"I don't see shit funny about a man letting a married dude crash at his spot without encouraging him to stay home with his family. Why are you staying with him until things are good? Things are good where? What's going on?" she demanded. He didn't satisfy her with an answer, so she got right in front of him. "You're not going anywhere, K.P."

"Kimberly, move. This is not gon' get ugly. I'm not going to allow this to get ugly. Now, it will save some drama *and* time if you'd just not get in my way." He walked around her and continued to get some of the things that he needed. He didn't want to leave any of his stuff behind because he knew she'd probably destroy them, but he couldn't worry about that. Although he had tailor-made suits, expensive shoes, and name-brand ties, he could only get the essentials.

She watched him put his favorite suits into a garment bag and couldn't think of anything to say to stop him. He ran down to the basement closet and got another suit-case, and she was looking at him as if she were in shock he was actually leaving. He was packing more clothes than just for a couple of days. She watched him go from his closet to the bathroom to the luggage, and he was sure she wanted to unpack his things and put them back where she thought they belonged.

"You're going to be sorry if you leave, K.P. I promise you that."

"Well, Kim, I think I'll be sorrier if I stay," he said and zipped up the garment bag.

"Kerry, what do you want me to do—beg? Okay, then, I'll beg," she said and moved closer to him. "Please don't go. Don't leave us. I'm begging you," she said, and a tear rolled down her cheek.

K.P. wasn't buying the bullshit she was selling. "Cut the dramatics, Kimberly." He walked back to the closet, grabbed a few more things, and added them to his bag.

"You are not going to need those suits and ties if you leave here today. I'll call my father the moment you leave, and you will *not* be allowed on the premises if you go."

He threw the strap of his garment bag over his shoulder and pulled the handle up on the suitcase.

"Go ahead, Kimberly, call him. You'll be doing me a favor. That way, I won't have to call him myself." He walked away and left her standing there looking dumb-founded. The old "you need your job card" was dealt with. He no longer cared about his position at her dad's company. He was his own man and had a promising future with or without Grayson Financial Services. He had things lined up, so big little "Miss Got to Have It All's" weave would spin if she only knew.

"You are *not* leaving me, dammit," she yelled, running behind him as he walked out of their bedroom. She ranted and raved, but he ignored her. He went out to his truck and loaded his things. Reality hit her dead in her face as she now realized that she couldn't get or have anything she wanted because what she wanted most was on his way out the door.

She got close to him and began to pull him back, but her five-foot, size-five body was nothing to his six-foot-four, 237-pound frame. "Please don't go. Don't leave us, K.P.," she begged, and he basically dragged her around with his movements because she refused to release him.

"I'll be by tomorrow to talk to my kids myself about what's going on, so I suggest that you not put any more of your foolish and evil ideas of what I'm doing to you and them in their heads," he said firmly. She then threw herself in front of the driver-side door, not allowing him to open it.

"Okay, Kerry, I get it. I'm a spoiled, controlling bitch. I don't deserve half the shit I have, but without you, I'll die, K.P."

"No, you won't. You're just putting on another show, and it's not entertaining anymore, so move."

"K.P., I swear if you give me a chance, I can change. I can *make* you love me."

"Kim, I'm asking you to move." He spoke firmly to her, letting her know he meant what he was saying. Nothing she could do or say would change his leaving her. He was confident that his harsh tone infuriated her. There was no way that something was happening to her beyond her control, and he knew that angered her.

"K.P., if you leave me, I swear to God, I will kill that bitch," she spat at him. "I will snatch Janiece's head off her shoulders with my bare hands," she tried to threaten, and before he knew it, he grabbed her little ass and pinned her to the truck.

"You stay away from Janiece, do you hear me? This is between you and me. Don't even entertain the thought of hurting her, you hear me? If you go near her or even try anything, Kimberly, you'll be sorry. Now, get your crazy ass outta my way," he said coldly and let her down gently. The fear in Kimberly's eyes told him that she believed his words to be true. "It's over between you and me, and there ain't shit you can do to make me stay with you. No money in the world could make me love you," he declared.

She finally moved and let him leave. Her mind was working overtime on what she would do to make them pay for ruining her life. "I'm gon' get you, Ms. Janiece, just watch. You done fucked with the wrong bitch. You will regret crossing Kimberly Renee Paxton, this I promise you," she said out loud as she watched her husband back out of their driveway.

Chapter Twenty

K.P. drove downtown to Marcus's office to get the key to his loft. He called Janiece at her office but couldn't get her. However, he was determined to see her that day. He went by Marcus's place to shower and change. It was almost four, and since Janiece was getting off at five, he decided to meet her in the lobby at her job. He hurried out because he wanted to stop and get her some flowers before seeing her. He looked at the clock on the dash. He was losing his mind because it was twenty 'til five, and traffic was a monster.

He grabbed his phone and realized he had fifteen missed calls. He had forgotten to turn the ringer volume up after he had left his house a few hours earlier. When he saw that they were all from Kimberly, he was relieved. He called his mailbox to get his messages. He had ten waiting on him. He hadn't checked messages over the weekend, so he didn't know that Janiece had returned any of his calls. When he heard the numbers from his home, he automatically deleted them without listening.

When he got to the ones from Janiece, he listened carefully. He was happy to hear her voice and delighted to know that she was concerned about him and his kids' well-being. He smiled because that gave him some relief. At least she was thinking about him.

He got to her building three minutes before five and parked and waited for her in the lobby by the information desk. When he saw Shawnee get off the elevator, he knew that Janiece wouldn't be too much longer. Shawnee saw him and licked her lips, walking over to where he was standing.

He hoped she would speak quickly and keep going because she was the last person he wanted to be caught talking to when Janiece came down, but, of course, that wasn't what happened.

"Hey, good looking, how are you?" she asked, giving him seductive eyes.

"Things are fine. How are you?" he asked, being polite. He wanted to tell her that he didn't have time to be flirted with today, but he figured he'd stay on the friendly note and not satisfy her efforts to make him say or do anything to disrespect Janiece.

"I'm good, *real* good," she said like she was describing her pussy.

"That's good to know. Do you know if Janiece is on her way down?"

"I'm not sure," she said, then quickly changed her story. "As a matter of fact, I think she may have already left," she said, with a straight face, but he knew she was lying through her teeth. He just went along with her.

"Well, I've been down here for a few minutes, and I didn't see her. I'll give her a few more minutes. I'm sure she'll be down soon."

"Okay, suit yourself, but you're probably too late. She may have left with her friend, Isaiah."

"Excuse me?" he asked to make sure he heard her say that his woman may have left with another man.

"You know, her friend, Isaiah, the one she was out with at Houston's the other night. She didn't tell you that I'd be calling you soon about some business for my brother?"

"No, she didn't tell me. I was out of town for a couple of days, and my cousin Isaiah came into town. I'm sure she was just hanging out with him for a little bit. And I know he didn't pick her up because I'd have known that," he said, playing it off. He didn't have a clue about Isaiah or Houston's, but he wasn't about to let her know that he didn't know what his woman was doing.

"Oh, so you know she was out with Isaiah," Shawnee asked him, not able to distinguish if he was serious or not.

"Of course, why would you think otherwise?"

"Well, because she said he was her date."

"Oh yeah," he said and smiled. "She was just messing with you, I guess. I don't know what to tell you—oh, there she is now," he said when he saw her getting off the elevator. Shawnee quickly turned and walked out of the revolving door. Janiece was smiling and talking to one of her coworkers, but she froze when she saw him. He knew she was surprised. That was his plan.

He walked over to her, greeted her with a kiss, and gave her the flowers. She took them, and they walked toward the door. "What are you doing, K.P.? What's going on?" she asked him when they got on the street.

"Nothing, baby. Can't I show up at your job? Were you expecting someone else?" he asked as he opened the door and helped her in.

"No, I was just asking. I didn't expect to see you, that's all."

"Well, I'm going to take you out to dinner and show you how much I've missed you," he said, then walked over to the other side of his truck and got in. He leaned over to kiss her. She smiled, and he knew she loved him so deeply. He knew that she couldn't leave him alone, and they would work it all out.

"I've missed you too, baby. I was worried about you, K.P. What happened to Kimberly? What's going on? I called you all weekend."

"I'll tell you when we get to Nick's. It is a long story, trust me."

He took the ticket from the valet, and they went inside and were seated at a table.

Janiece excused herself to the restroom to freshen up her face and wash her hands. She counted to ten and looked at herself in the mirror and wanted to cry. She felt like shit for sleeping with Isaiah now that K.P. was trying to make their thing work. She knew if K.P. found out, he'd be devastated, and she felt like the words "I fucked Isaiah" were written all over her face.

She straightened her clothes, went back to the table, and took her seat, hoping that he couldn't see the nervousness on her face. She felt sorry for what had happened, and she wished she hadn't gone as far as she had with Isaiah. She wanted to take it back, so bad, but she couldn't. She sat down with a nervous look on her face.

"So, baby, how was your day?" he asked.

"It was fine, a little hectic, but I made it through."

"That's why you're looking so stressed?"

"Am I? That's not good," she said and picked up the glass of wine he had ordered for her and took a swallow.

"And how was your weekend?"

"My weekend was okay, nothing big," she said nervously. "How was yours? I was concerned with the hospital thing," she said and took another swallow of her wine, hoping the conversation would turn to his weekend and not hers.

"Well, mine was interesting, actually. I moved out, and Kimberly tried to kill herself. I also found out you were at Houston's with another man," he said, and she almost choked on her wine. She was coughing, trying to catch her breath, and the waiter offered her some water.

She shook her head and tried to say, "No, I'm fine," but her pipes were blocked with the wine. She hurried to the bathroom to cough out all of the wine from her throat and get some air. Then she grabbed a Kleenex and wiped the tears from her face that formed from her near-death episode.

She looked at herself again and said, "Shawnee. That bitch," and she tossed the Kleenex into the trash. A few moments later, she went back to the table. After she sat down, K.P. looked at her with curious eyes before he asked, "Are you okay?"

"I'm fine," she said, trying to sound calm.

"Are you sure, Jai?"

"Yes, and I know that hot-ass Shawnee is the one who told you about my date."

"Oh? So it *was* a date?" he asked, and she wished she had not used that word.

"Well, if that's what you call a guy and a girl having dinner."

"Yeah, I guess that's what we can call it then," he commented, and the waiter came over for their dinner order. Janiece was relieved because that took the focus off her. She took awhile to order, trying to get her story straight. As soon as the waiter took their menus and walked away, she jumped in to change the subject.

"So, Kimberly tried to kill herself?"

"Yep, I'm afraid she is crazier than I gave her credit for. I know it was just a stunt, so I'm not sweating it."

"And you moved out?" she asked and took another sip of her wine. She wanted to talk about anything other than her and Isaiah.

"Yes, I moved out, and I'm not going back. I told you that I was going forward with my divorce, and I see you didn't believe me."

"Why do you think I didn't believe you, K.P.?"

"Well, I'm not sure. Maybe if you hadda believed me, you might not have gone out with ole boy Saturday night."

"Well, K.P., you are *not* my man, and I have a right to go out with whomever I choose," Janiece said with attitude and sipped her drink like she was in charge, and K.P. looked at her like she had lost her mind.

"Oh, so it's like that now? You can go out with whomever now? Although you promised me that you'd never date another guy as long as we were together?"

"Well, things have changed. I'm tired of coming in second."

"Janiece, don't even go there with me. You have known the circumstance with us for a long time. Now that things will be different and we have a chance to be together, you're ready to see other men? Did you sleep with him, Janiece?" he asked, and she didn't want to answer that question. Not then, not there in the restaurant, but he asked again. "Janiece, did you sleep with him?"

"Why, K.P.? What difference does it make? Do you sleep with Kimberly?"

"Don't play games with me, Jai." He leaned in closer, trying to remain calm, and Janiece knew that that situation would only get ugly.

"I'm *not* playing games with you, K.P. I've loved you for all of these years, and I'm stuck on hold—and for what? You don't love me, K.P."

"Jai, how could you say that? You know damn well I love you. I've been going through hell at home because of how much I love you. Do you think that I get home and just *forget* about you? Do you think for one minute I would've stayed with you if I didn't love you? I traded everything because of how much I love you."

"Traded what? Your crazy-ass wife knows about us, and she has known forever, so you are not giving up anything because she would rather me convince you to stay with her and continue to be your mistress, and then we'll all be happy."

"Whoa whoa whoa. You talked to Kimberly? Did Kimberly threaten you? Is *that* why you suddenly want to move on and just forget about us? Are you worried about Kimberly?"

"No, I'm not worried about her crazy ass, and yes, we talked. She's gone as far as sending me a back-off card. That crazy bitch knows where I live, K.P., and I told you before I didn't want to be in no drama. I ain't ever fucked with her, and as long as you and I don't take our relationship too far, she's cool with it. Imagine that," she said and took a sip of her wine.

"And you have it so damn hard? Two women who love you and want you so much 'til they sacrifice their morals and beliefs to be with you, and I don't want to sacrifice myself anymore. I'm tired of playing myself."

"I hear you, Janiece, and, baby, I'm sorry that you feel like I got it so good because I don't. Yes, two women are involved, but I only love one of them. You don't have to worry about Kimberly. I've filed for my divorce, and she can't keep me away from you no matter how many suicide attempts she takes. Again, I only love you, and all the changes I'm making in my life are for you and me to be together."

"Don't make any life changes for me, K.P. Do it for you—not me," Janiece said, looking at him. She wanted to believe that they had a future, but it was hard to think that things would be better now that he had actually left his wife. It seemed like it would worsen, especially with Isaiah across the hall and crazy-ass Kimberly on the loose.

"Well, it's too late. Even if you and I are no longer going to be together, Jai, I'm not going back to Kimberly. I'm moving on, and if you don't want to be a part of my future, you need to tell me now." He wanted to know what

Janiece intended to do because whatever she decided, he was still moving to Las Vegas—with or without her.

"I need some time," she said, and that didn't make him happy. He wanted to hear her say that she still loved him and was anxious for them to create a new life with each other.

"What? Time, Janiece? Are you digging this dude that much you are saying no to me?" he asked furiously. "I thought that you'd be overjoyed that I had finally handled my business and made an honest effort to make you number one in my life. I want to marry you, but now you need *time?*"

"Right now, K.P., I need time to figure things out, okay?"

"I can't believe my ears. You know what? Fine. You want time. I'll give you time." She knew her answer made him angry. He waved for the server and told him to put their dinners in to-go containers. When he brought their food out, K.P. paid and got up from the table. He was so furious he didn't say another word to her. The valet brought his truck around, and they rode out to Janiece's condo in silence.

She was afraid to say anything to him. When they pulled on her block, she saw Isaiah's car parked in her guest stall, and she knew K.P. saw it too. He pulled up to the steps and looked over his shoulder at the Chrysler 300.

"Jai, did you sleep with him?" he asked, and she didn't answer. They sat there for a moment, and he repeated, "Did you?" and she nodded her head, giving him a yes. He turned away from her and hit the steering wheel. She sat there for a moment, scared to open the door. She didn't know what to say. She saw his eyes water, and she wanted to disappear.

"I'm sorry I took so long to come through for you. Call me when you've figured your shit out," he said, and she knew that was her cue to get the hell out.

"I'm sorry, K.P.," she said, and he didn't even look at her.

"Yeah, I guess we both are."

She opened the door and climbed down from the seat. She looked at him once more before shutting the door, but he didn't look her way. Then she closed the door and walked up the steps.

He sat there for a moment until she got in. His eyes were burning with tears as he drove off.

"Damn, Jai, why did you do that?" he said out loud and drove down Ninety-Fifth Street. He had never been hurt by a woman before, and he hated Janiece at that moment for sleeping with Isaiah. He was so devastated that he said to hell with her too.

He was getting his divorce, his kids, and rolling out to Las Vegas. There was no reason for him to stay. He made it to Marcus's loft and took the ring out of his pocket. He put it into one of his bags. He didn't want to cry, but he couldn't hold back. He walked over to the window and thought about how much he loved the city of Chicago, but for his woman, he was willing to leave to make her happy. His thoughts were interrupted when he heard a set of keys. He hated that Marcus was coming in. He wanted to be alone, but it was Marcus's loft, and he had no right to demand to be alone in someone else's place.

"Hey, dude, what's up?" Marcus asked when he walked in.

"Hey, man, what's going on?" he replied dryly.

"I told Tracy that you were over, and I had to come home and check you out 'cause you going through the divorce and all."

"Aw, man, you could have stayed with your woman. I'm good."

"Naw, dude, she wore me out. Shit, I'll be able to get some good sleep tonight." They laughed, and Marcus went to pour them both a drink. "So, man, what's the deal?"

"You know, same ole, same ole. Kimberly's crazy-ass gon' make me choke the shit outta her, and Janiece fucking another man," he said and took the drink out of Marcus's hand.

Chapter Twenty-One

Janiece walked into her condo feeling worse than she had ever felt. She didn't know what she had done, but she wished she hadn't. K.P. was the only man she had ever been in love with, and she never wanted to hurt him. He did love her, but since she was into moving on and making all of her so-called life changes, she really hadn't stopped to think if she was truly ready to give him up.

She walked over to the cordless and dialed his number to ask him to come back so that they could talk, but he didn't pick up. She hung up, feeling like a fool because she wished she had just lied and not told him the truth about sleeping with Isaiah. She loved him too long just to let him slip through her fingers. She knew she had to show him how sorry she was for messing around with another man. She had to tell Isaiah that she could no longer see him.

Suddenly, she heard someone knocking. She put the phone down and made a mad dash to the door. *I knew he'd come back,* she thought to herself as she snatched open the door. To her unpleasant surprise, it was Isaiah, and the disappointed look on her face told him she wasn't too happy to see him.

"Hey, did I come at a bad time?"

"No . . . no . . . Not at all. Come on in." She stepped out of the doorway to allow him space to enter. He was dressed casually and looking good. He leaned over and kissed her, and that made her feel uncomfortable. He sensed that something was definitely not right.

"Is everything okay?"

"Everything is fine," she said and closed the door. She walked past him and went into the living room. He followed her with a baffled look on his face. He knew that things weren't right, and he knew it was because of the married dude.

"So, what's going on, Janiece?"

"Nothing, and why didn't you call first?"

"I'm sorry. I heard you come up the stairs, and I just wanted to say hi," he said. "I didn't know it would be a problem."

"What if I weren't alone?" she snapped.

"Hey, Janiece, baby, I'm sorry. I didn't think about that. I apologize, and it will never happen again."

"Thank you," she said, giving him more attitude.

"What's bothering you, babe?" he asked, moving closer to her.

"Nothing. Just had a long day. I'm sorry for snapping on you like that," she said, trying to avoid eye contact.

"It's more than that. You seemed stressed. Did something happen today?"

"No, Isaiah, I said I was fine," she spat and walked away. She went into the kitchen to pour herself a glass of wine to try to calm her nerves. She looked out of the kitchen window to see if K.P. had come back. She tried not to cry because she didn't want to deal with Isaiah just yet. She just wanted to be alone so that she could think.

"Look, Janiece, it's obvious something *is* bothering you. Let's just talk about it. Maybe I can help you feel better," he said, coming up and hugging her from behind.

"Isaiah, I'm sorry, but I would like to be alone for a while."

"Listen to me, Janiece—don't let him get you upset like this. You know you don't want to be his other woman. It's time for you to move on and do what makes *you* happy and what makes you feel good." He turned her to face him and began to kiss her. She allowed his soft lips and wet tongue to pleasure her mouth until she snapped back and realized what she was doing. One of the reasons she was hurting K.P. was standing right in front of her looking, smelling, and tasting so good.

"Isaiah, please, I know you think I should just tell him it's over, but it's not that simple. I don't know what to do right now. I don't like being confused. I want not to love him and not allow him to keep me hanging on, but it's so hard for me to do that right now."

"Janiece, don't do this to yourself. Let me help you forget about him. I want to help you forget about all the things he's put you through, baby. Come on, now, don't let him just show up and set you back."

"You can't help me just get over him, Isaiah. I know you want to, but it's not that simple. Things are complicated, and I don't want to lead you on or hurt you. So, please, Isaiah, just let me figure some things out on my own."

"So you want me to back off?"

"No, Isaiah, I'm not saying that. I just need some space to sort things out in my head."

"You know I'm leaving soon to go back to Texas, so I don't have a lot of time, and I don't want to spend the rest of my time here without you, Janiece." He was so genuine and so sweet. Janiece knew that he really did care for her, and that was the main reason she had to pull away from him because she didn't want to drag him into her world of disarray and misery.

"Isaiah, I do know that your time here is limited, but I don't wanna hurt you. I'm not completely done with K.P. You are too good of a person, and you deserve better than what I can give you right now."

"Sounds to me like your mind is already made up." He stepped back and looked at her with disappointment on his face. She didn't know if her mind was made up, but she did know she didn't want to hurt Isaiah. He was one of the good guys and treated her like silk. He possessed all the qualities she wanted in a man, but her heart was stuck on Kerry Paxton. She couldn't shake him off. Part of her wanted to allow Isaiah the opportunity to be in her life and just let the time needed for her to get over K.P. go by, and one part of her wanted to stay and allow K.P. to make things right.

"Look, Isaiah, you can't possibly understand what I'm going through right now. My heart says to stay and continue to love him, but my mind tells me to choose what's right in front of me. I'm just not sure, Isaiah, and I'm sorry. I want to look you in the eyes and tell you that I'm done with him, and from now on, it's just you and me, but if I do, I would not only be lying to you, but I'd also be lying to myself."

"Listen, Janiece, I understand more than you know, and I'm not mad. Just a little disappointed but not mad. I want you to do what makes you happy. I may not be what you need, and I'm willing to deal with that if that's your decision, but I'm not going to just walk out the door without you knowing how much I want you and how bad I want to be with you. You see," he said, moving close to her, "I recognize how special you are. You need a man that's always going to put you first." He kissed her again, and before she knew it, he raised her onto the counter.

He was standing between her legs with his erection pressed against her pleasure point, and she could feel it through her pants. His kisses were so good that she couldn't resist him. His hands found their way to the buttons on her blouse, and he began to unbutton them one by one. She leaned back a little and let him kiss her down her neck and lick the center of her chest. He raised her bra and began to suck on her erect nipples, and she rubbed the back of his head.

He was so sexy, and he knew how to wake up all the senses in her body. She moaned as she enjoyed the suction of his mouth over her nipples. Her body responded to the warm breath from his mouth, causing her spot to clench. The throbbing began to activate her juices, and she started getting wet.

"Oh, Isaiah, why are you doing this to me?" she asked, as he made circles around her right nipple with his seducing tongue.

"Do you want me to stop?" he whispered, and she didn't respond. Saying no would only make her feel bad about what she was doing to K.P. Saying yes would make the good feeling stop. He made his way back to her lips and gently grabbed her hair. He sucked on her chin hungrily and licked down her neck, making his way back to her tits. She tilted her head back slightly and opened her eyes, looking at him.

Why is he so fine? Why does he have to feel so good? Why do I want him inside of me? were all the questions that ran across her mind. She was in bad shape, and she didn't know how she would be able to resist Isaiah's sweet charm and thoughtful ways.

"What do you wanna do?" he asked when he saw that she was watching him suck on her hard nipples.

"What do *you* wanna do?" she asked him back, still not wanting to be the one to organize her crime of passion.

"I wanna take you in there," he said, pointing toward her bedroom door, "and make you feel good."

"Okay," she said before she could say no. He helped her down from the counter, and they went into her bedroom, undressed, and did what made them feel good. Janiece felt guilty again, but she tried to put it out of her mind.

They lay together in her bed afterward, and her back was facing him, so he caressed her skin gently as she fought the tears. She wasn't cheating on K.P., but

she knew she couldn't continue to mess around with
Isaiah if she wanted to work things out with K.P.

Her phone rang, which made her jump. She reached
for it on the nightstand and looked at the ID. It was K.P.
Her heart started beating fast, and she thought she was
busted. Was he outside, on his way over, or what? She
sat up in bed and held the phone until it stopped ringing.
Her hands began to tremble, and she was shaking like a
leaf.

She grabbed her robe and went into the kitchen to look
out the window for K.P.'s truck. Finally, she could relax a
little when she didn't see it.

"Isaiah, you have to go," she said when she walked back
into her bedroom. He sat up and looked at her and didn't
say anything. He just grabbed his boxers, dressed in
silence, and she followed him to the kitchen and watched
him unlock the door.

"You know how to find me when you're ready," he said
and walked out without another word. She was sure he
was angry and felt that Janiece was shortchanging herself to continue to be involved with a married man. Little
did he know how bad she wanted things to be different
from what they were. The truth was, he didn't know K.P.
for the good things. He only heard the bad things. He
didn't know what lengths K.P. would go to make Janiece
happy. Hell, Janiece didn't know either. He was just a
typical-minded person when it came to a woman that he
wanted that may have wanted someone else, even if K.P.
were a single man. He wanted Janiece and had had ill
feelings for K.P. anyway.

Janiece went back into her room, picked up the condom wrapper from the nightstand, and flushed it down
the toilet. When she got into the shower, she shampooed
her hair and noticed she had started her period. No
wonder she didn't put up much of a fight because her

hormones would not have allowed her to say no even if she wanted to. She got out of the shower, put on her robe, and blow-dried her hair.

When she finished drying her hair, she went into the kitchen to pour another glass of wine. She glanced out the window and could have sworn she saw K.P.'s truck rolling down the street. She closed the curtain and figured her mind was playing tricks on her because if he had come by, he would have used his key. After all, she hadn't changed the locks yet. Then she wrapped her hair and settled on the sofa to watch a little TV.

When she finished her wine, she got up to take her glass into the kitchen, put it into the dishwasher, and put the food on the stove from Nick's in the fridge. She had forgotten about her grilled salmon and vegetables. She didn't touch it at the restaurant because K.P. ordered the waiter to put their food into to-go containers, and when she got home, she was too frustrated to eat.

Then Mr. Isaiah took her mind entirely off food, so she didn't bother eating. She went to bed and decided to call K.P. again, but it went straight to voicemail when she called. She didn't leave him a message because she didn't know what to say to him after sleeping with Isaiah once more. She turned in and prayed for guidance and strength. She was madly in love with K.P. but was too weak to resist Isaiah.

That was a situation she didn't want to venture into any longer. Isaiah going back to Texas was something she wanted to come quickly because her situation probably would only worsen if he were around.

Chapter Twenty-Two

Friday rolled around, and still, there was no word from K.P. She hadn't seen or heard from Isaiah either. She decided to go out to Janelle's house for a while after work because she was in no mood to be alone at her condo. First, she stopped by her place to change clothes, get her car, and then went to her mailbox to pick up her mail. A letter with no return address on it awaited her. Quickly, a knot formed in the pit of her stomach. She sat down and opened it anyway. It was from the one and only Kimberly Paxton. She braced herself and read the evilness that Kimberly had sent to her. It read:

Are you satisfied? He has left my two kids and me for you—you dick-sucking tramp. You will not get away with this, and you will not live happily ever after. You will pay for destroying my marriage. How can you sleep at night knowing you have ruined someone's marriage? But don't worry, Ms. Dick-Sucker Janiece, payback is a mother, and you are going to get yours, you fat, gold-digging, greedy ho.

Do you think you are better than me? Maybe because you give him head on a regular or let him fuck you in the ass. I don't know what nasty hoes like you do to steal a woman's husband. Maybe those are the reason why he wants you. Enjoy him for now because I assure you, he will leave you too for the next nasty bitch that comes along. I actually feel sorry for your broke ass. You couldn't find a man of your own, so you schemed and plotted to get mine, but you will see how I get down. Nobody takes anything from Kimberly Renee Paxton and gets away with it. There will be consequences, Janiece Hawkins, believe that. If I were you, I'd watch my back from now on.

Yours truly,

Mrs. Kimberly R. Paxton

Janiece stuffed the letter back into the envelope and shook her head. *This bitch is outta her damn mind,* she said to herself and grabbed her keys to leave. Who in the hell did Kimberly think she was trying to scare because all the threats in the world wouldn't keep her from K.P. if she wanted to be with him. She can call her all the names she could come up with, and K.P. *still* wouldn't want to be with her. Janiece was not worried about that little, twisted woman. She put the letter into her purse to take with her to Janelle's, so she could get her to laugh too.

Janiece headed out the door and walked down the steps, and just for the sake of being careful, she looked out at the parking lot and up the street before reaching the bottom of the steps. Everything looked safe, so she proceeded to her car. She got into the car, and when she pulled out of the parking lot, she noticed a vehicle off to the left with a woman sitting in the driver's seat. She had on dark shades even though the sun had gone down, and Janiece could see she had on black gloves.

The woman looked in Janiece's direction for a moment, and Janiece returned the look. Then Janice decided to go on her way and not even think about crazy-ass Kimberly and her threats. She had to talk to K.P. about his nutty-ass wife because he had to do something about her. She was obviously mad at the wrong person. It wasn't her fault K.P. was leaving. She never asked him to do that or even thought he would, so all the anger was directed at the wrong person.

Janiece thought about the idea of him and her being together exclusively, and it made her smile. To actually have him all to herself wasn't such a bad idea.

When she got to Janelle's and showed her the letter, Janelle was furious and took the threats more seriously than Janiece. She insisted that Janiece go to the authorities and put a restraining order out on Kimberly, but Janiece wouldn't hear of it.

"Nellie, ain't nobody afraid of her," she said and went into the fridge to get a bottle of water.

"You being afraid of her is *not* the issue, sis. She's crazy and unpredictable. She's an evil, bold bitch to send shit to your house and then go as far as signing it. She ain't afraid of shit either. She's badass to send this shit to your home," she said, looking at Janiece like *she* was the crazy one.

"I know. Do you really think I need to get a restraining order, Nellie? I mean, she can't be serious," Janiece said, making it out to be no big deal.

Janelle grabbed the letter from the counter and read, *"Payback is a mother, and you are going to get yours. If I were you, I'd watch my back from now on."* "Duh, hell, yeah, you need a restraining order," she said and dipped her banana into a bowl of chocolate syrup.

"What the hell are you eating?"

"Girl, this baby got me craving shit already. I can eat bananas and chocolate all day long. That's all he or she wants."

"That ain't my niece craving that mess. That's *you* being a pig," Janiece joked.

"But for real, little sissy, you're staying here tonight, and we're getting you an alarm system, got that?" Janelle said, standing up to get another banana. "And you are changing your damn locks tomorrow too."

"Okay, okay, now get off my back," Janiece said, agreeing and giving in. Janelle was too, too much like their mom, and Janiece knew she wasn't going to let up.

"So, how is Mr. Isaiah?"

"Mad," Janiece said, trying some of the bananas and chocolate.

"Mad about what?"

"Because I fucked him and put him out."

"Why? I thought you said his dick was good," Janelle asked, making sure she got a hefty amount of chocolate on her piece of banana.

"It is, but that wasn't why I put him out."

"Then why did you?"

"Because things are not done with K.P. and me, and to be honest, I hate I got involved with him in the first place."

"Jai, what do you *really* want to do? Be honest. Either you like Isaiah and wanna move on, or you are in love with K.P. and want to give him a chance. How much time do you need to be honest with yourself?"

"You know, that's a good question, Sherlock, and if it were just that simple, I wouldn't be over here looking crazy watching you eat bananas and chocolate. I'd be with K.P. or Isaiah enjoying myself on this Friday night."

"Oh, so you are *not* enjoying yourself with me?" Janelle asked because she was always so sensitive, and since she had become pregnant, it was sensitive to the nth degree.

"No, Nellie, I didn't mean it like that. I just meant if I were sure of what to do, I'd be doing it with one of them."

"Well, my gut tells me you wanna be with K.P., but you're afraid." That one actually took Janiece by total surprise because she didn't expect her sister to say anything in favor of K.P.

"Why would you say that?"

"Well, for one, you've loved him forever, and he is your first love, Janiece, and I think you are a little afraid because he's a man that cheated on his wife with you, and you are a little concerned that same thing will happen to you."

"Yeah, I do wonder that a lot, and it makes me a little scared."

"Jai, he's taking a huge step by leaving his wife and family. If a man leaves his home and gives up everything, that should let you know that he cares and wants to make you a priority."

"Yeah, but what if I get with K.P., and he starts cheating on me with another woman?"

"Well, li'l sis, we can't worry about that, can we? All we can do is hope for the best and keep going. Even if you hadda met K.P. before he married Kimberly, and he had been with you the entire time, we would never know if he would, or wouldn't have, cheated on you, Janiece. Just because of the situation with K.P. and Kimberly doesn't mean he will cheat on you. Chile, people are unpredictable, even Greg. I love and trust him, but at the same time, I'm not naïve.

"We are all capable of being unfaithful, so if you truly love K.P., Janiece, that is who you should be with. Don't waste time on love. Let him know it and start fresh with the man you love. Think about it . . . There was a time when you couldn't see yourself sharing your bed with another man, and now what? You just slept with Isaiah, so never say never. We just got to roll with it," Janelle said and got up to go get herself something from the fridge.

Janiece couldn't believe her eyes when her sister came back to the table loaded with cheese and crackers. Janelle never ate stuff like that before. Janiece just looked at it but didn't say a word. She thought that her sister would be a big pregnant cow if she kept eating like she was.

"So, you telling me after all these years you've hated on K.P., you're suggesting I get with him?"

"Well, I'm not entirely okay with him. That part is going to take some time. But if it makes you happy, Janiece, I don't mind it one bit." She smiled at her sister, and Janiece thought that baby was making her sister crazy because she had never given K.P. credit before, not even if he had found the cure for cancer.

"Oh, Nellie," she said and got up to hug her sister. She was so happy to have her support she didn't know what to say. She stayed over at Janelle's house that night, and the next day, they met the locksmith at her condo. He couldn't install the alarm system until the following week, so she was concerned about having to take off a day of work to wait for them to come, but Janelle agreed to come over for her, so she wouldn't have to take off.

Afterward, they went shopping and looked at baby clothes and furniture. Janiece was glad to be out. In fact, she felt better than she had in the last few days. She thought about K.P. and Isaiah a little but not enough to spoil her day out with Janelle.

She got in around seven, and Janelle went home because she was exhausted from the day in the mall. She also got sick for the first time, and it was so funny to Janiece, but Janelle didn't see the humor in her getting sick from the smell of gourmet popcorn. That was one of her favorite things to eat before the pregnancy. Now, she couldn't be in the same room with the smell.

No way did Janiece want to think of having a baby after watching Janelle blow chunks in a nearby trash can because she couldn't make it to the bathroom in time. She was happy at the moment that K.P. already had two kids. That way, there wouldn't be any pressure on her. She looked at the clock. It was only ten after seven.

She wasn't tired, and she wanted to go out. She called her girlfriend Tia, and they caught up for a few minutes. Then Tia made it clear that if they were going out, Rick would be going too, and Janiece was not in the mood to be a third wheel, so she told her that was okay. She called K.P. before attempting to call Isaiah to see if there was a chance they could get together and at least talk, but he didn't answer his phone.

She didn't leave a message. She just figured he'd see the missed call and call her back. She hoped he'd call because she wanted to tell him that he was the one, and she was sure that she wanted to be with him and nobody else.

She put some of her things away to keep from calling Isaiah. She knew that she would be doing a bad thing by contacting him, but she didn't want to be alone on a Saturday night with nothing to do. She wished she still had Marcus's number to call him, so he could have gotten a hold of K.P. for her, to tell him to call her because it was important.

A few moments later, her phone rang, and when she saw K&K Paxton on the ID, she got excited but sad because if it was K.P., he calling from home, meaning he may have decided to go back to Kimberly.

"Hello," Janiece said.

"Is Kerry there?" Kimberly asked.

"You have the wrong number," Janiece said and hung up. Why Kimberly was playing on the phone, she didn't know, but she wasn't going to go there with her. Before she walked away, the phone rang again. It was from K.P.'s house.

"Hello," Janiece said, irritated.

"May I speak with Kerry, please?"

"Again, Kerry doesn't live here. You have the wrong number."

"Is this 773-555-0648?"

"Yes, it is, but Kerry doesn't live here."

"Cut the shit, Janiece, and put him on the damn phone," the evil one said.

"Look, Kimberly, Kerry doesn't live here, okay? And don't call my house again." She hung up, and that crazy trick called back. Janiece yanked the phone from the base and pressed the TALK button. This time, she wasn't going to be so nice.

"Hello," she said, frustrated.

"Look, bitch, don't hang up on me again. I *know* Kerry is over there. Now put that Negro on the phone because he needs to come here and pick up his kids. I got somewhere to go, and he needs to keep them."

"Look, Kimberly, he's not here, okay? If he were, I'd be more than happy to let you speak to him concerning the kids, but I'm telling you for the last time, he is *not* here, and he doesn't live here, and don't call my motherfucking house again."

"I don't want to call your *apartment,* Janiece; I'm just looking for my husband. Unfortunately, I cannot reach him. That's the only reason why I'm calling."

"Well, try him on his phone, Kimberly."

"Duh, you dumb bitch, don't you think I've tried that? He's not answering. That's why I'm calling *your* apartment."

"Well, Kimberly, I don't know what to tell you, but he is *not* here."

"Well, I tell you what. Since you want to take my place so badly, why don't you keep his kids?"

"Are you outta your mind, Kimberly? You are *not* serious."

"Like hell, I ain't. We'll be there in about thirty minutes. So get in touch with their daddy, or *you* will be keeping his kids tonight," she said and hung up.

That bitch is out of her mind, Janiece thought to herself. She grabbed her phone and texted K.P. because she knew he wouldn't pick up if she called. The text message said, "Urgent. I know you are not speaking to me, but your crazy-ass wife is on her way over here to bring your kids."

Within five minutes, her phone was ringing.

Chapter Twenty-Three

"What? Kimberly said, *what?*" he asked in disbelief.

"She just called here talking about having something to do and not being able to reach you, and she's bringing the kids to me."

"You're kidding, right?"

"No, K.P. Why would I joke with something like this?"

"Let me call you right back."

"Okay, but, K.P., please call me back. I *really* need to talk to you," she said and exhaled. He agreed to call her when he finished talking to "Crazy."

"Okay, baby, I will. Just let me handle Kimberly before she does something off-the-wall." He hung up with Janiece and hit the speed dial to call his house. Kimberly answered on the first ring.

"Oh, so you can't answer when *I* call, but when I called your bitch, you hurry up and ring?"

"Nope. I'm calling because I want to know why you're harassing Janiece, and what is this bullshit about you dropping my kids off to her?"

"I'm not harassing her. If you weren't over there laid up with yo' ho and picked up your damn phone, I wouldn't have called her."

"Kimberly, I'm not at Janiece's house, and I didn't pick up my phone because I had no desire to talk to your ass. Where are my kids?"

"They're here, and you need to come get them because I wanna go out."

"Go out where, Kim?"

"None of your damn business, K.P.," she said with much attitude.

"Look, Kim, I don't have a problem with watching my kids, and I really don't care where the hell you're going, but don't ever call Janiece again for *any* reason. You got that?"

"You can't tell me what to do, you jackass. Do you think that I'm going to be nice to that tramp bitch? I'll call her 'til I'm satisfied. I'm not happy, so why should she be happy?"

"Yes, that's right. Misery loves company. I'll be there in twenty minutes to pick up my kids," he said and hung up the phone, not allowing her to say anything else. He drove to the house, pissed off at Kimberly. He was so disgusted with her he hated he had to see her. He had gone by his home earlier that week to talk to the kids, and she purposely didn't pick them up from her parents, so they were not there when he arrived. It was just a plot to get him out there so she could try to seduce him, but it didn't work.

Now, he had no clue what he might walk into once he arrived. He hoped she didn't try that dumb shit again because he may have to slap her face this time. He pulled into the garage, and the kids rushed him when he walked through the garage door. They were so happy to see him, and he was just as excited to see them. They were talking a mile a minute, asking him question after question. He let them get out what they wanted to say and then asked where their mom was.

"She's in her room putting on pretty-girl clothes," KJ said, making faces.

"Oh, is she?"

"Yep, and she smells really good too, Daddy. Are you and Mommy going to a fancy place?" Kayla asked.

"No, your mommy has other plans."

"So, where are we going tonight? Back to Grandpa and Grandma's house?"

"No. You guys are going with me over to Uncle Marc's."

"Why, Daddy? Why can't you stay here?"

"Because Daddy won't be staying here anymore."

"I told you he would leave us, KJ," Kayla told her little brother, looking sad.

"No, Kayla, I'm *not* leaving you. Your mom and I just have some grown-up stuff that we have to work out, but Daddy could never leave you guys."

"You promise?"

"I promise," he said and hugged his kids. He loved them more than he loved anyone, including Janiece.

"Okay," they both said and let him move around the house.

"Now, let me go and talk to your mommy for a minute. When I'm finished, we'll be going." He walked up the stairs. Kimberly had the music playing loud and had a glass of something on the bathroom vanity. She was sitting down in her lace thong and bra, applying her makeup.

"I got the kids, and I'll bring them back tomorrow evening," he said, trying not to look at her in her undergarments.

"Call first to make sure I'm here," she said and got up off her little bench and walked by him, giving him more than an eyeful of her sexy body. She wore one of his old favorites. He used to love that number, he thought to himself as he tried to avoid looking at her.

"Okay, whatever, Kimberly. I'll call you," he said and chuckled a little.

"What's so funny, K.P.?"

"Nothing. Nothing. Do your thing," he said as he watched her step into one of the sexiest dresses that she owned.

"So . . . What you saying, you can move around and do your thang, but *I* can't?" she said, as she sashayed past him, sat back at her vanity, and took a sip of her drink.

"Naw, you can do what you like. Drop like it's hot, or whatever you want. I'm cool," he said because he really didn't care what she did. He was actually happy to see her doing something with herself and not whining over him.

"I was gon' say," she said and applied her lipstick.

"You look nice," he said sincerely. He didn't want her, but she was a beautiful woman.

"This old thing, K.P.? You know you've seen this dress before."

"I know, but it looks good. Have fun tonight."

"Thanks. Just make sure you call before you come tomorrow."

"I will," he said and was out the door.

That was the first time things ended on a civil note. He was relieved that nothing ugly was said. He was on his way down when Kimberly called after him. He knew it was too good to be true.

"Yeah?" he said, answering her.

"Don't take my kids around that bitch, you got me?"

"Oh, it's okay for you to call Janiece and tell her you're going to drop my kids off on her, but I can't take them around her?"

"You know I wasn't going to drop my kids over at her house. You know me better than that."

"So, you're just doing what you do to make others miserable?"

"No. I'm doing it because she's a tramp bitch."

"Whatever. Just know this. Whenever my kids are with me, I take them where *I* want to take them, and I can have them around whomever I want as long as no one hurts them, so *don't* tell me who I can have around them."

"Yeah, do it and see me act a fool."

"You *always* act a fool, Kimberly. That's *nothing* new."
He walked away and called Janiece as soon as he pulled
out of the drive. She answered, and her voice was like a
breath of fresh air.

"Hello," she said.

"Hey, baby, is this a good time?"

"Yeah, did you work things out with Kimberly?"

"Yes, as a matter of fact, I have my crumb snatchers
with me now."

"You do?" she asked, feeling bad because that meant he
wouldn't be coming by, and she wasn't going to be able to
talk to him.

"Yep, you want to meet them?" he asked, and Janiece
got quiet. She didn't know if she was ready to meet his
kids, and at the rate things were going with Kimberly, she
wasn't sure if it was a good idea. "Baby, are you there?"

"Yeah," she responded.

"So, what do you say? Do you want to meet my little
ones?"

"Yeah, sure. If you think it's okay, it's okay with me."

"Good, we'll be there in about thirty minutes. Do me
a favor. Order some pizza from Fox's for us. They like
cheese only and get the usual for us, okay?"

"Okay, baby, see you in a few," she said, and they hung
up.

Chapter Twenty-Four

Janiece ordered the pizza and ran into the bathroom to freshen up. She was happy that she would see K.P. but meeting his kids made her nervous. She had heard so much about them, and now that she was finally going to see his seeds, she was scared she would say or do something wrong.

She walked into the kitchen to open the door after hearing K.P. outside with his keys. She had forgotten that the locksmith had changed the locks earlier that day.

"What's going on? My key didn't work."

"Oh, Janelle insisted I change the locks. Come in, and I'll tell you what I mean," she said, trying to keep him from getting upset about the key situation. She shut the door behind them and introduced herself to Kayla and KJ.

"Hi, you must be Kayla."

"Yes, and this is my little brother, Kerry, but we all call him KJ."

"Hi, how are you, KJ?" Janiece asked, extending her hand to shake hands with the young man.

"Thirsty. Do you have apple juice?"

"Humph, let's see. I have orange and cranberry," she said, looking in the fridge for him.

"But I really like apple juice," he whined.

"So do I, but I'm all out right now. How about you have some orange juice for now, and when we go get the pizza, we can stop for some apple juice?"

"Okay," he said, and she poured him a small cup of orange juice. She chatted with them for a few before they all loaded up in K.P.'s truck to go pick up the pizza. She reminded K.P. to stop at the store for apple juice. He ran into the convenience store and got the juice and some candy. Then they went back to Janiece's condo and ate and watched the Disney channel. When the kids fell asleep on the floor, Janiece stood up, got a blanket, and covered them. She was a bit nervous because it was time for her and K.P. to talk.

"Your kids are beautiful."

"Thanks. They are the best thing that happened to me. The only thing I can say I love Kimberly for."

"Yeah, I can see what you mean. Guess what?"

"What?"

"My sister is pregnant."

"Is she?"

"Yep."

"That's great. Maybe she'll be nicer to me since she's pregnant."

"K.P., Janelle doesn't hate you. She just wants what's best for me. She's going to support me in whatever I do that makes me happy, and you going between Kimberly and me didn't make me happy."

"You know I'm done with her, Janiece."

"I know, but—"

"What is it? I thought you'd be thrilled that I've finally stepped up to the plate and showed you how much I want to be with you."

"I am, K.P., but I'm scared."

"Scared of what? You know I love you, and I'd never hurt you, Janiece."

"That's not it. Do you *really* love me, K.P.? Are you *certain* you can be faithful to me? Are you *sure* you won't do to me what you did to Kimberly?"

"Janiece, Kimberly and I should have never gotten married. To sit here and tell you why I married her is something I can't explain. Back then, I wasn't making decisions on what I wanted. I made choices based on what others wanted me to do. I'm so tired of doing things based on what others want me to do or think I should do. This is the first time I have done something based on what I wanted. And I want you, Jai."

"What do you want from me, K.P.?"

"Your love, your understanding. I want you to love me back and love my kids. I need you *and* them and want you and them more than money, success, and popularity. I want you as my wife, Janiece. You are my match. I married Kimberly for all the wrong reasons, and that is something I will have to deal with for the rest of my life, but I can't imagine my life without you."

She sat there in silence for a few moments. She didn't know what to say. He had never before spoken to her that way.

"So, you're sure you're ready to leave your home, your marriage, and be in a committed relationship with me?"

"Janiece, I want you to marry me."

"K.P., you're *still* married."

"Not for long. I told you, I've filed for divorce, and it's only a matter of time before it goes through. I've moved out, Jai. I'm not going back."

"Let me show you something," she said and got up and went to the dining room table and got the letter and card that Kimberly had sent her. She handed them to him.

"What's this?" he asked out of curiosity.

"Just open them and read them," she said, and he did. He shook his head and laughed out loud. "Janiece, I'm sorry, baby, but I can guarantee you that she is all talk. You don't have to worry about Kimberly."

"Why shouldn't I worry about her, K.P.? It's obvious that she thinks *I'm* the evil one that took her husband."

"Trust me, baby, you *don't* have to worry about her. I'll never let her or anyone hurt you."

"Well, K.P., I'm not afraid, but this is *exactly* the BS I never wanted to go through."

"I know, baby, and it'll be over soon. I got so many plans for us, and I know you're going to be happy."

"Oh yeah, like what?"

"Well, first, remember how you always talked about going away and starting our lives over in Las Vegas?"

"Yes," she said, sitting up, so she could look at him in the eye.

"Well, I've worked so hard the last year to make that possible for us."

"What are you saying, K.P.?"

"I wanted to surprise you, but I guess now is the perfect time to tell you."

"Tell me what?"

"I want us to move out to Las Vegas."

"Las Vegas? Are you serious?"

"Jai, you have begged me and said to me so many times how you wish we could just go back to Vegas and start over, and the last year I've been making plans for us to move. I'll be opening my own business there, and I want you to go with me."

"To Las Vegas?"

"Yes. I can't start my new life without you. I want to marry you, Jai. I have left Grayson Financial, and the grand opening of Paxton Mortgages will be in three weeks. I want you to go out there with me for the grand opening, and while we're there, we can look for a house."

Janiece was in total shock.

"When, how . . . How did you start your own business? I mean, starting a business takes money—a lot of money."

"I know, and trust me, it wasn't easy, but it all worked out."

Janiece was still confused and amazed at the same time.

"Oh my God, K.P. I don't know what to say. Las Vegas is far. I mean, Janelle's expecting her first baby and just moving out of Chicago is . . . I mean . . . wow."

"All you have to do is say yes. I'm going, Jai, with or without you. I want a new start and a new life. It was perfect when we took our trip out there, and I want to have a life with you and my kids. I mean, I love Chicago too, baby, and I understand that your sister is having her first child, but this is *our* lives at hand, and we have to live out *our* lives and what makes *us* happy."

"I know, K.P., and I'm not saying no. I just didn't expect to hear something this big from you. I mean, I don't have money to move to Las Vegas. I have things to consider."

"Like what?"

"First, I'm not financially set to make a move like that, to ship my stuff and start over. I'm not loaded, you know."

"Yes, I do know that, but let me worry about all of that. You don't have to worry about work, money, or shipping your things. All you have to do is say you'll be there with me and for me, and I'll take care of the rest," he said sincerely.

Janiece had no idea he was financially well-off and had a great deal of money and investments so that he wasn't going to have to struggle with anything. K.P. was a brilliant man, and he invested and made many wise money decisions when working for Kimberly's dad. He took advantage of all the opportunities that came his way. In fact, he had wealth even Kimberly had no idea about.

"K.P., you say that, but you know I work hard, and I don't have all of this and all of that, and I would only be a burden right now. I have no money saved, and I just don't know—"

"Shhhh, listen, Jai. *I'll* take care of us. Money is the last thing you need to worry yourself about. We're going to be okay. You don't have to worry about working if you don't want to because I got us. If you want to go to school, pick up a hobby, whatever, I'll take care of us."

"But how, K.P.? How can you afford to—"

"Baby, I'm not Donald Trump, but trust me when I say we ain't broke."

"When you say 'we ain't broke,' do you mean we ain't broke as far as me having to work for you doing all the office work until the business gets off the ground or we ain't broke like I can have a house just as pretty as the one we stayed in when we went for my birthday a couple of years ago?"

"Well, baby, to answer that, you don't have to work if you don't want to work, and we can get a house *twice* as big as the one we stayed in when we went for your birthday."

"Bullshit," she said in disbelief.

"Nope, baby, no bullshit. If you go out to Vegas with me for the grand opening, we can look at houses, and after the divorce is final, we can be married."

"Just like that?"

"If you want to do this."

"K.P., I do love you, and I have loved you for a long time. I really want to get excited and be happy, but I'm scared."

"Why, baby?"

"Because this all seems so unreal. Things this great never happen to people like me," she said with her eyes watering.

"That's where you're wrong, Jai. Good things happen to good people. You are the most humble, selfless, loving woman I know. You have loved me for me from the beginning, and you have never tried to be a bitch or vindictive. So *I'm* the lucky one. I'm ready to do this, babe."

"K.P., I am so sorry, baby," Janice said, breaking down. She started to sob loudly. He grabbed her and put his arms around her.

"Come on, let's go into the other room so we don't wake the kids."

"Okay," she said, whimpering. Why did she sleep with Isaiah? She had to tell him how sorry she was for doing that. She followed him into the bedroom, and he closed the door. She sat down on the plush purple velvet chaise, and K.P. sat down at the chaise's foot to finish their conversation.

"K.P., I'm sorry for hooking up with Isaiah. I didn't want things to go down like they did. I promise you I never intended to hurt you. I was so confused, and I thought I wanted to move on, and I . . ." she said, now crying uncontrollably.

"Shhhh, Jai, baby, it's okay. I understand why you did what you did, and I'm not mad about that anymore. I just want us to start fresh, baby." He moved closer to comfort her.

"I just . . . didn't know what—"

"Baby, it's okay. We're going to be fine," he said, and she looked at him, trying to find some reassurance. He touched her face and pulled her close to kiss her. He missed her, and he didn't care what happened last week or the day before. He started touching her, and Janiece lay back and allowed him to kiss her and stroke her breast. Then she remembered it was that time of the month.

"Baby, wait," she said, stopping him.

"What? What is it? What's wrong?" he asked.

"We can't, baby," she said, and he was looking at her like she was out of her mind.

"Why? What do you mean we 'can't'?"

"The curse," she said.

"Damn, how long?"

"Yesterday."

"Ooookkkkaaayyy. That's not good," he said, and she giggled. "It's okay. I want to, trust me, but I'm just happy that we're together again. And this time, Janiece, I'm not leaving your side," he said earnestly.

"Are you sure that's how you want it?" she asked.

"I wouldn't have it any other way," he replied and wished he had the diamond with him. They got in the bed. Janiece just rested in his arms. She felt good about her decision to be with him but going to Las Vegas was still scary. She wasn't a freeloader, and she was concerned about going there as broke as she was.

"I love you, Janiece," K.P. said softly in her ear.

"I love you too," she responded.

He pulled her closer and squeezed her tighter. She slowly relaxed and stopped worrying about Las Vegas. She decided she'd cross that bridge when she got to it. Right now, she was content to nestle in his arms. Before drifting off to sleep, she wondered how she would tell Isaiah the truth. She had a few flashes of *his* body, *his* kisses, and *his* laughter. She liked him, no doubt, but she loved K.P., and that was her choice.

Chapter Twenty-Five

K.P. woke up to find KJ in bed on the other side of Janiece. He smiled and was delighted to have his kids and the woman he loved under the same roof. He looked at Janiece sleeping so peacefully with his son beside her, lying on her arm. He didn't wake them because it was still early. Quietly, he arose and went to the bathroom, and when he came out, he was surprised to see Kayla up and sitting on the couch. He went over and sat down beside her, but she didn't look up at him. She was so wrapped up in the program she was watching on the television.

"Hey, princess," he said, brushing her hair away from her face.

"Hey, Daddy," she said, not taking her eyes off the tube.

"How'd you sleep?"

"Okay, but I like sleeping in my bed much better, though," she said, still focused on the children's program she was watching.

"I know, princess. Daddy didn't intend for us to stay all night."

"Daddy, are you going to marry Ms. Janiece now?"

"Well, Kayla, I dunno. Janiece and I have a lot to work out first."

"You don't love my mommy anymore, do you?"

"Princess, I do love your mommy, and I will always love your mom. She's the reason why I have you and your li'l brother. But things are just different for your mommy and me, and it's a different type of love."

"How so?" she asked, and K.P. took a moment to think of how to answer that question.

"Well, Daddy loves your mommy for being a good person and being your mother. Daddy loves Janiece like wanting to kiss her and hold her hand. It's kinda complicated, princess, and you are too young to really understand."

"I understand, Daddy. You like Janiece like Mommy likes Mr. Rodney, right?"

"Mr. who?" he questioned.

"Mr. Rodney. He came over to our house the other day when Kami came over to babysit, and he kissed Mommy before they got in the car."

"Oh . . . Tell me, did he kiss Mommy right in front of you?"

"No, I was watching from my room window, and I saw him kiss her and touch her bottom. I remember you telling me never to let anyone touch my bottom, Daddy," she told him.

"That's right. No one is allowed to touch your bottom, don't forget that. Now, when you saw Mr. Rodney kiss Mommy, did he kiss her like Uncle Marc kisses her when he greets her, or did he kiss her like I kiss Mommy?"

"It was like the way you kiss Mommy when your head goes like this," she said, showing him head moments as she kissed her hand to show him what she saw. After seeing that, K.P. decided to leave it alone and not probe Kayla for any more information.

He went down to his SUV to get the kids' overnight bag. He saw a guy looking at him coming down the steps. He nodded and went back upstairs. When he saw him get into the silver 300, he remembered that car in Janiece's guest parking stall. Naw, that can't be him. Must be the chick across the hall's man, he thought to himself.

He put Kayla in the tub first since she was up, and then he showered. Janiece and KJ were still sleeping, but he had to wake her because his dresser drawer was empty.

"Jai, where are my things?" he asked, and she sat up confused because he woke her up out of her sleep.

"Huh?" she said, rubbing her eyes.

"My things . . . my boxers, my tanks, socks, and shit," he said, standing next to the chest.

"Um . . . before you get mad, let me explain," she said, getting out of the bed. She stood and tried not to talk loudly because KJ was still sleeping. "I was upset, okay? And I didn't know if we were over or if we'd get back together or what," she said nervously.

"Okay, but what did you do with my things, Jai?" he asked, hoping, for argument's sake, that she hadn't done anything foolish like throwing them out or burning them. That was behavior he'd expect to get from Kimberly, not his precious Janiece.

"They're in the bag in the hall near the front door," she said, and he walked past her to retrieve the bag. Then he came back into the room in his towel and just started putting his things back into the drawer. He was smiling, and she wondered why he was smiling. She thought he'd be pissed, but he wasn't.

"Why are you smiling?" she asked him.

"I just never pictured you putting my stuff out like trash," he said in disbelief. He wasn't mad, though, just surprised.

"It wasn't like that, K.P."

"Yeah, whatever," he said and stepped into a pair of boxers. He looked so fine standing there, rubbing lotion on his arms. Janiece wished she wasn't on her menstrual, and KJ was not lying in her bed sleeping. She shook away that image of him hitting her from behind and went back to the subject.

"Come on, K.P., you were not speaking to me at the time, and I didn't know where we stood. I'm sorry, but I wasn't going to throw your things out. I had given them to you."

"I know you had, baby. I'm not mad, okay? I'm not sweating the small stuff," he said and kissed her on the forehead. He continued putting the rest of his stuff back. Janiece went to the bathroom, and he woke up his son. They all dressed and went out for breakfast. Then they went to the mall and shopped and ended up going to Hollywood Park to let the kids eat pizza again and play games.

They had a blast, and Janiece enjoyed his kids. They were intelligent, polite, and funny. They had Janiece cracking up, and she got to thinking about having one of her own one day. K.P. was feeling so good to have Janiece and his kids together. He was no longer afraid to be seen in public with her, and he was glad that everything was finally out in the open. They held hands, kissed, and did all the things that were never before possible to do in Chicago.

They got back to Janiece's condo around six, and when they were coming up the steps, Isaiah was coming down. Isaiah and Janiece didn't speak, but their eyes locked as K.P. unlocked the door. Isaiah shook his head, and she turned away from him. He didn't understand what she and K.P. had, and he didn't understand how much she loved K.P. She knew she should not have started messing around with him. She wished she hadn't gotten involved with him at all.

She was wrong, but she was curious about where he was going smelling and looking as good as he did. She couldn't help but wonder if he would be with another woman or what he had going on that Sunday night.

They got inside, and she tried to shake the thoughts of Isaiah because she didn't want K.P. to detect that anything was wrong.

K.P. tried calling Kimberly so that he could take the kids home, but she wasn't answering. He tried her phone, and she didn't answer it either. He gave it a few more minutes and then called again. After what seemed to him like the tenth attempt, she finally picked up and gave much attitude.

"Damn, K.P., why are you blowing up my phone?"

"Kimberly, ain't nobody blowing up your phone. I'm trying to bring the kids home. Where are you?"

"Where I am is none of your business. What time do you want to bring the kids?"

"Well, because it's a school night, Kimberly, I was thinking now, so they don't go to bed too late."

"Again, Kerry, what time do you want me to be home," she snapped. He hated her ass, and he wanted to ask her if she was with Mr. Rodney, but he didn't go there.

"In thirty minutes," he said and hung up. He knew she would start another argument, and he wasn't in the mood to go there with her. He had had a wonderful day with his woman and kids, and he didn't want to ruin his mood.

"Hey, baby, come ride with me to take my kids home," he said, and Janiece's mouth almost hit the floor.

"Are you crazy or high?"

"Neither," he answered, looking at her like, *what's the problem?*

"Then why do you think it's a good idea to ride with you to your house?"

"Because she has her man picking her up from the house to go on dates, so I can bring my woman to the house with me to take my kids home."

"How you know she has guys coming over to the house, K.P.?"

"Kayla told me."

"K.P., you got your kids spying on their mom for you and telling their mom's business?"

"No, I didn't ask her, nor do I have them reporting to me what happens at the house. She told me on her own about some cat named Rodney kissing her mom and groping her in the driveway. True, that is her business, but you are *my* business, and she can't tell me who I can and cannot bring with me. You'll have to be around Kimberly sooner or later."

"Well, I'd prefer later, *after* your divorce."

"Oh, so you're scared of Kimberly now? She has control over what you do?"

"K.P., you know damn well I'm not afraid of her. I just think it's not a good idea for me to go to her house. That causes problems for you, me, and the kids. Come on, K.P., use your head," she said, trying to make sense of the situation, but he was adamant about taking her with him.

"Look, Jai, I'm not going to put myself, you, or my kids in any bad situations, okay? I know how to handle Kimberly. You have nothing to worry about. I want you to ride with me," he said, and she finally agreed to go. The idea of her going to that woman's house was terrible, but she did what he asked her to do.

"Okay, K.P., come on, let's go, but I'm telling you that this is a bad idea."

They got in the Escalade and headed out to Kimberly's house. Janiece was a little nervous, but K.P. held her hand to assure her that everything would be fine. He pulled into the front of the garage, but he didn't park inside. Instead, he just went through the garage door, and Janiece stayed in the truck. He left the truck running with the lights on, and she told him to hurry because she had a bad feeling about being there.

She was on Kimberly's property, and Janiece knew that she had a right to kill any unauthorized persons that came on her property, and she didn't want any shit to go down. It seemed like K.P. was taking forever to come out. She sat there and peered at the little door over to the left that he went into, wishing he'd hurry. She was relieved to see him come out and before she knew it, "Crazy" came rushing out of the house behind him.

She was yelling and screaming as she ran up to the truck. "Oh shit," Janiece said out loud. I knew this crazy bitch was gon' act up. *I told K.P.* was her thought. When she saw Kimberly approaching her side, she froze. She wasn't anything like she expected. Kimberly was a small woman with a big roar.

"Get out, you bitch!" she yelled, coming closer to Janiece's side. Janiece sat up straight, and she couldn't react fast enough to stop Kimberly from snatching open her door. She was yelling at the top of her lungs, telling Janiece to get out of the truck. Janiece was too busy trying to position herself for defense, and before she could block, she felt a sting on the left side of her face when Kimberly slapped the shit out of her. She struck her so hard that Janiece's eyes watered. Janiece blinked to focus, and K.P. was pulling Kimberly away.

"Aw, naw, K.P. Let her ass go," Janiece yelled after she undid her seat belt and jumped out of the truck. Kimberly was struggling to try to break free from K.P.'s strong hold. Janiece was two feet away from her, and she told K.P. to let her go.

"No, Janiece, get back in the truck," he snapped.

"No, K.P. That li'l bitch hit me, and if she bad enough to put her hands on me, she bad enough to get her little ass whipped!" Janiece yelled. She was mad as hell.

"Jai, baby, get back into the truck," he pleaded.

"No, K.P. Let that bitch loose," Janiece shouted as Kimberly was trying to break free, all the while yelling and talking shit while she struggled.

"Kerry, let me go," Kimberly screamed.

"I will *not* let you go. Jai, get back in the truck," he instructed her again.

"Kerry, let me go," Kimberly demanded while she squirmed, but she couldn't break free.

"Jai," he said, looking at her with pleading eyes.

"Let her go, K.P.," Janiece told him again.

"Yeah, let me go so I can fuck up that bitch," Kimberly spat, but K.P. would not release her, and Janiece just stood there waiting for him to do so. Kimberly continued to try to break free, but it was useless. Janiece knew K.P. would not let her go, and he was looking at her with pleading eyes, so she finally turned to get back in the truck.

"Yeah, bitch, you betta do what Kerry said and get your fat ass back in the truck."

"Kim, shut up!" K.P. yelled. "When I let you go, you carry your ass into the house," he said as he watched Janiece climb back in the truck. When Janiece touched the door handle, he released Kimberly, and she immediately ran and tried to hit Janiece from behind, but Janiece was no fool. As soon as she ran up on her, Janiece turned and punched her dead square in her nose. Blood immediately gushed from her face. Kimberly grabbed her nose, tilting her head back.

Janiece didn't budge. She waited to see what Kimberly's next move would be. She hated it had come to that, but Kimberly asked for it.

"You bitch. You fucking bitch," Kimberly screamed, realizing that her nose was busted. K.P. grabbed Janiece to keep her from hitting Kimberly again and forced Janiece into the truck. Then he took Kimberly into the house and went into a kitchen drawer to get a towel. He ran cold water over it and tried to clean her face.

"Let me see," he said, trying to help her.

"I'm fine," she snapped, snatching the towel from his hand.

"Look, Kim, let me see if you're okay," he said, grabbing the towel from her. He ran some more cold water on it and started to wipe her face for her.

"Stop it. I'm fine," she said, getting up and not letting him see how bad it was. "You get out and get your ho outta my driveway and away from my house," she spat.

"Kimberly, you should not have gone out there in the first place trying to be all bad and shit, fucking with her."

"No, K.P. *You* should not have brought that bitch to *my* house. Why would you bring her here, K.P.?" she asked, with tears in her eyes. He felt terrible and now knew that it was a bad idea, but she had guys coming over, and he couldn't tell her who to have and not have at the house, so he felt like he could bring Janiece if he chose to. It's not like he invited her in.

"Kim, I'm sorry. I didn't think it was a big deal for her to ride out here with me. You got cats like Rodney picking you up here, so why can't I bring her with me?"

"So *this* is what this is about? You moved out. This is where *I* live, K.P. If I have a man pick me up here, it's not your damn business. *You're* the one who moved out. If you think it's okay to bring yo' hoover here, keep bringing her. It's gon' be some shit every time that bitch comes around my house."

"Yeah, if you want Janiece to whip yo' ass, you keep fucking with her. She's *my* woman, and she's going to be around for a long time. She's going to be around my kids, and you may see her again, and I don't want this bullshit to keep going on, Kim. So you have to control yourself and act like an adult. She didn't want to come, Kim, but I convinced her that it would be okay, and then you come out clowning and showing your ass. And look, you got your nose all busted up for what, Kim? I'm sorry for bringing her out here and disrespecting you, but you have to accept that's who I'm going to be with."

"I accept, now get the hell out and stay outta my business. I have who I want in this house because you don't want to be here anymore. So if that's your decree, stay outta my life. You got it?"

"Yep, I'll call you tomorrow about seeing the kids," he said and walked out.

"Fine," she yelled behind him. He hated that things escalated to that level. He walked to the truck thinking now he had to hear it from Janiece.

Chapter Twenty-Six

"K.P., I told you that this was a bad idea," Janiece said, looking in the visor mirror at her face. She was dark-skinned, but the slap left an ugly burgundy bruise on her face. "That crazy-ass woman is outta control. Then she hit me, and you thought I was just gon' get back in the truck? *Look* at my face," she spat, and K.P. glanced over and saw the bruise on her left cheek. He was sorry for taking Janiece out there, putting her in a bad situation. He had never seen Janiece that angry before.

"Jai, baby, I'm sorry. I didn't want her even to know you were in the truck. One of the kids must have said something when I walked out. I just wanted to drop them off and roll. I didn't intend for her to know you were outside, Jai. I promise you."

"Regardless of who said what, K.P., that nut hit me, and I would have beat the snot outta her ass if you weren't holding her. You should have let her go," she said, still examining her face.

"I didn't because I didn't want y'all scrapping in the driveway. The kids were in the house, Jai. I didn't want them coming out seeing y'all fighting and shit."

"Yeah, I know that, K.P., but do you think she cared? Do you think she was thinking about her children being in the house when she slapped the shit outta me?"

"That's exactly why I'm suing her for custody, Jai."

"K.P., you are *not* innocent in all this," she said as she finally closed the visor. "I shoulda stayed my black ass at home, but no . . . 'It's cool, Jai. I'm not gon' let you get hurt,'" she said, mocking him. "Then this little midget-ass woman weighing five pounds and two ounces jumps back and smacks the shit outta me, K.P."

"Okay, I know that was wild, and I'm sorry, but you did hit her ass pretty hard."

"She deserved it. I had to defend myself," she said, looking at her clothes to make sure she didn't get blood on them.

"True, but damn, girl, her nose is fucked up," he said, shaking his head. Kimberly thought she was prettier than Halle Berry, and that nose is going to be a jack for a little while, he thought.

"I don't give a damn about her nose. Look at *my* face. She shoulda kept her hands to herself." Janiece was on fire. She was so mad she could have beat K.P.'s ass. But on the other hand, she was happy to finally see the evil one behind all the harassing calls and malicious letters. She smiled because she knew there was nothing to fear with that lightweight. She was rugged, accurate, but Janiece wasn't worried about her pint-size ass anymore.

They rode the rest of the way in silence. When they got to her condo, Janiece was still on fire and mad as hell at K.P. They walked up and saw a note on her door. At least Jai knew it wasn't from Kimberly because she was at home with a busted nose, but knowing it was from Isaiah made it much worse.

"Who is that from?" K.P. asked.

"Well, K.P., I don't know. I haven't opened it yet," she replied with an attitude. She was still mad at him for taking her out to the evil one's house and getting her face slapped.

"Ha-ha, don't be a smart-ass." He walked in and went into the living room, but Janiece stayed in the kitchen to open the note. It was from Isaiah, and she got sad as she read it.

Hey, Janiece, how are you? I'm doing okay, just missing you. I know it's been a brief moment for us, and I know you have other things going on in your life, but I want you to know that I care for you and hope you haven't decided to stop talking to me. I have been trying to keep my cool for the last couple of days, but it's super hard to maintain when you can't stop thinking of someone. I know you feel like you still love him, but if you want to start fresh and try something new, you ought to do that. Don't continue to sell yourself short because you are worth so much more. You are beautiful, and I really miss spending time with you. I hope we can get together soon.

She folded the note, and K.P. walked into the kitchen. "So, when you gon' handle that?" he asked.

"Handle what?" she responded, acting like she had no idea what he was talking about.

"Isaiah. When are you going to tell him that we're back together?"

"K.P., don't start."

"Don't start what?" he asked, confused. All he did was ask a simple question.

"Don't start drilling me about when *I'm* gonna take care of *my* business. I'll handle him *and* my situation soon." She wasn't in any kind of mood to explain anything to K.P. She was just attacked by his crazy wife, making her feel a little different about the K.P. situation. She didn't want to face all the drama with K.P. and moving to Las Vegas. She did love him, and she didn't want to tell him no, but the bullshit she was going through was pissing her off.

"Jai, I'm not trying to drill you. I just want you to tell this cat that we're back together, and he needs to back off."

"K.P., you and I still have things to iron out."

"Okay, but what does that have to do with telling him to back off, Janiece? Either you want to be with me and work it out, or you don't," he yelled.

"I wanna be with you, K.P., and I do want things to work out for us, but right now, our shit is not tight, and I don't want you concerned or worrying about when and how *I'm* gon' deal with Isaiah. All you should be concerned about right now is *your* shit with Kimberly."

"Janiece, I got my situation with my wife under control. It's you that I'm worried about now because the look on your face tells me that this guy is a little more than you're leading me to believe. It's not hard to tell him that you can't see him anymore if you truly don't want to see him anymore, Jai," he said, and she was quiet. She turned away and didn't look at him because part of what he said was true. She didn't know how she had gotten to that point where she thought about a man other than K.P.

"Jai, look at me," he said, turning her to face him. "Tell me what's going on in your head, babe. I know we have our problems, Janiece, but things are going to be better and different, I promise," he said. He was genuine and honest with her, and he knew that he was ready to make a life for her and treat her the way she deserved, but if she had doubts, she needed to tell him.

"Do you care about this dude, Jai?" he asked, looking her in the eyes. She turned her head. She didn't want to lie, but she couldn't tell him the truth either.

"K.P., that's absurd. I haven't known him that long. I just don't want to hurt anybody. He's a nice person, and he doesn't deserve to get hurt behind me. I'm not the one to play with people's hearts."

"Then it shouldn't be a problem with telling him the truth," he said, waiting for her to confirm.

"I guess it won't."

"I love you, Jai, and, baby, you will *not* regret this. I'm going to give you all that I got and better than I was with Kimberly," he said, and she did believe him, but at the same time, she was not happy. It was just too much drama, and the mess with Kimberly made her stomach ache. She knew she didn't have the appetite for the bullshit that was ahead, and although she wanted not to, she cared about Isaiah.

"I'm going to take a shower," he said and kissed her on the forehead. After that, he headed for the bathroom, and Janiece went into her bedroom and took off her clothes. She walked around in her underwear, waiting for K.P. to finish showering so that she could get in.

She peeped out her kitchen window. Isaiah's car wasn't there. She poured herself a drink because the eventful day had her stressed. Then she went back into her bedroom and looked in her top drawer for a set of pj's, and she caught a glimpse of the bruise on her face. She was definitely not going to work the next day with that bruise on her cheek. She had to take a few days off until it healed.

She went back into the living room and pressed PLAY on her machine to listen to her messages. One was from her sister, and the other was from her girlfriend, Tia. There was a third message, but whoever it was just held the phone and didn't say anything.

She got chills and thought about crazy-ass Kimberly, so she hit STOP and went to get her drink on the counter. She dialed her sister back, but Greg said she was already asleep. Then finally, K.P. came out of the shower and found her in the kitchen, pouring herself another drink.

"You wanna drink?" she asked him as he walked up behind her.

"Yeah, a scotch will be fine," he said. She went over to the bar, grabbed the Chivas, and fixed him a scotch on the rocks. After handing it to him, she gave him a soft kiss and went to take a long-awaited shower. With the water cascading over her, she thought about Isaiah and how he felt to her body. She closed her eyes and thought about how he sucked on her nipples, so soft and good. She washed her body, imagining his hands gliding over it. Then she took the showerhead and let the water massage her clit, imagining it was Isaiah's tongue.

Since she still had her monthly visitor, she knew she and K.P. wouldn't be able to get any action that night, but she'd be straight the next day. Since she was on the pill, her period only lasted two days, if that. She touched her nipples and let the water vibrate on her clit 'til she was near her orgasm. Suddenly, she was interrupted before getting what she was working for by tapping on the bathroom door.

"Baby, Tia's on the phone. She said it's an emergency."

"Tell her I'm in the shower, K.P.," she said.

"I did, but she said it's urgent," he told her. Quickly, she turned off the water, grabbed a towel, and wrapped it around her body. She stepped out of the shower and opened the bathroom door, took the phone from K.P.'s hand, concerned with what was going on with her friend.

"Hello," she said.

"We broke up," Tia said, crying on the phone.

"What! What happened?" Janiece asked with concern. Tia was crying so bad she couldn't understand her explanation of why they broke up. She went on to tell Janiece how her boyfriend said he wanted some space and that they needed to slow down. Janiece could tell she was devastated. She had a feeling that Tia was probably smothering him because ever since she and Rick got together, she saw and heard from Tia less and less.

"Can you come over? I can't be alone tonight," she begged.

"Tia, K.P. is here right now."

"Well, when he leaves, will you come over, or can I come by there?"

"He won't be leaving. I can come by for a little while, but K.P. will be here for the night."

"On a Sunday?" she asked, shocked.

"Yes. I'll slip on some clothes and come by, but I won't stay long, okay?" she said, and K.P. was looking at her strangely. She slipped on a pair of jeans and a sweatshirt. K.P. was still looking at her like she was up to something. When she was putting on her tennis shoes, he finally said what was on his mind.

"Are you sure you're going to Tia's?" he asked suspiciously.

"K.P., please, don't even go there. I am not going to wait 'til now to start lying to you. She and Rick broke up, and I'm just going over for a few hours," she said and went into the bathroom. She combed her hair and put some gloss on her lips.

"If you are going to Tia's, why are you getting all prettied up?" he demanded, standing at the bathroom door.

"K.P., stop it," she said, squeezing by him. She went to the closet and grabbed a jacket.

"You want me to drive you?"

"No. I can drive myself," she said and headed for the door.

"Here, take the truck. I think your rear left tire looks a little low," he said, handing her the keys.

"You gon' let me drive the Escalade?" she asked him in disbelief.

"Sure, why not?"

"Okay, I'll be back soon," she said and took the keys and kissed him. She went down the stairs and got in the truck. She still didn't believe she was driving his Escalade, but it felt good. She jumped on the expressway and headed over to Eighty-Seventh and Torrence. Tia lived in her mom's house. Her mom had died two months after Janiece's dad passed away, so she inherited the three-bedroom home and lived there alone. Before she could park, her phone was going off. It was K.P.

Chapter Twenty-Seven

K.P. was asleep on the sofa and heard a tap on the front door. He got up, walked to the door, and looked through the peephole. It was the same dude he had seen earlier that day. He looked down at his watch—after midnight. He wondered why the man was tapping on Janiece's door at that hour. He opened the door, and the shocked look on Isaiah's face told K.P. that he didn't expect to see him there.

"Can I help you?" K.P. asked.

"Sorry, man, I was looking for Janiece."

"And you are?" K.P. asked, standing up straight. They were both about the same height, and although K.P. wasn't in the military, his body was just as tight as Isaiah's, but Isaiah wasn't intimidated by him one bit.

"I'm Isaiah," he said, extending his hand. K.P. didn't bother to shake it.

"Well, I'm K.P., Janiece's fiancé. She's not here right now."

"Okay, can you tell her that I stopped by?"

"Sorry, man, I won't be able to do that. I don't know if she told you, but she and I are back together, and it would be better if you didn't come by anymore," K.P. said and gave him a look to let him know that he should back the fuck off.

"Well, you don't have to let her know I stopped by, and until she tells me it will be better for me not to stop by, that's when I won't be stopping by anymore," Isaiah retorted. He had no clue that K.P. was there because his truck wasn't there when he pulled up. He had debated whether he should go over, and now, he wished he had not.

"Look, man, I know you been hanging out with Janiece because we were going through some things, but we're working our things out, and it would be better if you would leave my woman alone. I read the little note you left hanging on our door, and I understand that Janiece has shared some things with you, but I'm telling you to back off and leave her alone," K.P. said sternly. He didn't want to take their conversation to the next level. Janiece and Kimberly already fought earlier, and if he and Isaiah had to scrap in that little-ass hallway, so be it.

"Oh, so you're divorced now?" Isaiah asked, and K.P. stepped out the door.

"Man, you don't know me, and you don't know shit about my situation, so you need to tend to your own business and leave my woman alone. She is *not* interested in you and all this shit you trying to put in her head about moving on and starting fresh. That's just what she's going to do, but with me . . . partner," K.P. said, but Isaiah didn't back down.

"Look, K.P. I ain't putting nothing in your woman's head. She's an intelligent woman, and evidently, you didn't realize what you had. You would not have kept her on the side for over five years if you did. Trust me, I didn't have to spit too much game to have her calling out my name, playa," Isaiah said, and before K.P. could catch himself, he punched Isaiah in the mouth. Isaiah swung back quickly, but he didn't hit K.P. as hard as he wanted to.

They were tussling until Janiece yelled from the door for them to stop. She had come home and heard them thumping in the hall. She ran to see what was happening and saw K.P. and Isaiah wrestling.

"K.P., stop it! Stop it! Let him go!" she yelled, and he backed up. He and Isaiah were breathing hard. Now she stood between them.

"Jai, tell him that y'all are done and not to come by here ever again," K.P. demanded. Janiece was shaking. She wanted to touch Isaiah's lip and wipe the blood away.

"Isaiah, I'm sorry," she said. He straightened his shirt and walked back into his sister's condo. He didn't say one word to her.

"K.P., what the hell is going on?" she demanded.

He walked away, went over to her liquor cart, and poured himself a scotch. Then quickly swallowing it, he poured another.

"Jai, you stay the fuck away from that cat. Do you hear me?" his voice thundered at her, and she visibly started shaking. She had never once in their entire affair heard that tone from him.

"K.P., what happened? Tell me what's going on. How did you end up in the hall fighting with Isaiah?" she asked. She wanted to know how it all started. She wanted to go and check on Isaiah, but she knew K.P. wouldn't let her out the door.

"That motherfucker got the nerve to talk to me about how he fucked you, Jai. He doesn't know who the fuck he dealing with. I didn't need to hear that shit from him, and I'm telling you, Jai, you betta stay away from him— do you understand?" he yelled and hit the wall. Janiece stood there, too scared to move. She hated what she had done. She hated that she had caused this much drama for Isaiah. She wanted so bad to check on him.

She went into her bedroom to undress, but K.P. was so fired up he walked around like he would explode.

"K.P., baby, sit down, please, and calm your nerves, baby. You're making me nervous," she said, pulling her nightgown over her head.

"Why are you nervous, Jai? You think I'm going to do something to you?" he said, getting in her face. "You think I'm gon' hurt you for fucking that cat, huh?" he snapped, and Janiece jumped. He realized that he needed to calm down. He looked at her and at the bruise that she had on her cheek and thought about all the drama and bullshit he had put her through, and now he was mad because, after all those years, she fucked one dude. Finally, he calmed himself and apologized to her.

"Jai, I'm sorry, baby. Forgive me for yelling at you. You're the best thing that ever happened to me. And I can't stand the fact that he touched your body and then gon' stand in my face and brag about it like you were his woman. I lost my mind, okay? Please forgive me, baby," he said and held her close.

"Jai, let's go. Let's fly to Las Vegas tomorrow and buy a house and start over."

"K.P., you're still married," she reminded him.

"I know, and I'll just have to commute back and forth 'til it's final, but we just have to leave this place. I don't want to be surrounded by all of this drama and negativity. I want us to be away from everything."

"Baby, we can't run away from our problems. That isn't going to make them go away."

"Well, let's just take a vacation, wherever you want to go. I can call the travel agent in the morning. Just say you want to get away with me," he pleaded, and she agreed that they should. She figured if she left for a few days, maybe by the time she returned, Isaiah would be gone, and she wouldn't have to go through the motions with him.

"Yes, let's take a trip. Let's go away. We need to get away and be alone," she said.

"Good. I'll call my travel agent in the morning, and we'll go wherever just to get out of Chicago, okay, baby?"

"Okay," she said, and they kissed. He rubbed her back, and his dick started to swell. He pulled her closer to him. Janiece knew he was horny and wanted her, but she wasn't quite free from her "visitor," Aunt Flow, so she pulled his boxers down and kneeled on the floor. She stroked him gently and then took him inside of her mouth. The warmth of her mouth made him moan. He rubbed the back of her head while she teased his dick with her tongue. She played with his balls while making circular motions with her tongue around the head.

She paused for a second, and he went over to her bed. He lay back and rested on his elbows, so he could watch as she sucked him like a porn star. He had ten inches of thick steel, and Janiece was a pro at pleasing him with her dick-sucking skills. Now, she stood and removed her gown, exposing her erect nipples, which turned him on more.

She spit on the tip and then rubbed his dick in the center of her breasts. He reached and squeezed on one of her nipples while she stroked his dick while rubbing it over the other nipple. After a few moments of playing around her breasts, she put her mouth back on it. He was ready to climax, and when he gave her the signal, she jerked him and let his hot juice squirt all over her breasts.

K.P. was out of breath by the time she finished. Janiece got up and went into the bathroom to clean herself up, and when she came back, she took the hot towel and wiped him down. After that, they climbed into bed, and he pulled her close to him and silently vowed never to let her go. There would never be an opportunity for another man to slip inside his woman. She was too fine, too intelligent, and too good for him to lose.

As K.P. thought about Isaiah and cringed, he prayed that he'd never come across that cat again because he was liable to kick his ass. He definitely had to get Janiece away from that cat because he could give K.P. a little competition. They were built the same, had the same complexion, and the brotha looked like he could dress. K.P. didn't want him around persuading Janiece to do anything else. That slick bastard was trying to snatch Janiece from him, and K.P. vowed that that shit wasn't going to happen.

The sooner he got Janiece out of Chicago, the better. He didn't want to go out every day wondering if Isaiah was somewhere lurking around her place. He already knew that Janiece had feelings for him, and he wasn't going to lose her, not after all they had been through and how close he was to marrying her. Isaiah was messing with the wrong man's woman, and K.P. would ensure he didn't go anywhere near Janiece ever again.

Chapter Twenty-Eight

Janiece set her alarm for six a.m. to make sure she got up to call into work. First, she went to the bathroom. After that, she went into the kitchen to get a drink of juice. As she did so, she looked out and saw Isaiah getting out of his car. She wondered what he was doing so early, and then she thought about his sleep still being off. She wanted so badly to open the door and say something to him, but she knew if K.P. caught her talking to him, it would be hell.

She stood there watching him for a moment until she could not see him any longer as she finished her apple juice, and then went back to bed. She tried to go back to sleep, but her mind wouldn't rest. Thoughts of Isaiah flooded her mind. She got back up and got her phone out of her purse, went into the bathroom, and sent him a text message. When she hit the OK button to send the message, she looked up and noticed herself in the mirror.

The bruise on her face was an ugly, darker shade, and she got pissed all over again. When she touched it, it still had a sting—"crazy-ass nut," she said to herself. She was getting ready to walk out of the bathroom when her phone went off. She hurried to silent the ring tone because she didn't want to wake K.P.

It was Isaiah responding to her text. She said that she was sorry for the previous night's events. His response was, "Janiece, I need to see you," and she responded to him, saying, "I can't because K.P. is here," and he texted her back asking if she could get out and meet him somewhere. She stood there with her mind racing. She wanted to go and meet him, but she had no idea what she would say to K.P. to get out, plus her tire was flat, and she had to use K.P.'s truck again.

She texted him back, telling him she needed time to figure out how she would meet him. His response was, "No matter what time, I'll wait for you because I gotta see you." She closed her phone, put it into her purse, and walked away but hurried back to make sure it was on vibrate, just in case.

When she went back into the bedroom, she was relieved to see K.P. still asleep. She climbed back into bed, trying to develop a plan to get out and see Isaiah. She couldn't come up with anything. She wasn't used to lying to K.P., and she wasn't really comfortable with the idea of starting to lie to him. She now knew what K.P. went through to get out of the house. She had a little more insight on how he used to tell her that "he would try" because she had to try now to come up with something that wouldn't make her look suspicious, and then, *bam,* it hit her.

She got up and grabbed her jeans off the chaise and her sweatshirt she had on the night before. Silently, she went into the bathroom, brushed her teeth, and washed her face. Silently, she combed her hair, making sure she covered the bruise on her left cheek. After applying a little lip gloss, she went back into the bedroom.

"K.P.," she whispered and shook him a little. Finally, he opened his eyes and said, "What is it, baby?"

"I need to run down to Walgreen's and get a box of tampons. I'll be right back."

"You driving the truck?" he asked, sounding groggy.

"No, I'm gonna walk," she said so that she could be by herself for a little while.

"You sure? It's probably cool this morning, babe," he said, turning over on his stomach.

"Yeah, don't worry. I'll be back shortly."

"Okay," he said and fell right back asleep. She jetted out the door and called Isaiah as soon as she was out of the window sight. He picked up on the first ring, it seemed.

"Hello, Janiece," he said, smooth as always.

"Hey, can you meet me at Walgreen's?"

"I'm on my way," he replied.

She quickly got into his car after he stopped where she was walking, and he pulled off. He drove down Ninety-Fifth Street, passing up Walgreen's. Janiece didn't want to go too far because she didn't have much time. He pulled up into an empty parking lot and turned off the car. He looked so fucking sexy to her with his fresh-cut, shaved face. He had on dark jeans and a Bears hoodie. Her heart was thumping so hard she thought he could feel the vibration.

"It's good to see you," he told her.

"It's good to see you too," she said to him, and they were looking at each other with no words. Janiece figured he too didn't know what to say next.

"Look, Isaiah, I'm really sorry—"

"Hey, don't worry about it. It's not your fault. He's starting to realize how good of a woman you are, and if I were him, I'd done the same."

"Isaiah, I should have never gotten involved with you because now, I can't stop thinking of you, and I miss—" she tried to say, but he kissed her. It sent tingles through her body, and she knew she should have stopped him, but she was too weak to break loose. He grabbed her face, causing her to cringe because of the sting.

"What's wrong?" he asked, and Janiece touched the area where she put on a little press power to conceal. "Did that asshole hit you, Janiece?" he asked, assuming the worst, and she could tell he was angry the way his brow almost became one.

"No, Isaiah, nothing like that. K.P. loves me. He would never hit me," she said, defending him. K.P. was a pistol, but Janiece felt safe with him, and he'd never physically abused her.

"Well, what happened to your face, and please tell me the truth?" he requested.

"I had a little altercation with his wife, but that's another story, and I don't have that long."

"Damn, I'm sorry," he said, touching her face gently.

"I'm cool. You should see *her* nose," Janiece said with a chuckle.

"Look, I know you're going to be with K.P. I don't see you leaving him any time soon. I hate that, but I know you love this dude, but at the same time, Janiece, I want you, and I miss you like crazy, girl, and it's killing me not being able to see you."

"I know, Isaiah, but I don't know what to do. I love him, yes, but there is something about you that I can't let go of. I think of you all the time, and I do miss spending time with you."

"Well, I only have a little over a week left here. I'm going back to Texas next week, Wednesday, so can you manage to squeeze me in sometime between now and then . . . ?"

"Isaiah, I don't know. K.P. is trying to take me out of town for a few days."

"Where?"

"I'm not sure. He'll be calling his travel agent today, and then I'll know."

"Well, for how long?"

"I don't even know that."

"Janiece, you can't. Tell him it's not a good time that you can't take off work. Just don't leave. I don't have much time left."

"Isaiah, how? I don't know how to lie to him. K.P. is smart, and he's not just gon' go for that. I agreed to go last night, and if I back out now, he's gonna be suspicious."

"Well, he doesn't know I'm going back to Texas, so if you go and I'm gone when you come back, can you get away to go to Texas?"

"You want me to visit you in Texas?" she asked him in astonishment.

"Yes, I'll buy your ticket. Just say you'll come," he asked with desperation in his voice.

"I think I can do that if you really want me to."

"Yes, I do," he said and kissed her again. The kiss turned into a long, passionate kiss, and Janiece knew she had to get back. "Baby," she said, pulling away, "I gotta go because I still have to run in the store and pick up something."

"Five more minutes, Janiece. I promise I won't let you get into trouble with your man." Janiece could see a slight bruise on the corner of his mouth, and she touched it.

"Are you okay?"

"Yeah, boo, I'm a soldier," he said and smiled. She kissed him again, and then he ran her down to the Walgreens. He let her walk back because she didn't want to take any chances of K.P. catching her with him. She walked, smiling ear to ear because she was glad she had gotten a chance to see Isaiah. Even if it was only for ten minutes, it was worth every moment.

When she turned on her street, his car was already parked. She tried to hurry past when she saw him sitting in the car. "Now he knows he's wrong for that," she said to herself because he got out at the exact same time she walked past.

Isaiah walked up the steps behind her, whispering naughty things about licking her clit and nibbling on her nipples, making her smile. She was determined to get away from him. He brushed up against her when he passed her to get to his sister's condo door. She paused and let him get completely in before she opened her door. She was happy to see K.P. still sound asleep when she entered. She went into the bathroom and took a shower and was surprised to see her menstrual was done when she removed the spot-free tampon that she had on.

She quickly checked her phone and read the text from Isaiah, telling her to enjoy the rest of her day. Then she went into her room and crawled back into bed with K.P. She had on a tank top and panties, and when he repositioned himself to hold her, he felt her skin, which gave him an erection. Turning, he grabbed her breast, but she stopped him.

"No, baby, I'm still on," she lied because she just went and bought a new box of tampons, so she had to play it off.

He didn't put up a fight. He just left it alone. They stayed in bed 'til about eleven, and when he got up, he was on the phone with his travel agent to see what was good. He decided they would go to Florida for a few days. Lucky for Janiece, she thought they wouldn't leave until the next day. This would give her a chance to see Isaiah again, but she didn't know where or how.

They planned to go for five days. They would return on Saturday so that Janiece could go back to work the following week. Today, she had to get away from K.P. At first, she thought she'd tell him she would get her nails done. She needed to, but she also needed a plan to give her a few hours with Isaiah.

K.P. walked around, chilling, and she walked around on pins and needles because she *had* to see Isaiah before they went to Florida. And how in the hell was she going to be able to visit him in Texas? she wondered. She was already taking this week off from work and trying to take a few more days off would be impossible.

"Hey, baby, I'm going to go over to Marc's to get a few things for our trip tomorrow. Do you want to come with me?" he asked, and she quickly said no. She thought about Isaiah being across the hall, and if K.P. would be gone for a couple of hours, she could at least talk to him.

"Naw, baby, I got to do some things around here myself for our trip tomorrow. First, I need to do laundry, and you know I have to get my hair done early in the morning."

"Why can't you get your hair done today?"

"Because there are no salons open on Monday, baby, and I'm gonna need some money because my direct deposit won't go in 'til Friday."

"No problem. I'll give it to you when I get back. I gotta stop at the cash machine. As a matter of fact, here," he said, going into his wallet and giving her his Visa debit card. "This account has money in it, and you can hold on to this one to get whatever you need. The pin is 7226," he said, handing her the card.

"Baby, are you sure because I can wait 'til you give me what I need later," she said, holding the card for him to take back.

"No, there's a few hundred in that account. I'm not worried," he said and kissed her on the forehead. He went into the bedroom, and Janiece sat there looking at the card. She felt funny because K.P. had always given her cash. Never before had he trusted her with a debit card, and then she remembered her tire.

"Oh, baby, do you think you can fix my tire before tomorrow so that I can drive in the morning?" she asked as he walked back into the living room wearing a jersey and sweats.

"Yeah, no problem, and, Janiece, baby, you know I trust you, right?"

"Yes," she said, looking at him puzzled.

"I know Isaiah is that dude from across the hall, and I'm trusting that you won't do anything crazy."

"K.P., come on."

"I'm just saying, Jai."

"I know, but don't worry, okay? I'm where I wanna be," she said and touched his face because he was leaning over her.

"I love you, Jai. Always remember that, and I am gonna do right by you."

"I know, baby, and I love you too. I have always loved you. That hasn't changed."

"Okay, I'll see you in a few hours. Call me if you need anything," he said and kissed her on the cheek. Janiece walked him to the door, and they embraced. She loved him, but something about Isaiah had her head. She watched him pull off and fought the urge to call Isaiah. She put the debit card in her purse and went to pick out the things she would pack for their trip to Florida tomorrow.

Chapter Twenty-Nine

Janiece was on her way down the steps with a basket of clothes. She decided she'd take her suitcase out of her storage while she was in the basement. So she started one load and went inside her storage cage to get her luggage. That's when she heard a noise and came out of her storage and looked around. She didn't see anyone, so she turned slowly and went back in. She continued to move stuff around to get to her luggage when she heard the door open and shut once more.

She walked out of her storage cage and looked to see who had come in, but she didn't see anybody. She stood still for a moment and waited to see if she'd hear the same sound again, but nothing. She hardly ever went downstairs when it was dark because it used to creep her out, but it was a little after one in the afternoon right now. She walked over to the door, opened it, and walked up the five steps but saw no one.

She looked around. No one was on the street either. K.P. wasn't back yet, and she suddenly wished he was so that he could come downstairs with her. She shook it off, went back into the basement, and entered her storage cage. She tried to move things quickly to get to her luggage so she could get out of there and once again, heard the door open and shut. After that, she heard whoever it was locking the door. She froze at first, and then she grabbed the bat that she had in the cage and moved slowly toward the door. She knew not to say anything because that would tell the perpetrator exactly where she was.

Taking a deep breath, she moved silently toward the cage door and almost knocked Isaiah's head off when he stepped in front of her storage cage.

"Isaiah, what in the hell are you doing? You scared the shit outta me," she said, putting the bat down, her heart thumping wildly in her chest.

"I'm sorry, baby. I didn't mean to scare you. I saw you walk down with the basket of clothes, and when I saw his truck gone. Well, I thought this would be a good opportunity to get a little time in with you," he said. She was still holding her pounding chest, thanking God that it was only Isaiah.

"Well, you should have said something or called out my name. You almost gave me a heart attack."

"I'm sorry. I had no idea you'd be in your storage cage. I thought you'd be out by the machines," he said, moving close to her. He touched her arms, and she began to shake. She knew she was doing K.P. wrong, but she couldn't help herself when it came to Isaiah. She was trembling from the kiss that he planted on her lips.

"What are you doing, Isaiah?" she asked, knowing where he was going, but she wanted to hear it from him.

"I'm doing exactly what you want me to do," he told her.

"How do you know this?" she asked with her eyes closed.

"Because I can read your mind," he said and kissed her passionately. Her nipples immediately hardened. She was mesmerized by him, and she wanted him to take her body and make her explode like he had done before. He lifted her sweatshirt, revealing her breasts because she wasn't wearing a bra. Leaning over, he took one into his mouth, and Janiece grabbed the back of his head and let his tongue probe her erect nipple.

The more he sucked, the wetter she got. He started to rub her through her jeans, and she wanted him to strip them off to touch her without any interference. He came back up to kiss her lips, took her hand, and put it on his erection. It was so stiff and solid. She *wanted* to please him. She undid his pants, took his dick in her hands, and stroked it while they played around each other's mouths with their tongues. Janiece wanted to please Isaiah, so she knelt down and took him inside her mouth.

His skin was so clean and fresh that it made her give him the expert mode head job. She was sucking on his dick like it was familiar territory. Like she had been sucking his dick for the last decade, and he was on cloud nine with the feeling she was giving him. It was so pleasing he thought that he would bust right there, and he didn't want to do that just yet, so he pulled back and began to kiss her passionately again. He undid her jeans and motioned her to go over to the laundry table.

She didn't object. She just allowed him to take her hand and lead her to the table. After he removed her jeans, he sat her on the table. She wore a purple thong. Isaiah didn't bother to remove it. He just moved it aside and tested her wetness with his finger. Of course, she was good because Janiece had no problems when it came to getting wet. He took the condom from his pocket and opened it.

She had second thoughts as she watched him roll it over his dick, but she had come this far. No way was she going to stop him. As soon as he was completely protected, she spread her legs, giving him an open invitation to penetrate her love nest. He slid inside her tight, juicy hole and found a rhythm to which they both began to moan.

Janiece closed her eyes, enjoyed Isaiah's sensations, and secretly didn't want it to end. She tried to keep her moans low, but he pumped her harder and harder, causing her to cry to erupt louder and louder. Then he leaned over and sucked on her nipples as he pumped his pelvis, giving her feelings of pure ecstasy.

"Stand up, baby," he suggested, and she did just what he said. He turned her back to him and gave her a slight push, bending her over the table. Then he planted his feet firmly on the concrete basement floor so that he could pound her correctly. She was screaming his name and had to bite her bottom lip by now. His dick was feeling so good inside of her she forgot where she was.

The machine changed cycles, bringing her back to reality. She opened her eyes and looked over her shoulder at him, and their eyes locked.

That look made them both realize how much they cared for each other. He stopped and turned her to face him. Passionately, he grabbed her head and kissed her deeply. His erection was between them, touching her stomach, and she wanted it back inside of her body.

"Come on, baby, I wanna feel you some more," she begged and sat back on the table. He watched as she spread her legs. Then she took her fingers and opened her lips so that he could get a good look.

It was shining with loads of juice, causing his erection to jump. Eagerly, he slid back in, and she grabbed him around his neck and worked her hips back on him. They were rocking so hard the table was making a loud thumping noise against the floor. She sucked on his earlobe because she was there, where she wanted to be. Her body gave him the response that it was supposed to give from all of his excellent penetration. He felt her juice rain down on him, and he let go of what he had been trying to hold back from the moment he entered her body.

The way he groaned and the way she moaned confirmed to them that their mission had been accomplished.

She didn't let go of his neck right away. She waited until his dick was no longer erect before she released him.
They looked at each other and wondered what to say
or do next. He kissed her, and she smiled. He knew he
should have left this woman alone, but he couldn't resist her. He didn't *want* to resist her. He was so into
Janiece that he knew he couldn't walk away or just let her
go. He was just as determined as K.P. was to get her, and
he didn't care if he had to go head to head with K.P. He
wanted Janiece, and he had to find a way to convince her
to leave her situation with K.P. and start fresh with him.

"Are you okay, baby?" he asked, making sure she was
all right with what just went down.

"Yes, I'm fine," she smiled. "I would like my clothes
because it's kinda chilly down here, though," she said,
and they laughed. He stepped back and let her get up. He
looked at her curvy body as she stepped into her jeans.
He pulled his jeans up from his ankles, and she went over
to her storage cage to get her sweatshirt. She felt so good
and so guilty at the same time. If K.P. knew what was
going on he, would kill her. K.P. was doing everything so
right, and now she was getting it all wrong.

"Can I see you later, Janiece?" he asked.

"I don't know, Isaiah. K.P. will be back soon, and I
know he'll be on me like white on rice. We leave to go to
Florida tomorrow and won't be back 'til Saturday night."

"Janiece, you have to try because I don't want this to
be my last time seeing you," he said and stepped closer
to her.

"I know, Isaiah, but it is gon' be hard. Trust me, I don't
want this to be the last time I see you either, but I'm with
K.P., and he loves me, Isaiah. I can't start this sneaking
around. I mean, I adore you, but I love him, and the last
thing I wanna do is hurt him."

"Listen, Janiece, I know you're stuck on this dude, and I can't make you not be stuck on him, but I do feel like you are shortchanging yourself. If you were my woman, no way would I be between you and another woman."

"Isaiah, that's our shit. Please don't try to analyze our shit. I'm not perfect. I just fucked you in the laundry room, so I'm no better than he is, so if you know what the real deal is, you got to accept it for what it is, or if you can't, you need to back off because right now, I'm not ready to walk away from him . . ." she said, sounding like K.P. in the beginning when they had their first conversation about their situation. Like she knew K.P. had a wife, Isaiah knows she has a man.

"Damn, it's like that now, huh, Janiece?"

"No, and I'm not trying to be mean. I'm just honest because I don't have time to play games. K.P. is finally stepping up to the plate and willing to give me everything I ever wanted from him, and I just can't walk away from him, so please, try to understand, Isaiah. I wish I could shake you, but I can't. That's why I'm right here right now with you, but I'm not over him," she said, being honest.

"I see," he said and scratched his forehead. "You enjoy your trip to Florida," he said and just walked away and left her standing there.

She felt more confused than ever at that moment because she didn't want to hurt Isaiah either, but she had to tell him the truth. Finally, she went into her storage cage and retrieved her luggage. Then she walked up the steps, and when she got inside, she saw she had a missed call on her phone from K.P., so she called him back.

"Hey, baby," she said when he picked up.

"Hey, where were you? I'm on my way back, and I wanted to know if you wanted anything to eat," he said, being considerate. His mind led him to believe other things, but he wanted to trust Janiece. He had trusted her all these years, and he didn't want to consider the worst now.

"I was down in the basement putting clothes in the machine, and I got my luggage from the storage cage."

"Oh, okay. Do you want a bite?"

"Yes, a bite of you," she teased.

"Oh, that can definitely be arranged," he smiled a devilish grin.

"Just one more day, daddy, and I'm going to take care of you," she said, having a flashback of what just occurred in the basement with Isaiah.

"I can't wait, trust me. I need some of that gushy-gushy," he said, and she smiled. "Hey, I'm close. What do you want to eat, babe?"

"Well, since we can go where we please now, I'd like to go out to get something, if that's okay with you."

"No problem. I'll be there in twenty."

"Okay," she said, and they hung up. She ran, jumped in the shower, and did a five-minute heavy-duty wash on her essential parts. Then she put on some fresh clothes and applied a little makeup to camouflage her bruise. In twenty minutes, she was ready, and K.P. walked through the door with a couple of bags of clothes.

She knew he was moving in because of all the stuff he brought with him. She didn't object because she had wanted him with her from the beginning. She kissed him at the door and then helped him put his things in the bedroom.

"I love you, K.P. You don't know how happy I am to have you here," she said sincerely. Although she was wrong for messing around with Isaiah, she was glad to have the man she had loved for the last five years to herself.

"I'm glad to be here with you too, baby, and I have something for you," he said and gave her the ring. She was speechless. He slid it on her finger, and all Janiece could do was stare at it. It was gorgeous, and the only thing that came into her mind was what had just gone down in the basement with Isaiah. She blinked back her tears. How did she get there, and what was she going to do now?

Chapter Thirty

Kimberly was calling K.P. back-to-back, and his phone just went straight to voicemail. She was furious because she hated trying to reach him, and he didn't pick up, or he'd power off his phone like he had no cares in the world. She was so angry that he was gone and off with Janiece livin' la vida loca, and all she had was the kids to use as leverage. There were plenty of sitters she could afford to pay, but she wanted to put them on Kerry just to play the single momma with no life role to try to make him feel some type of remorse for leaving her with two kids to raise alone.

She had her sitter on standby just in case she couldn't make Kerry come and take them off her hands. She instantly dialed Janiece's home number and got the answering machine. Since Kerry had neglected to respond to the ten messages she had left him on his phone, she figured he knew she was serious after she left a message on Janiece's machine saying, *"I know y'all are there probably laid up or, some shit. I've been trying to talk to you for the last couple of days, and I don't intend on spending my Saturday night cooped up in the house with your kids, so call me back, you jackass."*

She attempted to call his phone again, but she knew it was useless. She wondered why she hadn't talked to K.P. for three days. He called on Wednesday to talk to the kids, and she hadn't heard from him since. She had a hot date with her man Rodney, millionaire and heir to his daddy's empire, so she cared less what Kerry was really doing. She just wanted to be evil and didn't want folks looking down on her for not being able to keep her man. Rodney was first class all the way, and as long as she served him up and made him feel like a king, he didn't hold back on spoiling her.

Rodney did all the things K.P. didn't do. He was generous and not cheap like K.P., so he never shopped at JC Penney's like her tight-ass husband. K.P. had the money but always tried to control her spending. All the things that K.P. thought were superfluous, she would just go to Mr. Rodney, and he'd give it to her without question.

Half of the things K.P. thought her daddy was buying her came from the generosity of her lover. She didn't intend to cheat on K.P. with Rodney, but when she met him, he was so charming. It was almost two years ago when she was at one of her father's parties. In addition to that, Rodney was with some young woman who looked like he had taken her out of Mattel's toy package because everything on her was utterly fake.

Kimberly, always the center of attention, was a little bit jealous of this juvenile because all the men in the room were taking notice of her every move, so Kimberly's mission was to find out who she was and who she was with, so they could be dismissed from her daddy's party. K.P. had already gotten out of the party with some lame excuse, so she was solo. She was trying to catch one of the servers to get a glass of champagne, and Rodney stopped one of them for her. He took a champagne flute from the tray and handed it to her.

"Thanks," she said, taking it from him.

"My pleasure," he replied in a deep voice, and instead of him walking away, he struck up a conversation. "So, do you know the host?" he asked her and took a sip of his drink.

"Yes, I do. However, I wish I knew who the young lady in black is."

"Over there at the bar?" he said, looking in that direction.

"Yes," Kimberly answered in an irritated tone.

"Why? Is she making trouble?"

"No. She's just a little underdressed for such an occasion," Kimberly said, looking at her with an evil eye.

"Yeah, you can say that. Her dress is a bit much, but you, my dear, are looking positively stunning," he said, looking at Kimberly with a smile.

"Well, thank you. I guess we all didn't get the invitation that said, formal, not trashy," she said, and they snickered.

"If she's too inappropriate, I can have my driver take her home," the handsome stranger continued, and Kimberly's jaw dropped.

"I take it you know her?" she asked, feeling embarrassed for talking about his date.

"Yeah, that's my date, and trust me, I did tell her formal attire. My driver picked her up first, and when I got into the limo, that is what she had on," he said with an apologetic smile. His teeth were perfect and white. Kimberly looked at his fingernails and shoes and knew she talked to a quality man. She wanted to get to the core of what he did and his worth before she insisted he send little Barbie home.

After finding out a few details and his status, she batted her eyes, slipped him a little note, and they found themselves in the coat closet. After the party, he gave her his card and told her to call him. When she got home and opened the garage to find K.P. not there, she pulled out her phone and Rodney's card. She asked him if his "naked girlfriend" had been dropped off yet, and he said, "Pulling away from her driveway as we speak."

After that, he invited her to his home. She didn't mention her marriage, nor did she mention she was the daughter of Mr. Grayson. When she made it out to his beautiful mansion, her eyes lit up at the sight of his estate.

She pulled up to the gate and pressed the button. No one spoke, but the gate opened. She pulled into the circular driveway and parked her car. When she made it to the front door, a butler let her in and led her to the study. She imagined what it would be like to live in an elegant and luxurious home like his . . . like her parents. She admired all the paintings and artwork and couldn't resist touching the fabric on the drapes that covered the grand windows.

The butler walked back in to offer her something to drink and snapped her out of her fantasy of being the madam of that miniature mansion. She asked for an apple martini, and he told her to make herself at home. Mr. Armstrong would be with her momentarily.

Rodney came in a few moments later with her drink and joined her on the leather sofa. He didn't ask her any questions. He just handed her the drink, took her feet in his hands, and removed her shoes.

"You have a beautiful home," she said, and he didn't respond as if to say, "I already know."

It didn't take her long to realize that he didn't want to talk, so she sipped her martini while he massaged her feet and calves. Rodney was so smooth. By the time she finished her drink, all she wore was a diamond necklace, earrings, and thigh highs. He gave a new meaning to oral sex because he had her shaking from the oral magic he performed.

She never experienced that type of pleasure with K.P. because K.P. barely looked at her. The times they did make love, it was routine. They did the same, dull-ass positions they started doing from the beginning of their relationship, and K.P. usually didn't go down on her. He never asked her to go down on him either, so Rodney was definitely a person she had to make a return visit to. He was a man of highly refined, expert skills.

Rodney had her on top of the desk in the study pumping her to ecstasy when his butler walked in on them. Kimberly jumped, but Rodney continued to fuck her as if nobody were in the room with them.

"Rodney, baby, someone's—" she tried to say, but he put his hand over her mouth and kept on doing his thing. The butler set a tray on the coffee table and walked out as if nothing were going on.

Kimberly felt confused and embarrassed at first, but Rodney's dick was feeling so good she let it go. They went from the desk to the chair, then back to the sofa. They walked naked through the foyer and up the spiral steps to his colossal master suite. He laid Kimberly down and gave her some more, and her mind was totally gone. Once he finally collapsed, she realized it was after three in the morning, and she knew K.P. was home.

"Rodney, I'm sorry, but I gotta go," she said, getting up from the bed.

"Oh, so your husband got you on a curfew?" he asked, and she looked at him confused.

"What'd you say?" she asked in astonishment.

"Come on, Kimberly, I know you're married, and I know who your daddy is," he told her, and she was shocked. She had never seen him before in her life, so how did he know all of this about her?

"Come again, how do you know these things about me?"

"Well, for one, I am Rodney Armstrong, Samuel Armstrong's son," he said, and Kimberly paused for a moment. The name Samuel Armstrong was familiar to her, but she couldn't put her finger on it.

"Come on, Kimberly, your memory can't be that bad. Your dad and my dad used to play golf together when we were little. I went away to boarding school when we were 15," he told her, and it started coming back. Her dad and Mr. Armstrong were still buddies, but why didn't she remember his son, Rodney?

"Well, I know your father, but I definitely don't remember you," she said, looking around for something to put on because her clothes were on the floor downstairs in the study.

"I was at your wedding with my folks. I guess you wouldn't have time to notice another man on your wedding day," he joked.

"You know what? I *do* remember you. I remember when your dad brought you over to me, and he said that he thought you would be the lucky one to marry me," she said, with it all coming back to her now. She was so into K.P. she didn't give Rodney a good glance when his daddy said that. Finally, she sat down on the bed next to him because she felt awkward standing there naked.

"Yep, that was me, and you barely made eye contact with me," he said, like, now, who's the man?

"Well, Rodney, things aren't that way anymore," she said sadly.

"I see," he said and gently rubbed her back.

"Since my secret's out, I must go home," she said, standing.

He got up, handed her a silk robe, and walked her downstairs. "I've always had a crush on you, Kimberly," he said, and she looked up at him. Now she recalled that the two of them played together most of her childhood. She remembered how she was upset when his parents sent him away. She liked him when they were kids.

"I know. I remember you were my first kiss," she said, looking at him. She didn't know how or why she didn't recognize him earlier. His daddy was a millionaire, and Rodney wasn't doing too badly himself from the looks of it.

"Yeah, I had no clue what I was doing back then."

"Well, you sure know what you're doing now," she said with a shy smile.

"Come on, let me walk you out," he said and grabbed her hand. When they got to the door, he kissed her softly. "I know you're married, Kimmie, but I *must* see you again," he said, and she hadn't heard that in so long. That's what her parents and her really close friends called her, and it brought back so many memories. Her heart skipped a beat at the sound of him calling her that name.

"Rodney, let me call you, and we'll see," she said because she wasn't sure if it had been a good idea to start seeing him. He had it bad for her back then, but she was so popular that she played with him. She knew he really liked her, and she used to take advantage of him, and now he was all grown up. No more braces, no more pimples, just sexy as he wanna be. His body was tight, and his tongue was a breath-taker.

"Baby, you have my card, and you know where I am and that I'll be waiting to hear from you," he said, and she walked away. She didn't know what to feel when she got in her car. She drove home, letting her mind take her back to her childhood when they lived in the pool together at her parents' home. Her parents were not short of a few million, so she grew up living in luxury and had everything.

When she fell in love with K.P., she didn't expect him to turn out to be basically a cheapskate. K.P. made way more money than they spent. He had so much money invested, and it would piss her off that he didn't want to devote ex-amount to certain things.

Like their house. They could have gotten a place twice as big—but no, he wanted to wait a few years after making a certain amount of money before purchasing the house she wanted. He fussed when she splurged a little on jewelry or designer brands, so all the things she liked that he refused to get for her came from Rodney. Rodney didn't tell her no. Whatever she wanted, he just gave it to her.

She just couldn't make herself love Rodney the way he loved her. She couldn't help herself. She still loved K.P. Even though she knew about Janiece, she still loved that man. She always got everything she wanted, and she never wanted people to know that her husband had a mistress. To know that he was leaving her for a broke-ass bitch like Janiece was so embarrassing.

No matter how much Rodney had and could give her, money can't buy you love. She enjoyed all the gifts and fancy things Rodney offered her, but she wished he was K.P. Now that things were over for them and he was leaving, she was more comfortable with Rodney. Not seeing him that week made her miss him for a change, and now she wanted to go out, and K.P. was ignoring her.

She called him again on Janiece's house phone, and when she got the answering machine, she said, "I'm on my way over with your damn kids, and you better not leave." Then she called the kids downstairs, hopped in her Jaguar, and drove to Ninety-Fifth Street.

Chapter Thirty-One

As bold and brave as Kimberly was, she felt a little nervous as she pulled on Janiece's street. She saw K.P.'s truck and Janiece's old, raggedy Honda parked outside. She parked and called K.P.'s phone again, and then Janiece's house phone before she opened the door and got out. She told the kids to hold on a moment while she walked up the steps.

She knocked, but no one answered. She pulled out her phone and redialed Janiece's home, and she could hear the phone ringing, but no one moved around in the condo. She stood there and listened, but no sounds were coming from the inside.

She looked out at the parking lot and wondered what was going on. Isaiah came out of his sister's condo before she walked away, said hello, and proceeded down the steps. When Kimberly started knocking again, he stopped. "They're not there."

"How do you know?" she asked, like . . . *Why are you in my business?*

"They're in Florida," he said, giving her information on their whereabouts.

"When did they leave to go to Florida?" she asked, now wanting to hear what he had to say.

"I believe they left on Tuesday."

"Are you sure?" she asked.

"Yeah, who are you anyway? Maybe I could tell Janiece you were looking for her."

"I'm Kimberly, her man's wife," she said smartly.

"Ooookay, I guess I won't be telling her you stopped by," he said fretfully.

"And why not . . .? You didn't have a problem telling me that they were out of town. So, you can tell them I stopped by. I don't care," she said and walked down the steps. She was mad as hell and wanted to scream. She got into her car and watched Isaiah get into his vehicle. She waited until he pulled off and then got back out of her Jag. Determined, she walked over to Janiece's car and keyed the word "bitch" on the trunk. When she got back into the car, her daughter asked her what she was doing and was promptly told to "Stay outta grown folks' business."

She pulled out her phone, called her babysitter, and asked her to come by in twenty minutes so that she could dress in peace without the kids asking her a million-and-one question. Seething, she drove back to her house feeling like she wanted to kill K.P. and Janiece. She was thinking of ways actually to kill them both and get away with it. Her kids were the reason why K.P. stayed as long as he did, so she was grateful to be blessed with them. Even though her motivation was to have a houseful of children, he didn't go for that. She wasn't supposed to get pregnant with Kayla as soon as she did or KJ as quickly as she did after Kayla was born.

K.P. didn't believe she was taking her pills because she had lied to him about taking them when she had gotten pregnant with KJ, so he started to use condoms with her. She thought it was absolutely ridiculous for her husband to be using condoms.

Truthfully, since she had been seeing Rodney, she didn't miss a day of taking her pills because that was a definite no-no to get pregnant by your lover. Rodney was so nasty and good in bed that he had her going home performing better with K.P. whenever they connected.

Although she and K.P. rarely made love, she showed him how she could get down when they did.

Rodney had her turned out sexually, but K.P. had her heart, and she knew loving a man was stronger than just fucking a man. She knew that two wrongs didn't make it right, but what was she supposed to do all the lonely nights her husband was lying to her and not coming home?

He would come home, sometimes five or six hours after work. The times she used to come in, and K.P. was already home, he didn't bother asking her where she had been or what she was out doing. So she knew he didn't care if she was out doing her thing because any concerned man would raise hell if his wife came in after three in the morning, saying she was at Chelsea's or her parents' house.

The week he was supposed to be out of town on business when she knew he was in Las Vegas with Janiece, she loved it because she spent every night with Rodney. Rodney showed her a wonderful time that week: shopping, good eating, and incredible sex. When K.P. came home after being gone for a week, neither one made a move for the other. A typical married couple would be tearing each other apart after being away for a whole week, but not K.P. and Kimberly.

She didn't know why she couldn't let K.P. go because he was right. They were miserable, but that selfish pride and the fact that her parents had been married for thirty-six years and her grandparents for over fifty years before her granny passed meant something to her. She didn't want to be the first Grayson to have a failed marriage. No one in the Grayson family divorced.

What went on in their house stayed in their home, and if they had parties or went anywhere, no one had looked at them to be less than perfect, and *that* is how she wanted it to remain.

She still hadn't told her father that K.P. wasn't going to be returning to work. She had her parents thinking that they were just taking time off for themselves, and she had threatened her children's behinds if they told Grandma or Grandpa that Daddy had moved out. They lived by the same rule: "What goes on in our house stays in our house." Why was she so embarrassed about K.P. leaving her? She couldn't understand, and she didn't want to be that way.

She pulled into her driveway, and they all went inside. Going upstairs, she entered her walk-in closet and picked out a nice pair of slacks and a cashmere sweater. After a long, relaxing bath, she dressed slowly while waiting for Kami. She was trying not to think of K.P. while she rubbed lotion on her calves, but she couldn't help but think back to when he used to massage her feet when she was pregnant with her babies.

That was the only time he was ever sweet, considerate, and patient with her. He treated her like a queen, which is why she wanted to have a house full of children for him. When she first came home from the hospital with Kayla, K.P. was so attentive. She didn't have to move a muscle. He probably would have nursed the baby for her if it were possible. That is how good he was.

Once he met that damn Janiece, he changed. He stopped asking her how her day was, and he stopped standing by his words. He would tell Kimberly he'd be home by nine and wouldn't show his face 'til after one or two in the morning. He would take the kids out on Sunday for family day, but that was more daddy and kids' day because he never took Kimberly along. He'd say he wanted to spend Sunday with his kids, and Kimberly used to ask, "What about me? What about taking time out for me?" but he'd brush her off, or he'd take her to dinner and talk about work, movies, and current events . . . never anything romantic about them and their relationship.

That's why Kimberly didn't feel bad when giving her goods to Rodney. She had it down pat. She'd come home on Friday nights by two because K.P. always walked in about two thirty or two forty-five. On Saturday nights, it was the same thing. She had a trusted babysitter named Carmen that she hated to see move away because she kept her mouth shut. Rodney paid her well to watch the kids, and she'd get a few hundred for her hours of service and pull away before K.P. made it onto his street.

In a few instances, K.P. had come home before Kimberly, and Carmen would tell him that she was out with Chelsea and text Kimberly with a code 34, letting her know K.P. was home. Shit was perfect for her back then, she thought to herself because she had a good sitter who knew how to keep her dirt concealed, with a man spoiling her and giving her the best dick she had ever had, and still had the perfect family appearance. Nothing could have been better . . . until Carmen told her that she was moving to Detroit and K.P. decided to leave.

Why did he have to leave? He had everything—a ho giving him all the ass and blow jobs he wanted and a wife who learned to turn the other cheek. What else could a man ask for? He was making lots of paper because of her, and he was the son-in-law to Mr. Eric T. Grayson. Kimberly thought it couldn't get any better than that, but she found out she was wrong.

She wished she could leave it alone and not be vengeful and want to hurt Janiece, but she couldn't. Now that K.P. had filed for divorce, she had to come to terms with being without him, but she wasn't sure if she would make it without causing Janiece any bodily harm for taking her husband away. She didn't know how or what she would do, but she would do something to destroy her.

Chapter Thirty-Two

Janiece was on a plane on her way to Texas. Instead of going to Las Vegas with K.P. for his new company's grand opening, she decided to take the Texas trip to see Isaiah. When they got back from their trip to Florida, she didn't have the opportunity to see Isaiah one-on-one at all, only in passing because K.P. was no longer working. He was home all the time, and when they got back to Chicago, he didn't allow her one moment alone without him. One reason was that her car was vandalized, and he thought he had to protect her from whoever it was that thought it was cool to mess up her car.

Janiece lived in a safe and quiet neighborhood, so she could not understand how her car ended up being keyed and having all her tires flattened. Not only was the word "bitch" keyed on the trunk of her car, but the windows were also smashed, and the paint job was ruined with spray paint. K.P. told her he would just get her a new car, but she was so mad because her daddy had bought that car for her before he passed away, and that car had a lot of sentimental value to her. She knew deep down inside that Kimberly was behind it, but she didn't go there with K.P. to accuse her.

K.P. was so nonchalant about it and his solution, like to all things—just get another one. He didn't understand why Janiece wanted to have her car fixed, and Janiece was worn out trying to explain it to him. The insurance company totaled it because the damage was more than it was worth. She knew it was because of the splattered paint all over the interior.

They had decided to wait until they moved to Vegas to look for another one, and since he chauffeured Janiece to wherever she wanted to go, she didn't complain. She continued to ride the metro back and forth to work, and everywhere else she went, she drove the Escalade, or he took her.

Three weeks had gone by, and she managed to sneak around talking to Isaiah on the phone. Now she finally found an opportunity to visit him. She had told K.P. that her company was sending her to Texas for some type of training for four days, and that is why she couldn't go with him to Las Vegas.

Of course, he tried to convince her that it was pointless for her to go to the training considering she was leaving the company anyway, but she insisted that she wanted to go. He didn't argue anymore, but he was very disappointed that she would go to a training class with a company she was leaving instead of going to share the most important day of his life in Las Vegas.

She was unhappy with not sharing her man's company's grand opening with him, but she just *had* to see Isaiah. She missed him, and she couldn't wait to see him. From the moment she agreed to go, she was anxious.

When she landed in Killeen, Isaiah was waiting for her outside her gate with a bouquet of roses. They were red roses, and she blushed when he handed them to her. To keep K.P. from being so suspicious, she got a room at the Hampton Inn to allow him to have another way of reaching her beside her phone.

As soon as they checked into her room, they were all over each other, like they had been apart for years. He kissed her greedily as if he were trying to consume her. After they had incredible sex, they showered, and he took her to his apartment, where they were going to spend most of their time anyway. Although the hotel was $110, plus tax, a night, Isaiah didn't care. He would pay it so that she could be in Texas with him.

When they got to his apartment, Janiece felt a little more comfortable. Her nerves had been bad since K.P. had taken her to the airport. His flight was scheduled to leave the next morning, so he tried to convince Janiece to go with him instead. He even called her phone right before she boarded to make sure she hadn't changed her mind about going to Vegas with him.

Isaiah's apartment was neat and clean, and Janiece was relieved because she had to be in a clean environment or wouldn't have been able to stay. He poured her some Merlot in a wineglass, and she sat on the sofa with the remote while he prepared lunch for her. They sat and ate and talked for a while before he took her out to the base for a tour of Fort Hood. There were so many men and women walking around in uniform, and it was strange because you didn't see that in Chicago.

She had never been to a military town before, and to see so many soldiers was a new and exciting experience for her. He took her to his battalion to show her his office and where he worked. He introduced her to everyone as his lady, and she felt special, but she knew deep down that she wasn't his woman and probably never would be, but she decided to go with the flow. She did wish, just a little bit, that she was, and instead of going to Las Vegas to start a new life with K.P., she could move to Texas to begin a new life with Isaiah.

They left the base and headed to the mall because Janiece had packed the wrong clothes. Although it was November, it was hot in Texas, and she had packed her warmest winter items. She found and picked out a few cute little knit tops and skirts at Old Navy and Dillard's.

Dillard's was a store similar to Carson's in Chicago, so she found some cute stuff there, and Isaiah paid the bill again. She felt special, and what he did for her was generous, just like K.P. Generous.

The debit card that K.P. had given her to get her hair and nails done had a balance on it that made her blink four times. She made three inquiries just to make sure that the balance was really $26,000. She wondered how K.P. had that kind of money just sitting in an account when she could barely keep a balance of one hundred in her account after paying all her bills and buying groceries.

She knew if she had to, she could have used the card that K.P. had given her to make her purchases, but she decided to let Isaiah be the man and do his thing. After they left the mall, he took her to a steak house called Texas Land and Cattle. It wasn't a Ruth's Chris Isaiah said, but their steaks were decent.

They stopped by the hotel to get some things from Janiece's room and found her message light was blinking. She paused to listen to it. It was K.P. He told her that he was just making sure she had made it safely and give him a call. Suddenly, she realized that she hadn't powered her phone back on since she had landed in Killeen earlier that day.

She asked Isaiah to excuse her, and then she went down to the lobby and called K.P. from her phone. He answered. He was half-asleep. She talked to him for over forty minutes 'til her battery started to beep. Finally, he decided to let her go since he had to get up to make an early flight. He was so trusting and so loving. She felt terrible for lying to him. He said all the right things and treated her like the honest Janiece he fell in love with.

She went over to the counter and asked Rosa, the front-desk person, if there was a way to check her voice-mail from a different location. Rosa explained how she could check it without being in the hotel. Janiece had to make sure she didn't miss any messages from K.P. If he called, she could promptly get back to him.

They made it back to Isaiah's apartment, and Janiece felt good. She couldn't help but smile every time Isaiah looked at her. After they showered and made love again, they were lying in his bed just enjoying each other.

"I'm glad you finally agreed to come," he said, stroking her hair.

"So am I," she said and smiled back at him.

"So, when are you coming down again?" he asked, and she thought he was insane for asking her that.

"Coming again? Hell, it was like breaking outta Fort Knox just getting K.P. to agree to let me come this time."

"So then, when are you gon' tell him that it's over?"

"Isaiah, come on, now. We talked about this a million times," she said, changing positions. She couldn't understand why he insisted on pushing her to break it off with K.P.

"I know, Janiece, but I know myself. I'm not going to be able to share you too much longer. I hate it when you're with him, and you know you don't wanna be with him anymore."

"I know, Isaiah, and I'm trying, but I just can't leave him like that."

"Why not, Janiece? Do you still love him?"

"Yes and no . . . I thought we weren't gonna discuss K.P. You said that we didn't have to have this discussion, Isaiah."

"I know what I said, Janiece, and I'm sorry, but when I picked you up from the airport, I was so happy to see you, and after spending today with you and making love to you, I want you and me to be just you and me," he said earnestly, and she knew where he was coming from. She remembered having those same thoughts about K.P. way back in the day when she was lonely and wanted him for herself.

"I know, but please, Isaiah, don't push, okay? Let's just enjoy ourselves and have fun with the time we have together. I'm gonna tell him soon. I'm just not ready right now, okay?" she said, and her phone rang. She made a mad dash to get it. It was K.P. She looked at Isaiah, and he knew what the deal was, so he didn't trip out when she went into the living room to talk to him.

Chapter Thirty-Three

"Home sweet home," Janiece said when she put down her bags. She had come in a few hours ago, and Janelle picked her up from the airport.

"So, when are you going to break up with K.P.?" Janelle asked, going into her fridge to scope out something to snack on.

"Not you too."

"What do you mean?"

"Isaiah asked me that a million times, and I didn't have an answer then, and I don't have one now."

"Well, you're gonna have to come up with something real soon, little sister, because K.P.'s going to want to move you to Las Vegas soon, and if you don't want him, you're gonna have to tell him."

"I know, Nellie. Why y'all sweatin' me?" she asked with attitude.

"Hey, now, what's *your* problem?"

"I'm sorry, sissy, I'm just so confused. I mean, when I'm with K.P., I'm happy, and when I'm with Isaiah, I'm happy. K.P. has been in my heart forever, and Isaiah . . . he's just so sweet and funny and sexy and, girl . . ." she smiled and gazed in the air.

"But the bottom line, Jai, is you can't keep this up. You're gonna be in a situation just like K.P. was, and you don't want that headache, trust me," she said and stuffed some chips into her mouth.

"I know, Janelle, but I don't know how to tell K.P. it's over."

"Oh, so you chose Isaiah?" she said and took a swallow of her Grape Crush.

"No . . . I mean . . . I don't know, and why are you eating so much?"

"Because the baby is hungry, Janiece . . . Do you think I'd be eating these chips like this was my last opportunity to eat if I weren't pregnant with this greedy little baby?"

"All right now, you gon' have more than baby pounds to drop if you keep it up."

"I know," she said and stuffed more in. "I just can't help it."

"You better. You gon' have hips and an ass like mine otherwise," she said, and they laughed.

"You need to leave me alone and worry about your own situation. I say when K.P. comes back into town, you better tell him."

"I know, Nellie, I just don't know how . . ." she said and took her suitcase into her room to unpack. Janelle hung around, and they talked for a while. After that, she took her to the grocery store since she was carless. She got a few items and used the card K.P. had given her. After she got home and settled in, Janelle left. As soon as she was about to take her shower, Isaiah called.

"Hey, woman, why didn't you call me when you got in?" he asked.

"Well, my sister was here, and we hung out for a while, and then I had to go to the grocery store, and I'm really just now getting settled in," she explained.

"Oh, I thought you forgot about me."

"No, I can't forget about you, boo," she said and sat on the sofa.

"I was gon' say . . ." he said, happy to hear her voice.

"So, what's going on?"

"Nothing too much. Just missing you already," he said, and she blushed.

"I'm missing you too."

"I can't wait to see you again," he said.

"I know," she replied. Suddenly, her other line rang. It was K.P. "Listen, I gotta give you a callback."

"K.P., right?" he asked, in a disappointed tone.

"Yes. I'll call you right back, I promise," she said, and he just hung up.

"Hello," she said, answering the other line.

"Hey, baby, I see you've made it home."

"Yes, Janelle just left about ten minutes ago."

"So, how is my favorite girl?"

"I thought Kayla was your favorite girl."

"She is, but you are my favorite *adult* girl," he said, with a smile in his voice.

"I'm good, babe. How's Vegas?"

"Vegas is Vegas. It would have been better if you had been by my side for my grand opening."

"I know, K.P., but you know I have responsibilities too."

"I know, I know, but I didn't think you'd go on a trip for a training course for a job you would be quitting."

"Well, K.P., I haven't made a decision yet on exactly what I'll be doing. That's why I went."

"So, are you saying that you're thinking of *not* coming to Vegas with me?"

"No, K.P. I haven't decided yet, okay? I'm still debating if I'm ready, you know?"

"Janiece, it's not hard. Either you want to be with me, or you don't."

"I wanna be with you, K.P., but you went and planned out this life in Las Vegas without asking me. You went and did all of these things without asking me how I felt or what I wanted to do, so now, I'm not sure, not that I don't wanna be with you."

"Jai, you've said a million times that you wanted us to move out here and start our lives together," he said, speaking the truth.

"Yes, I know, K.P., but never in a million years did I think you'd take it to heart and make that happen. I wish you had just let me in on your plans, so I could have said something, you know? But up and leaving wasn't how I planned it to be for me, and now Janelle is having a baby, and I just don't know."

"Well, Jai, you're gonna have to make some decisions because my business is open now, and I'm gon' have to be out here the majority of the time. I want you here with me. I want to share my life with you."

"I know, baby, and I wanna share my life with you, but I need some time," she said, and K.P. didn't want to hear those words. Instead, he wanted her to say that she would be there as soon as he could arrange to move her.

"Listen, Jai, I understand all of that, but if you want me like I want you, I don't see what's so hard," he said, frustrated.

"I do love you, K.P., and I want to be with you, but Vegas, baby? I just didn't know we would be moving to Vegas. I mean, I love Chicago. My sister is here, and Nellie is my only family."

"And when we get married, *I'll* be your family," he said, and Janiece's stomach got an aching feeling. She thought about Isaiah when he said, "married." No way could she marry K.P. without cutting Isaiah off completely.

"Baby, please, let's just talk about this when you get back," she said, and she wondered when he was actually coming back to Chicago. "When are you returning?"

"Well, right now, I'm not too sure because I need to get some things in order with Paxton Mortgages. I can't come home right now. I have a lot of work to do. So I was hoping you'd come out here with me for a few weeks."

"K.P., you know I can't take off work for that long."

"I know, Jai, so why don't you just quit?"

"I can't just quit, K.P. I haven't made up my mind if I'm actually leaving yet, and I can't quit my job."

"Something tells me, Jai, that you are not trying to be with me. Am I right?"

"No, K.P. I never said that. I just said I need some time. Can you give me that? Moving is a big step, and again, if you have forgotten, you're *still* married. I'm *not* your wife, K.P."

"No, Jai, I haven't forgotten. You seem to keep reminding me."

"I remind you because it's true. I would rather be your wife before I gave up my life and moved to another city."

"Oh, so it's like that, huh? I thought you loved me, Jai, and wanted to be with me? So why now do you decide to have all these conditions? I know you, and you know all I want is to be with you, and now you want to play me?"

"No . . . K.P., what are you talking about? All I'm saying is I don't feel comfortable with quitting my job and packing up to move to another state with a man that isn't divorced yet. These are things that I'm thinking about."

"Okay, Janiece, fine. Since you need time, take your time. You know the number," he said and hung up.

Janiece sat there and contemplated calling him back, but she decided not to. She waited a few moments and called Isaiah back, and when she did, *he* gave her attitude. She didn't talk to him too long because he was so short and aggravated with her, and she didn't want to deal with him either.

She let him go, got into the shower, and climbed into bed. She set her alarm for the following day. As she lay there, she wondered what she would do. She loved K.P., but she wanted Isaiah. She didn't want to hurt K.P., but the more she contemplated her life, she saw herself being with Isaiah and not K.P.

Chapter Thirty-Four

It was holiday break for K.P.'s children, and K.P. was in town. He had been with Janiece and his kids, going back and forth, because Kimberly refused to let them go anywhere with him, fearing having them around Janiece. Janiece didn't care one bit because she knew how Kimberly was feeling, and she didn't blame Kimberly for hating her so much.

K.P. was just about done moving to Vegas, except he didn't have Janiece. She kept avoiding the moving conversation and always had an excuse for her to push back the date. She was totally astounded at herself that she was no longer interested in living with K.P. for the rest of her life. Things were different now, and she didn't want what he had to offer her anymore.

Because she talked to Isaiah at least ten times a day, she had to change her phone plan and add unlimited text because between him and K.P. living out of state, her phone was her only connection to them. She couldn't figure it out, but she knew that she and K.P. didn't have a future together. She just couldn't bring herself to tell him that it was over.

Instead, she walked around faking the funk like it was all good. She missed Isaiah and wanted his time to be up so he could come back to Chicago and for them to be together. She was so high at the thought of him, and she often dreamt about them and their brief time together. She had to catch herself sometimes to keep from calling K.P. Isaiah.

There were moments that she sat in silence and tuned out everything K.P. would say to her because she was too busy thinking about Isaiah, like at that moment.

"Do you want this?" K.P. asked her for the second time, trying to hand her a glass of wine.

"Huh? What?" she said, turning her attention back to him. He stood over her with his arm extended, holding a glass of Chardonnay.

"Do you still want this?" he asked her again.

"Oh yes, thank you," she said and took the glass.

"What's really going on, Jai?" he asked, taking a seat beside her.

"What do you mean?"

"You know exactly what I mean. I've been asking you for weeks about coming to Vegas, and all you do is put me off. I try to talk to you about moving, but you evade the subject. So now I need to know, Janiece, what is going on?"

"Nothing, baby, nothing. I just . . . you know . . . since my sister is pregnant. I just . . . kinda . . . don't know if I should just up and leave."

"Jai, we've talked about this. We have *our* lives to live. Janelle is a grown woman with a husband that will be here for her and their child. This is us. Why are you not considering what's best for us?"

"I dunno, K.P. Maybe what I thought was best for us isn't what's best for me," she finally said.

"What?" he said and stood up. "What the hell does *that* mean, Jai? Forever and a day, you've wanted this. You've said, over and over again, how you wanted us to start over, and now we have that opportunity—and you want to back out?"

"No, K.P., I'm not backing out. It's just things are different now."

"How, Jai? Tell me how. I love you. That didn't change. The only thing that changed is that I finally left my wife, took a leap of faith, and started my own business. I've been living in a hotel, Jai, because I've been waiting on you to finally clear your busy schedule to come down and at least find a house, and now you trying to tell me some bullshit about your sister," he said angrily.

"No, K.P. Please, you don't understand. I love you. I loved you for so long and now things . . . you and I . . . things are . . . just different," she hesitated to say and turned away.

"Jai, tell me this, and I want you to be honest. Are you coming to Las Vegas?" he asked and stood there waiting for her to answer. Finally, after a few moments of silence, he walked away. He didn't want to face it, but he knew she wasn't.

The excited Janiece that he expected wasn't who he was looking at. He thought for sure she'd be on the first plane to Vegas, but she didn't seem happy or excited about the thought, and the way she didn't respond told him that there was more to it than what she was saying.

"I'll be back to get the rest of my things," he told her as he went into the closet to get his coat.

"K.P., where are you going? What do you mean?" she asked, scared that it was over. She wanted Isaiah, yes, but her future with K.P. was standing in front of her face. She had no clue if she and Isaiah had a future together, and she didn't want K.P. to walk out on her.

"You know what the hell I mean. I have a life and a dream to pursue, and if you don't want to be a part of that, fine. But I can't wait forever for you."

"Oh, so you gon' just walk out. I've waited for you and waited for you, K.P. For over *five* years, I've waited for you, and now, you just gon' walk out on me like I'm not worth the time. That goes to show how much you *really* love me," she spat, and he turned to her. The look in his eyes was fiery, and the flaring of his nostrils showed him pissed. Both of his hands were raised as if he wanted to reach out and shake the shit out of her.

"You know what, Janiece? You're right. You were my mistress for five years, and you knew what you had when you continued to let me come around here. So don't give me that bullshit about you waiting because even if I wouldn't have left Kimberly, you'd *still* be my mistress," he said, and that stung. The truth hurts, and Janiece was feeling her truth this time.

"Just know this . . . The reason I did any of what I did is that I wanted to show you how much I really do love you, and I see things have changed. Now, I don't know when you stopped loving me, but for the last few months, Janiece, I see that you've changed. You are not the same woman that you used to be. I feel it, and I see it. You act like I can't touch you, so you don't have to say it. I know, so do your thang, and I wish you the best," he said and walked away.

In a way, Janiece was relieved, but she was unsure if she was really ready to give up K.P. She had loved him for so long, and she was perplexed. Yes, she cared for Isaiah, but would he be the man she wanted him to be? Yet, despite it all, K.P. did love her, and in her heart, she knew that.

"K.P., wait, baby, please," she said, and he turned to her.

"Wait for what, Jai?" he yelled. She stood there and couldn't come up with anything.

"K.P., I love you, I do," she tried to say.

"Yeah, I'll be by before I leave for Vegas to get the rest of my stuff," he said, and it made her angry that he was leaving. She wasn't ready for this reality check. The truth had come, and she wasn't prepared to own up to it.

"So, what you gon' do now? Run back to Kimberly?" she yelled behind him.

"You know something, Jai? As much as I love you and wanted us to be together, I regret one thing," he said and walked closer to her. "And you know what that is?" he asked but didn't allow her to answer. "I regret setting up my future in a different state, away from my kids. I know that I'll end up getting custody of them, but I live more than a phone call away from my kids right now because of my love and sacrifices for you, so if you think that I am just gon' run back to Kimberly because you changed your mind about us, so be it. Think whatever you want to think," he said and walked out the door.

He got downstairs to his rental car and fought the tears. His heart was broken. He couldn't believe that Janiece would change on him. He cranked the engine and pulled out, and she watched him from the kitchen window. When he turned out of the parking lot, she began to cry.

What had she done? Did she make the right decision? Was she really ready to release him? She went into her bedroom and sat on the bed, and the pain hit her. It was over. She had just let him walk out. How would she be able to be with K.P. if she didn't move to Nevada?

If she were to do that, that meant she'd never see Isaiah again, and she didn't want that to be an option. No matter what she and K.P. had together, she had managed to fall in love with Isaiah, and it hurt her that she hurt K.P., but she wanted to be with one man, and the sad reality was that man was *not* K.P.

She grabbed her pillow and sobbed in it 'til her head was hurting. Moments later, she got up, went into the kitchen, and took an aspirin. Then she made sure she had locked her door and set the alarm. She turned out all the lights, went into her room, and dressed for bed. She tried calling K.P., not knowing what she'd say, and she was a bit relieved when he didn't answer.

The next morning, she got up and tried calling him again, but he still didn't answer. She decided not to leave him a message. Instead, she called her sister and told her what happened, and Janelle told her that she was proud of her for doing what she knew in her heart was right.

The next couple of days dragged by, and she still hadn't heard from K.P. She called him several times . . . but nothing. So finally, she stopped calling and waited for him to call her. She knew he'd be in town until after the New Year, and if he wanted the rest of his things, he'd call, sooner or later.

Chapter Thirty-Five

It was New Year's Eve, and Janiece was at home alone with no plans. She and K.P. had made plans to go out, but now they were shot because they had broken up. She had talked to Isaiah several times the past few days, and he was elated that she had finally let K.P. go. She knew why he was happy, but he still didn't say anything about them being any more than what they were.

It was around seven o'clock, and after Janiece attempted to call K.P. 500 times, she had finally given up. She called Isaiah, but she only got his voicemail on every attempt, which pissed her off. She knew he was probably down in Texas having a good ole time, waiting to bring the New Year in with another woman.

She got up and walked into the kitchen to pour herself another drink when she heard a knock on the door. She looked at the clock and wondered who'd be knocking on her door without calling her. Maybe it was K.P., she thought, and she smiled. At least she wouldn't be spending New Year's Eve alone.

She walked over to the door, and to her pleasant surprise, it was Isaiah.

"Oh my God, Isaiah, when did you get here?" she asked, hugging him, and they kissed.

"About three hours ago. I wanted to surprise you."

"Oh, baby, I'm so happy to see you," she said, and he squeezed her tightly.

"I'm happy to see you too," he said and kissed her passionately.

"Oh my goodness, you should have called me. I would have been more presentable," she said, looking at the faded pajamas she was wearing.

"No, baby, you look perfect," he said as she shut the door. He was up on her like she was the last woman on earth. "Oh, baby, I've missed you," he murmured, and they kissed some more.

"I know, me too," she said, and they quickly moved to her room to take care of their sexual business. After they were done, Janiece felt so relaxed and happy he was home.

"So, how long are you here for?"

"Till the fifth; not long."

"Damn, only five days," she said, whining.

"I know, baby, but that was the best I could do. I'm lucky to get that. Trust me, it wasn't easy. I just had to see you, though. I'm going crazy without you," he said, and she knew exactly how he felt.

"I know, babe. I can't wait 'til you come home for good."

"It's only a little while."

"Yes, but it seems like forever."

"I know, but don't worry. It'll be here before you know it."

"You promise?"

"Yes, baby, I promise," he said and kissed her. "Now, get up and get dressed because we're going out."

"This late . . .? Where are we gonna go to beat the countdown?" she asked, looking at the clock. She needed at least thirty minutes to get dressed.

"Don't worry. As long as you hurry up, we'll make it. My sister hooked us up with these tickets to Jay's, and you know Vi, right? He's performing there tonight."

"Really? He is?" she said, sitting up. He was one of Chicago's finest, and she loved him.

"Yep," he said, and she quickly hopped up.

"Oh yes, let me get dressed," she said. She turned on the light and went to the closet. Isaiah got up, grabbed his things, and told her he'd go across to his sister's to shower and dress to kill after she promised him she'd be ready in half an hour.

Janiece dressed and smiled the entire time. She didn't think about K.P. at all. Finally, they got to the club and were having a good time . . . 'til the unbelievable happened. It was K.P., and he was *not* alone. Janiece's stomach dropped when she saw him with his arms wrapped around a woman that wasn't Kimberly.

"I gotta go to the ladies' room," she told Isaiah, and he helped her down from her stool.

"Hurry, baby, the countdown is coming soon," he said, looking at his watch.

"Okay, I'll be right back," she said, and she moved quickly. She was hurt and confused. She was out with Isaiah, so why did it hurt her to see K.P. with another woman? She flushed the toilet, although she didn't tinkle. Since there was a line, she didn't want to get cussed out for taking a stall if she didn't have to go.

Then she stood in front of the mirror and prayed that her mind was playing tricks and that it wasn't him, but she knew what she saw. She washed her hands and hurried back over to the table, and just like she thought, it *was* him. He and his lady friend were obviously having a perfect time. He held her close and planted kisses on her neck. The look of disappointment on Janiece's face showed because she heard Isaiah ask, "Baby, what's wrong?" His voice dripped with concern.

"Nothing, I'm cool," she said and took a drink of her vodka and cranberry. She tried to toughen up and not show any emotions, but her insides were burning not to cry or walk over to him. She knew that wouldn't be wise since she was out with Isaiah, but she couldn't help it.

She tried to focus on Isaiah as they got ready for the countdown, but suddenly, she noticed that the woman with K.P. was a woman she knew. She almost passed out when she realized it was Shawnee, and before she could get her thoughts together, the countdown began. By the time they got to one, she was ready to explode.

She and Isaiah kissed as "Happy New Year" rang through the club. A few seconds later, Vi was on the stage, and the crowd gravitated toward him. Janiece took a seat and tried to get herself together, and Isaiah went to get them another round of drinks. She couldn't help but stare at Shawnee and K.P., and she wanted to fight.

She looked over her shoulder. Isaiah was still in line, so she hopped off her stool and marched right over to them.

"What the fuck is this, K.P.? We break up, and you go straight to this ho," she yelled, catching K.P. off guard.

"Jai," he said, surprised.

"Yes, Jai," she said with attitude.

"Listen, Jai, don't—" he tried to say.

"Don't what? Act a fool? How long have you been fucking this bitch?" she spat.

"Hold the fuck up, Janiece," Shawnee said, but Janiece didn't back down. She was tough and strong, and she was ready to take the opportunity to kick Shawnee's ass.

"What, you tramp bitch?" Janiece said, getting in Shawnee's face, and Shawnee backed down like the coward Janiece knew she was. "You've wanted him from day one," she yelled at Shawnee. "And as soon as we break up, K.P., you run after *this?*" she asked with attitude, pointing at Shawnee. Shawnee eased behind K.P. so he could be between the two of them.

"Listen, Janiece, you made it painfully obvious that we were done when you told me you were not coming to Nevada," he said as Isaiah walked up. He stood close enough to watch the scene with her up in K.P.'s face, but he said nothing.

"Because I asked you to wait and give me some time," she spat.

"Time for what, Janiece?" Isaiah asked from behind her, and Janiece wished he had not overheard her say that.

"Isaiah, listen, I need to talk to K.P. right now, all right?" she said nervously.

"No, that is *not* all right," he barked.

"Janiece, go back over there with your date and pretend we didn't see each other," K.P. said, and it hurt Janiece so bad. Tears burned her eyes.

"K.P., you can't talk to me?" she asked, and Shawnee was standing behind K.P., shaking. Isaiah just stood there witnessing her foolish moment with her ex.

"Janiece, let's go," Isaiah said.

"K.P.—" she said again, standing there looking at him with tears in her eyes, but he didn't even glance her way.

"Janiece," Isaiah said, his voice firmer, but she stood there waiting for K.P. to say something.

"K.P., please . . . You can't talk to me after what we had?" she said, standing there with a face full of tears. K.P. simply didn't respond, and she stood still waiting for him to turn to her and say something, but he didn't. Instead, he acted as if she weren't there, and that tore her heart into a million pieces. "Okay, fine, then. Fuck you," she blasted and stomped away.

Isaiah gave him a look that K.P. didn't bother to challenge. He just shook his head. Isaiah looked through the crowd, searching for Janiece, but she was nowhere to be found. He went over to their table. Her jacket was still there. He grabbed it and headed for the door. When he got outside, she was standing in the cold, crying. He didn't say anything. He just put her coat around her shoulders and walked her to the car.

They drove back to Ninety-Fifth Street in silence. When they got upstairs, he came in and didn't ask her any questions. She showered while he sat on the sofa, waiting for her to come out.

"You're still here?" she said softly. He knew she was surprised when she saw he was still there. She went into the kitchen and came back with a glass of water, then sat on the sofa. They sat there in silence for a while, and finally, he stood to leave.

"Listen, I'll catch you later," he said. She didn't want him to leave, but things were just not right.

"I know you think I'm pathetic," she said, not looking at him.

"No, I just think you got a lot to work out."

"Why does it have to be so complicated, Isaiah? I don't love him anymore, so why does it hurt?"

"Well, Janiece, I can't say that I believe that you don't love him anymore, and I know you thought you wanted me too, but maybe you're not ready for me. You need time, and I don't want to be in the middle like this anymore. I don't want to watch you go through the motions. I thought I could handle this, but after tonight . . ." he said and slowly walked away.

"Isaiah, don't leave, please. I don't want you to go," she said, getting up and going after him.

"Jai, you need some time. I think it's best for us if you and I just chill out."

"No, Isaiah, come on. I'm sorry I acted that way. I'm sorry for causing a scene. It just pissed me off to see him with that bitch Shawnee. I can't stand her, Isaiah, and when I saw them together . . ." she said, sobbing. "Please, baby, stay. You don't have long to be here, and I don't want you to go."

"Look, I'll see you tomorrow. You get some rest, and I will see you tomorrow," he said and tried to pull away.

"Trust all of me wants to stay, but I can't. You are not ready, baby. I want you to be mine, and I want to love you, but you are not ready," he said, and she still held on. Finally, he leaned in and kissed her forehead and her wet cheek before he pulled completely away from her grip on his jacket.

Once she heard the door shut, she fell back onto the sofa. She cried and sobbed so hard she thought she would hyperventilate. She finally calmed herself and got up to lock the door. Then despondently, she went into her bedroom and climbed into bed. She looked at the clock. It was a little after two.

She cringed at the thought of K.P. holding Shawnee in his arms. She was jealous and mad at him for getting with her. Of all the women in Chicago, he chose her. She would have felt better if it had been Kimberly, not Shawnee. How was she going to show her face at work after tonight?

She sobbed a little more until she finally fell asleep. She woke up the next morning, telling herself that it was time to let go and move on. She got up, brushed her teeth, and wondered how she would get Isaiah back and convince him that he was the one.

She prayed that he would talk to her again, and she also hoped that K.P. wouldn't ever come around her anymore. After seeing him with Shawnee, she had no respect for him and how he treated her. She knew that if she saw him again, she'd be tempted to slap the shit out of him.

Chapter Thirty-Six

After Janiece put all of K.P.'s things in trash bags, she cleaned her condo from top to bottom. Then she shampooed and blow-dried her hair while thinking what she would say to Isaiah. How would she get him to see that she wanted him and she was done with K.P.?

She dressed, and when her phone rang, she just knew Isaiah missed her and wanted to talk to her, but when she saw Private, an unlisted number, she got nervous.

"Hello," she said.

"Put him on the phone," Kimberly demanded.

"Listen, Crazy, I told you not to call my house again for your husband. He doesn't live here. So now, please, with all due respect, Mrs. Paxton, leave me the fuck alone," Janiece said and hung up. "Crazy" called her right back.

"Listen, you slut, as I told you before, I don't enjoy calling your funky-ass apartment looking for him, but when I can't get in touch with my husband, you are my last resort, so, please, with all due respect, you trifling bitch, put him on the phone," Kimberly spat.

"Look, K.P. is not here. We are not together, and he doesn't live here. Now, if you can't reach him, that's *your* problem, but please, leave me alone. I ain't done shit to you for you to keep calling my house."

"You really think you're innocent, Janiece? You've been fucking my husband for years, and you haven't done *anything?* I can't sleep at night because of you. My husband is gone . . . moved to an entirely different state because of you, and you don't think you're responsible?"

"Kimberly, K.P. is a man. He comes and goes as he pleases. He fucks whomever he wants as he pleases. So for crying out loud, stop acting like you're the victim."

"You stank bitch, how dare you!"

"How dare I what? Point out the obvious? It's women like you that allow men to do what K.P. did to you, and instead of saying no, I'm better than this and leave, you put up with it, and now, you're blaming me. You said it yourself. I've fucked your husband for five years, and you know what? You're right, but you allowed him to continue fucking me for five years, so you, my dear, are *not* a victim. Now, don't call my house anymore.

"Regardless of whether you believe it, I'm over him, and we are not together, and wherever he is and whoever he's doing, I hope that's what he wants because Janiece wants more for herself, and if you would wise up and stop running behind his two-timing ass, you'd stop fucking with me," Janiece said, and Kimberly got quiet for a moment.

"Well well well, I see you are just like me. You love him, and you know it. You're right. I was never the victim, Janiece. I stayed with Kerry because I wanted to, and yes, I allowed him to carry on a relationship with you for over five years, and you know what? I stayed. I could have walked, but I didn't.

"You can say what you want and try to throw me off with this 'we're not together, and I don't want him' bullshit, but I know how much K.P. loves you, and for that, my dear, you *will* pay for what you did. So now, when you see my husband, you lying bitch, tell him he needs to come and get his children," she said and slammed the phone down.

Janiece was in total disbelief that Kimberly still had it in for her even though she and K.P. weren't together anymore. She hung up and sat down for a moment or two before calling Isaiah. She didn't let Kimberly's threats interfere with her day. She had other things to handle, and Kimberly didn't have that kind of power over her. Janiece was not the type to be bullied by anyone. She called Isaiah and crossed her fingers, hoping he'd pick up.

Chapter Thirty-Seven

"You've got to help me," Kimberly said, taking a seat on Rodney's sofa. This look of disdain in his eyes showed proof that he thought the idea of doing something so crazy was so disgusting, but she asked anyway, giving all the reasons why she had to destroy the woman who killed her marriage.

"Are you really serious right now, Kimmie, or are you just kidding around because the idea is ridiculous and hearing you makes me question your sanity," he said with his brows furrowed. When she realized that he thought the idea was insane, she played it off as if she were only joking and laughed. She enjoyed her apple martinis with him and let him devour her body again. She felt like a love goddess when she was with him and wondered why she even had any type of sexual attraction to K.P. because the truth is, he didn't come close to Rodney.

The way he put it on her made her glad at times that she didn't have to get up in the middle of the night to creep home. She loved the single life, and now that everyone knew that she was separated and on the threshold of divorce, her whole lifestyle had changed.

Of course, she lied to everyone about why K.P. had left her. She never let a soul besides Rodney know that her husband had fallen in love with a low-class, dick-sucking, evil bitch. No way. She was too embarrassed to let her country club friends know something like that, so she told them that he wanted to relocate, and she didn't. End of story.

She dared anyone to challenge her explanation about their breakup. There were rumors, of course, but no one was brave enough to say it to Kimberly's face. Even though she was a pint-sized woman, most women were intimidated by her—but not Janiece, which pissed her off more.

No one had ever stood up to her before, and after she took a punch in the nose from Janiece, she knew she had to get somebody to handle the bitch for her.

She, of course, called Chelsea, and, of course, Chelsea, being the hot thang she was, had had a couple of rough-necks in her life. The kind Kimberly refused to let come within five feet of her. She knew Chelsea could get her to someone that knew someone who wouldn't mind beating a bitch to the floor for some quick dough.

After a few calls, Kimberly had found her man. A dude that was down on his luck that she told she'd pay him five grand if he just roughed up Janiece a little bit. All she had to do was come up with the when and where. Now that posed a problem because she knew K.P. was in town, and for the most part, she thought K.P. would be with Janiece since she no longer had a car.

So she told the guy she'd be in touch. She walked around numb and coldhearted and didn't feel one ounce of sympathy for Janiece. If she could hire someone to kill her, she would have, but she definitely couldn't afford a murder to come back on her, so she settled for a beatdown.

Chapter Thirty-Eight

Janiece repeatedly tried to get a hold of Isaiah, but he wasn't answering her calls. She finally went across the hall, but he wasn't there, Iyeshia told her. She asked her if she knew when he'd be back, but Iyeshia said she had no idea. Janiece was frustrated and angry, but she smiled and told Iyeshia to ask him to call her.

She went back inside, sat on the sofa, and turned on the tube, watching it until she dozed off. When she woke up after ten, she was disappointed to see that Isaiah hadn't attempted to call. She went into the kitchen to get something to drink and heard voices outside her door.

Janiece pulled the curtain back. It was Isaiah and a guy talking. She closed the curtain quickly and ran to wash her face and brush her teeth. She wanted so desperately to speak to him, so she would ask him if he could step in for a moment. As she opened the door, he looked at her, and so did his friend.

"Hi," she said, and both Isaiah and his friend greeted her. "Isaiah, when you're done, do you have a moment?" she asked nervously.

"Naw. Me and my boy 'bout to roll out."

"Okay, well, when you get back then?" she asked, sounding pitiful. She wanted to talk to him, knowing he was leaving soon.

"I . . . I . . . don't know. It'll probably be late," he said, not even looking at her.

"Isaiah, look at me," she pleaded. He hesitated before turning in her direction. "Listen, I made a mistake, okay? And I'm so sorry. I need to talk to you," she said, and his friend looked at him like, *Do you need to handle this?*

"Quentin, man, can you give me a sec? I'll be right down."

"Sure, man, I'll be in the truck," he replied and went down the steps.

"Janiece, I have to be honest with you, and please don't take this the wrong way. I don't think that we need to talk anymore, so, no, I can't come by tonight or any other night," he said.

"Isaiah . . . You can't mean that. You can't just cut me off like that."

"I'm not trying just to cut you off, and yes, I do mean that we can't see each other anymore. Last night, you made me realize that I'm not the guy, no matter what I do. You want him so much, Janiece, so why don't you just take the dude up on his offer and move to Vegas? I mean, that's what you really want."

"No, Isaiah, no, that's not true," Janiece said, stepping out on the porch with no coat on, and it was cold as hell. "Come on; we got to talk. I need you."

"No, you don't, and I can't keep holding on, hoping you'll cut this cat loose. I want what's best for you, Janiece. Believe me, I do, but I *know* what's best for me."

"Isaiah, no. *You're* what's best for me. I made a mistake, okay? I was stupid, but that will *never* happen again. I'm done with K.P. I'm not going anywhere. I want to be here with you. I want to wait right here for you to come home," she said, walking closer to him. She wanted him to hold her, but he just stepped back.

"Listen, Janiece, I gotta go. Take care," he said and walked down the steps.

"Isaiah . . . Isaiah . . . Isaiah, don't do this," she yelled after him. He didn't turn around. He just proceeded to his friend's truck and got into the passenger side. Janiece stood there in the cold and watched the Denali drive off. She was numb from the cold, but she couldn't move.

The tears were warm rolling down her cheeks, so she finally went inside. She was hurting, and she didn't understand how she had let this happen. Why did she have to confront K.P. last night? Why did she have to go and do that? She wished she could take it back because she was in love with Isaiah, and now she had lost him too and didn't know how she would get him back.

He didn't want to even talk to her, like it was just nothing for him to walk on by—like he didn't give a damn. Finally, she gave up trying to figure it all out. Instead, she crawled into bed and cried herself to sleep.

Chapter Thirty-Nine

"Jai, baby, come on. I'm sorry," K.P. said, and she just looked at him. After four days, he finally showed up at her condo to talk.

"K.P., you can save your apologies and your words. There's nothing left for you to say to me, and there's nothing left for me to say to you. It's over, and I want to be done with you, your wife, and this drama."

"Jai, come on. You know I love you, and I don't want to be with Shawnee. She kept calling me, I swear, and I finally gave in to her because she said she had these tickets. So since you and I had a falling out, Jai, I went, and that was that. You know damn well I don't want that woman."

"Well, K.P., the way you were all up on her the other night and the way you looked at me like *get the fuck out of my face* was enough for me to know that I'm not important to you. So just get your shit and go. I don't want you, K.P. I'm over you and this relationship, and you can fuck Shawnee, Kimberly, or whomever else you choose to. I don't care," she said and walked away, and he was right behind her.

"Jai, you don't mean that, baby. I know you don't. And come to think of it, you were out with that cat Isaiah anyway, so what was that, huh?"

"It was none of your damn business. I don't have to explain anything to you about my personal life, K.P. I should have let you go a long time ago, and now, I may have messed things up with Isaiah trying to hold on to you," she said and went into the kitchen.

"Because you still love me," he said, walking up and grabbing her from behind.

"K.P., you know what? The truth is, I don't. I don't love you anymore. I stopped loving you the day I met Isaiah. I have been walking around here lying to myself, and the truth is I love Isaiah," she said, and he backed up.

"You what? You gon' stand here in my face and tell me that bullshit?" he yelled.

"It's not bullshit. It's the truth. So I'm telling you again, K.P., get your things and get outta my life. I don't ever want to see you again. I held on and held up my life for too long for you, and now, it's my time to be honest with myself and you. I don't love you anymore, K.P., and I never thought it would be this easy to say it, but I love Isaiah, and he deserves all of me.

"I see now exactly what he meant because I was doing to him exactly what I let you do to me. And like me, he deserves better. I wish you well. Now, see your way out," she said and walked away. Janiece went into the living room, sat on the sofa, and waited to hear the door shut.

K.P. was so outdone with Janiece he didn't argue. Instead, he grabbed the black velvet ring box from the counter, got his things, and left. He walked down the steps, heartbroken because he'd lost. He lost his family *and* the woman he loved. He hated Shawnee for putting all that bullshit about Janiece in his ear. She had schemed and talked about Janiece so badly, he actually had a dumb moment and believed her. *That's* how he ended up going out with her.

He didn't like her because she was a fake, and after they left the club, he took her ass home, dropped her off, and was sure to tell her never to call him again. After that, he chilled out and hung out with his kids. He knew he was leaving, and he knew he had time to work on his relationship with Janiece, but now he knew that he was wrong.

He loaded his rental trunk and pulled out of the parking space, and as he was pulling out, Isaiah was pulling in. K.P. wanted to get out and knock his ass out, but he decided it wasn't worth it. Although he was hurt and upset, he sincerely loved Janiece, and he wanted her to be happy, and it was hard for him, but the truth is, if it was with Isaiah, then that's what he wanted.

Chapter Forty

"So, what are you gonna do now?" Janelle asked Janiece after putting her plate into the dishwasher. After K.P. had gone, Janiece called her to come over to help her work on getting Isaiah back.

"I don't know, sissy. He doesn't trust me, and I don't blame him, you know?"

"Yeah, you shouldn't have shown your ass the other night getting all crazy with K.P.," Janelle said with a sad smile.

"Yeah, I know."

"But it'll be all right, kiddo. Don't worry," Janelle said and got up. "Well, I'm going to be heading home. You know, once I eat, the baby and I want to nap."

"All right. Now I told you to slow it down. You my size now with all those hips," Janiece said, looking at Janelle. Since she was pregnant and put on some weight, they looked more alike.

"I know, girl, but I kinda like it. I hope I keep some of these hips after this baby. I betcha I'll look better in my jeans."

"I know that's right," Janiece said and got up. "Let me walk you down."

"Chile, please, it's freezing outside. I'll be okay. I'll call you when I get to the house."

"Are you sure?"

"Chile, yes. I parked in your parking stall anyway. It ain't like you got a car."

"I know, but I'll get one soon. K.P. was generous enough to write me a check for my down payment. He knew his crazy wife destroyed my car."

"Yes, we all knew, but that's good he at least helped you out."

"Yeah, he was nice about things like that, but, oh well, right?"

"Yes, you can say that again," Janelle said and opened the door.

"I love you, sis. Call me soon as you get home."

"I will, and I love you too. And, Jai, I'm proud of you, and I hope Isaiah comes around," she said, and they hugged.

"Me too," Janiece said, and they exchanged smiles. Janiece watched her sister go down the steps but closed the door quickly because it was bitterly cold and windy. She quickly ran into the bathroom to tinkle.

When Janelle got to her car, she dug in her purse for her keys. The wind was blowing so hard. She wished she had taken them out upstairs like she usually did.

"Excuse me, ma'am," a man said, walking up to her out of nowhere.

"Yes," she said, trying to see him clearly.

"Would you happen to know how to get to . . ." he said, getting closer, then suddenly, Janelle felt a blow to her face. The punch was so hard it knocked her pregnant body onto the pavement. She tried to focus and reach out, but she was in a daze. He hit her again . . . and again.

"Please . . . please . . . I'm pregnant . . ." she tried to say, but she felt another cruel blow. Now she was dazed and couldn't move, but she hazily saw him standing over her. She opened her mouth to plead for mercy, but she couldn't push the words out. She felt him kick her twice and quickly decided not to move. He bent over to get her purse, but she suddenly heard a man's voice from behind him.

"Hey! What are you doing?" the voice thundered. The guy jumped up and took off running, Janelle assumed. Then she blacked out.

As Isaiah got closer, he saw a woman lying on the ground. He rushed over to her. Her face was bloody, and she was not responding. For a second he thought it was Janiece, but he couldn't tell because her face was so messed up. He reached in his pocket to get his phone, and then he saw someone quickly pull off. He looked and realized it was K.P.'s wife's jag that pulled away just moments after the guy ran off.

He called 911. After that, he called Janiece. She ran down the steps and lost it when she saw her sister lying there severely beaten. She started screaming and shaking her to wake her up.

"Please . . . Nellie, wake up . . . please . . . please—just wake up, baby. Please, everything's okay . . . You just gotta open your eyes for me, sissy . . . Come on now," she said, crying and holding her sister closely. Isaiah tried to comfort her and calm her until the ambulance arrived, but she was too hysterical.

"No, Isaiah, she's all I got. My parents are gone, and Nellie is all I got," she cried, holding her. "Wake up, sissy, please, wake up," Janiece begged. "My sister is pregnant . . . Isaiah, and who . . . would do this . . . She's having a baby . . ." she continued to cry hysterically. By then, the ambulance had finally pulled up.

"Janiece, baby, come on. You gotta move so the medics can take care of her," Isaiah said, trying to get Janiece to let go, but she was holding on to Janelle too tightly.

"Janiece, come on, baby, they can't help her. Come on. You have to let her go, so they can help her, baby . . . Come on," he urged, and Janiece finally let go. The medics checked Janelle's vitals. She was alive. They lifted her onto the gurney, put her in the back of the ambulance, and got to work.

They told Janiece what hospital they were taking her to and told her she could follow.

"I don't have a car. How . . . Sir, I don't have a car," she said hysterically.

"Don't worry, sir, we'll be right behind you," Isaiah said, and the guy jumped into the truck, and they left. Janiece was crying and shaking. Isaiah hugged her tightly. "Baby, come on. Relax. They're going to take care of her. Shhh . . . Come on, baby, calm down, okay? She's gonna be fine. We have to go to the hospital."

"Isaiah, how did this happen to my sister? I told her I'd walk her down. My sister never goes without me walking her down, Isaiah. It's my fault. If I hadda walked her down, none of this would have happened," she said, crying.

"Baby, it's not your fault. Now, come on. Let's get her things," he said, picking up her purse and hat from the ground.

"I need my purse, Isaiah, and my phone. I need to call Greg."

"I'll get it. Come on, get in the car, and I'll go up and get it," he said and put Janiece into his truck. He ran up and got her purse, keys, and phone. He went into her closet and grabbed her coat too because she came down without one on. On his way back down, he couldn't help but think about the Jag. He knew that woman had something to do with it, but he wanted to make sure Janelle was okay before saying anything.

When they got to the emergency room, they were told to wait. Janiece explained to them that her sister was pregnant, and they told her just to sit tight. As soon as the doctor was done, he'd come for her. Shortly after that, Greg walked in, and Janiece ran into his arms.

"Somebody attacked her, Greg. Some evil person attacked my sissy," she cried, and Greg was in tears.

"What did the doctor say? Is she all right? Is my wife okay? How's my baby?" he asked frantically.

"I don't know, Greg. The doctor hasn't told me anything yet. It's my fault. I shoulda walked her down."

"Shhh, it's not your fault. Don't go blaming yourself."

"She has to be okay. I can't lose my sister, Greg."

"Shhh, don't think like that. She's gonna be fine," he said reassuringly, and Janiece finally calmed down a little. Isaiah was right there holding her and comforting her too, and she was so glad of that.

They waited for what seemed like hours, and finally, the doctor came out.

"Well, we have good news. She's going to be fine. The babies are okay too. She didn't suffer any injuries to her abdominal area. She's just bruised up pretty bad. The swelling is going to take a few days to go down, but your wife is one of the lucky ones," the doctor told Greg.

"When can I see her?"

"In a little while. She's being admitted, and then you and your family can see her. She's not going to be alert, though, and she is going to need plenty of rest."

"Doctor, I'm sorry, but did you say, 'the babies are fine'?"

"Yes, I thought you knew. It looks like a boy and a girl, and they're fine," he said, and Greg and Janiece were stunned. No wonder she was getting so big in such a short time. That explained it.

They sat down, and Janiece was relieved to know her sister would be okay. She sat beside Isaiah, still shaken but relieved. She let Greg go in first, and she told Isaiah he could go if he wanted to and that she'd get a ride home from her brother-in-law.

"No, I'll stay. I wanna make sure you're okay, and you get home safe tonight."

"Thank you, but I'll be fine. Greg will take me home."

"No, Janiece, I wanna stay. The horrifying thing is, when I came up the steps from the laundry room and saw that guy over your sister, I didn't know what to think. And when he ran, and I came around the car and saw Janelle lying on the ground, I thought it was you, and I thought I had lost you. It scared me so bad, Janiece, but when I looked closer, really looked, I realized it wasn't you. I was so relieved, but then I remembered meeting Janelle that night we went on our first date, so that's when I called 911."

"I thank God that you came when you did because whoever it was could have hurt her worse."

"You know, something, Janiece? I didn't want to say anything earlier, but I think I know who's behind this."

"What? What are you talking about? You *know* who did this, and you didn't say anything?"

"Listen, I know you were in no state of mind to be talking about that. I just wanted to make sure Janelle was okay first, baby. Believe me, I was more concerned about that and you than anything."

"Okay, then, who . . . Who would want to hurt Janelle?"

"It wasn't Janelle they were trying to get. I believe they were trying to go after you."

"What? Who—?" she asked, confused.

"Do you remember back when you and K.P. went on your trip?"

"Yeah . . ."

"Well, his wife Kimberly came by looking for him, and I saw her, and that same silver Jag was parked in front. Now, I know cars, and that Jag is not one that I could forget seeing. That was the same Jag that pulled away after I ran that guy off."

"What? You can't be serious," she said in disbelief.

"Dead serious. Now, I don't know what's going on, but I think she got somebody to attack you and wanted to watch, and in that coat and hat, you and Janelle look almost identical," he said.

Those words frightened and chilled Janiece. "Isaiah, we got to go to the police."

"With what? We gon' need some proof. It's not like she gon' confess."

"Then I need to go over to that bitch's house and beat *her* ass," Janiece said. She was angry. All she wanted to do was beat the shit out of Kimberly.

"Baby, come on; think. What is that gon' solve? We have to have proof."

"How are we gon' get proof?"

"I'm not sure, but we'll figure out something."

"Isaiah, I'm so grateful that you're here. I didn't want something like this to be the way we got a chance to talk, but since I have you here at this moment, I have to take a chance and tell you something."

"What is it?"

"I love you," she said. "I know I may have messed up any chance of us being together, and I can't say I blame you, but I love you, and I'm sorry for all the bullshit, lies, and drama that I've put you through. If I could redo it all over again, I'd change everything except for falling in love with you," she said, and he sat there in silence. She didn't know what he would say, but she was happy that she had gotten the chance to tell him her heart.

He turned away and took a deep breath. Janiece knew that it didn't matter because Isaiah was a straight-up, no-nonsense guy, and if he decided to end their relationship, that was what he'd do. She let out a breath, sat back in the seat, and fought the threatening tears. She didn't expect much, but she didn't expect him not to say a word.

"Janiece," he said, turning back to her. Her eyes had watered, but she didn't let a single tear drop. "Things have been good for us, and things have been bad for us. But you must understand that I want to be with a woman I can trust. I still have almost six months to be in Texas, and if you and I are together, I want to be able to trust you, and I can't lie and say that I do."

Now, she let the tears flow freely.

"However, I love you too, and I'm willing to try because you deserve a chance, and I deserve you. I want us to have a long life of happiness together, and I want to be with you. I want to come back home to you when I'm done, and if you still love me and you feel like putting up with me, I'm yours," he said.

Now she smiled.

She was so happy to hear him say that he loved her. She finally got it right. She had found someone just for her. No fighting, no scratching, no threats, just a man of her own that wanted her too.

They kissed and held hands until Greg came out to get Janiece to go in to see Janelle. When she walked in to see her sister lying in the hospital bed with a bruised face and IV in her arm, she covered her eyes. They burned so bad with tears, and she wished she was the one lying there instead of her sister. She was the one Kimberly targeted, and she was the one who fucked Kimberly's husband. Janelle did not deserve that. She dried her eyes and vowed that Kimberly would pay for what she had done.

She took a seat beside Greg and answered all the questions he had for her as best she could. But unfortunately, she didn't have anything solid, so finally, he stopped drilling her, and they sat in silence until the nurse said she had to leave.

Since Gregory was her husband, he was allowed to stay, so he did. Janiece was happy that Isaiah didn't leave because she would not have had a way home. She could have taken Greg's car, but she was scared to go home alone under the circumstances.

When they got back, it was late, and Janiece was tired. She and Isaiah climbed into bed and fell asleep. She felt safe in his arms and got an unsettling feeling when she remembered he was scheduled to leave the next day.

Chapter Forty-One

The following day, Janiece woke up and overheard Isaiah on the phone. She wondered who he was talking to so early, so she got up.

"I know, Captain, but my girl's sister was attacked last night, and whoever did this was trying to get my fiancée," he said, and Janiece wondered what fiancée he talked about. "I know, but can you just please cut me this one break? Under any other circumstances, I would never call and ask for an extension, sir, but I just can't leave right now," he said, and she stood there listening. Isaiah was unaware of her presence.

"Sure thing . . . I will have my fiancée get the paperwork and fax it over to you ASAP," he said, nodding. "Thank you, sir. One week is fine. I can assure you, I'll report back on the twelfth," he said and hung up.

"When did you get engaged?" she asked.

"Oh, baby, that was my commander. I just couldn't leave you here today. So I called to get an extension."

"And what did he say?"

"He said, fine, but I need some papers from the hospital to fax to him to prove that I'm not lying about Janelle."

"Why is all that necessary?"

"Trust me, baby, it's not, but sometimes they get that way. He probably won't even look at them. He just wants to give me a tough time."

"Oh, well, that shouldn't be a problem. I'll call my brother-in-law and tell him what we need, and when I go by the hospital today, I'll get the papers for you."

"Thanks, babe," he said and kissed her on the cheek.

"Oh, is my sister's purse still in your car? I have to get her keys and use her car until I can get me another one."

"No, we gave her purse to her husband, if I'm not mistaken. But I can take you to the hospital."

"Are you sure? Because I know I'm gon' be there probably the entire day."

"And I'll stay with you the whole day," he replied, and she smiled.

"You are too much," she said and went into the kitchen.

"Hey, when are you thinking about getting a car?"

"Well, I was gonna wait 'til spring, but I guess I need to start looking now."

"What kind of car do you want?"

"I don't know. I haven't thought about it much."

"Well, whenever you're ready, let me know."

"Why? You gon' buy me a car?"

"I could. Did you forget my family owns one of the largest car lots in Chicago?"

"Oh shit, I did forget about that. I remember you changing cars on me every other day."

"Yeah, that's the upside to it."

"There's a downside?"

"Yep, but like I told my dad a million times, I don't want to talk about it."

"Well, I think it would be neat to work for the family. I wish my daddy were here to get me to work with him. Just to have him here, I'd work with him in a heartbeat."

"I never thought of it that way."

"Think about this . . . Parents work hard to give their children something. Your daddy has one son. Who do you think he has hopes and dreams of taking over when he retires or passes? His only son. So don't give your dad a hard time. He's only doing what 99 percent of daddies do."

"That's true," he said. Suddenly, her phone rang. Janiece got up. It said Private. She paused for a second and didn't answer. Instead, she let the answering machine get it to see if she could get "Crazy" to leave an incriminating message.

Janiece figured that Kimberly believed that she had been attacked the previous night and was probably calling to boast, and sure enough, she was. Janiece and Isaiah listened to her message, and when they heard Kimberly's evil voice, it gave her chills.

"I guess you know now that I am who I say I am. The next time you decide to go after someone's man, you'll think twice. And I heard the sad news this morning that you and K.P. are over. I wish I had known the truth before I let loose on your ass last night, but let's just say that was your dose of reality. Now you know that Kimberly meant what she said. You were going to pay when she told you that you would. Enjoy your time in the hospital, bitch, and I hope the swelling goes down quickly. Ciao."

Janiece hit save, ran into her room, and got all Kimberly's cards and threatening letters. Then she and Isaiah got dressed and headed for the police department. Kimberly was the one who would get a dose of reality. Unfortunately, she would do some time because of her evil and vicious behavior.

It was a shame for Kimberly, though, to give up her freedom and wealth to be behind bars over a man. Janiece was relieved that she had not gone to any extremes to keep K.P. because he wasn't worth all the stress and drama she endured. She was glad to finally have a fresh start in a relationship with someone where she didn't have to compete for time and attention.

Isaiah was the best man for her, and she was thankful that she had finally owned up to her true feelings for him and let go of her dysfunctional, emotional feelings for K.P. The truth is, you *can* get over someone and start fresh again. Had Kimberly realized that too, Janelle might have never been hurt. And Kimberly Renee Paxton wouldn't have been taken from her uppity country club, in front of all of her peers . . . in handcuffs.

The End